The Square Moon

The
Square
Moon

Supernatural Tales

Ghada Samman

*Translated from the Arabic
by Issa J. Boullata*

The University of Arkansas Press
Fayetteville 1998

The title of this book in the original Arabic is *Al-Qamar Al-Murabbaʿ:Qiṣaṣ Gharāʾibiyya* by Ghāda Al-Sammān

Published by Manshūrāt Ghāda Al-Sammān

Beirut: December, 1994
© 1994 Manshūrāt Ghāda Al-Sammān

English translation © 1998 by the Board of Trustees
   of the University of Arkansas
02 01 00 99 98   5 4 3 2 1

Designer: Sheila Hart

∞ The paper used in this publication meets the minimum
requirements of the American National Standard for Permanence
of Paper for Printed Library Materials Z39.48-1984.

Library of Congress Cataloging-in-Publication Data

Sammān, Ghādah.
      [Qamar al-murabbaʿ . English]
      The square moon : supernatural tales / Ghada Samman ;
   translated from the Arabic by Issa J. Boullata.
         p.   cm.
      ISBN 1-55728-534-9 (alk. paper). — ISBN 1-55728-535-7
   (pbk. : alk. paper)
      I. Boullata, Issa J., 1929–   . II. Title.
PJ7862.A584Q2613   1998
892.7ʹ36—dc21
                                                      98-30084
                                                      CIP

This translation is dedicated to Marita, my wife,
who was the first to read and enjoy the stories
of this collection in English

Contents

Beheading the Cat

"**S**he's a rare bride-to-be, my son, quiet and obedient. No one but her mother has ever kissed her mouth. She'll never leave home without asking your permission—unless it is to her grave. She'll give birth only to boys. A maid by day, a slave girl by night, she'll be a ring on your finger which you can turn around as you wish and take off when you wish. And if you rub it, it will say, 'At your service, your slave is at your command.'"

Abdul listened, hardly able to believe that this was really happening to him here in the heart of the Trocadéro district in Paris six years before the year 2000. But here was a mysterious lady in her fifties, sitting in front of him with her plump face and her black scarf, which she threw back, revealing locks of hair dyed red with henna—the old women of his family in Beirut had used henna when he was a child. She had pleasant dimples and was adept at the art of discarding formality, right from the first meeting, as was customary in Lebanon, his motherland. *What made this matchmaker offer her services today in particular, when I had finally decided to ask Nadine this very evening to marry me?*

The mysterious lady continued, "'Abdul Razzaq, my son, this bride worships God in heaven and you on earth. You can marry a second, a third, a fourth wife, in addition to her, and she will live happily with her co-wives. She will even go out herself to ask the hand of a second bride for you if she can bear you no children. But it is important that your wedding night you behead a cat on the threshold of your home, in front of her, so she will see and understand that her fate will be that of the cat's, should she disobey you."

The matter would have appeared odd to Abdul had the lady not correctly pronounced his name, 'Abdul Razzaq. All his acquaintances in Paris called him Abdul for short, and without the guttural beginning. Therefore, the mysterious lady must really be a friend of his mother's, since she knew his original full name. *I was putting on my clothes and making ready to go out when the door bell rang. I was surprised, for I thought it was broken and had heard my father call the electrician to come by and fix it.*

I opened the door and saw her standing there, with a flood of light shining behind her. She looked like a pillar of black smoke in her black overcoat, which enveloped her like a cloak, and her black scarf, slanted to one side on her head as in the old Beirut photographs.

She asked in Arabic for my mother. I told her that she had gone out with my father for some purchases, and I inquired whether she had an appointment with her.

She laughed, "And since when do I need an appointment with your mother?"

I guessed she might be an old friend of my mother's whom I did not know because she had not visited Paris. Perhaps I had seen her in Beirut, for her face was familiar. But I was sure I had not seen her for at least ten years, that is, since we left Beirut and came to live in Paris.

She added, "You've grown up a lot, my dear. I almost did not recognize you."

Something in her look commanded me to invite her in. Something in her presence made me drop formality, contrary to my custom.

I apologized for the dust that covered the floor of the entrance hall. The carpenter, who had come by unexpectedly a little while earlier to hang the new hall mirror, had left behind some dust from drilling the wall. On the floor of the hall, he had also left behind a square pane of glass that he was supposed to use to replace the broken pane in the bathroom window, but he had forgotten to bring his tools and had promised to return on the following day.

When she sat on the soft sofa, I told her about my parents' regular visits to the popular vegetable stalls in certain Parisian districts, where they both were at that moment. I said, "Like most immigrants, we practice our Lebanese identity in the kitchen and through folklore."

She rose from her seat and took off her overcoat, as Beirut women do in the presence of those within the family whom they are legally forbidden to marry. I noticed that the soft sofa where she sat had not sunk under her weight, nor had the cushions changed shape. It was as though a bird had sat on the sofa, not a woman.

She began flicking the beads of an amber rosary. I felt I was in a dream. I usually boasted that I was a rationalist, one who accepted logic, a Cartesian as they would say here in Paris, that is, a follower of Descartes. I therefore began looking for logical answers to these questions: How could this lady know that my real name is 'Abdul Razzaq rather than Abdul? Why did the broken door bell ring under her finger's pressure? Why didn't the soft sofa sink under her weight as she sat? On the other hand, I was not sure that the door bell had rung. Perhaps I had heard her movement at the door and assumed that the bell had rung. As for the sofa, I could not be positive, in that weak light, about the extent of its sinking. To be sure, my nerves were exhausted. Making a decision to marry Nadine was not easy.

She continued to speak with exceeding seriousness as she handled the honey-colored beads of her rosary, "She's a rare white bride, as white as the inner heart of a turnip, as beautiful as the moon. She's illiterate, so that reading might not corrupt her morals. She'll watch television only under your orders. She'll wear red clothing only at home for you. She'd rather have her arm cut off than stretch it out of the doorway for a stranger to see. She'll hang the wash on the roof while veiled, for fear of people's gossip, and for fear of the neighbors' and the devil's eyes. You'll always see her laughing, others will see her frowning. She'll befriend only virtuous women whom you'll choose for her yourself, and she'll expel anyone who will not appeal to you even if it is her own mother. At home, the final word is yours; the duty of obedience is hers. Whatever you tell her, her answer will be, 'You command, master and crown of my head.' She'll not pick flowers from the balcony pots or look out of the window. She'll listen only to religious programs on the radio and to children's programs with her children. She does not smoke and has never even smelled alcoholic drinks. She'll never say words like 'banana,' 'cucumber,' or 'egg,' without adding 'Pardon me,' in order to clear herself of any suspicion of sexual insinuation. She's a fourteen-year-old, good for a lifetime's marriage."

He almost laughed as he imagined the mysterious lady's face if she were to see Nadine, the young woman he intended to ask that very evening to accept him as a husband. She would certainly faint, were she to hear their conversation or see them together. She would not believe it if she was told that girls like Nadine did find husbands. *At that gorgeous dawn, we stood on the bridge near Paris with friends from the sports club. Laughing, they tied Nadine's feet well with rubber ropes. She wanted to try bungee jumping, falling from the bridge into empty space, with her feet tied to rubber ropes that would return her upward like a human yo-yo before she hit the ground.*

She and her friends tried to persuade me to join them. I told them that I had become an old man at thirty-five and did not relish that kind of modern sport, while Nadine was a young woman twenty years old. They laughed at me, and I was ashamed of my cowardice, but I was not ashamed of my love for that beautiful genie called Nadine.

Her family had fled from the war in Lebanon when she was ten. She grew up in Paris and was a brilliant mixture of the magic of East and West. Her hair was like an ancestral cask of honey flowing on both sides of her face, shining with the hope, vitality, and defiant intelligence of a young woman; she was creative in her folly and soared high in her studies. She was a student at the famous institute H. E. C., taking courses in business administration and financial planning— she was not studying home economics and languages while waiting for a bridegroom, like the young women of my family did in Beirut when I was a little boy. I used to see them around me, studying things special to their minds, as my mother used to say, things such as English and French literature, which I myself studied up to the doctoral level.

Nadine, whose height equals mine, pulled me by the hand and forced me to lie down on the ground. She held down my slender, weak body with her strong arms and asked her friends to tie my feet with rubber ropes as I looked up with amazement at her. Her height appeared to be greater and she stood more erect than usual. Her beautiful and firm muscular legs had sport socks covering her knees, so that part of her thighs, between her shorts and socks, were left bare and luscious.

It was another kind of beauty, which did not resemble the semi-flaccid, dough-like beauty of the old cinema stars whose pictures I used to pin up in my Beirut room when I was an adolescent. She appeared to me to be a woman of another kind. I love her because she is so, and I am also apprehensive of her because she is so. What attracts me to her is the same thing that makes me afraid of her. And all that impels me to love her impels me also to fear marrying her.

They bound my feet, laughing, as they shouted in French, "Abdul will jump." Nadine's friend Colette said jokingly that she dreamt of binding all the professors' feet and throwing them from the bridge, provided that the rubber ropes were not good and would snap. They laughed, but I was overwhelmed by a secret terror: I could not jump into empty space that way, even though I was tied to the rubber umbilical cord. Yes, I was afraid. A man and afraid. I had no spirit of adventure. I hated being caught in surprises.

Nadine said, "Give me your hand so that we may jump together."

I said to her, "You jump first and let me think . . . I don't believe you really want to jump. Think how dangerous that is. To jump or not to jump, that is the question."

She said, teasing, "Fine, you Lebanese Hamlet, au revoir." And she stretched out her arms like a bird and jumped into space shouting in French, which she spoke all the time, "Liberté . . ."

She soared in a moment of absolute freedom and appeared to me to be a new kind of sea gull. Then she dropped as though hit by a bullet, finally subject to the law of gravity. She did not utter a sound. My heart sank. What if the rubber rope snapped? Human error was always possible. What if she was to be a victim of human error?

She continued to fall and fall and fall. My heart sank as it always did when I felt things were obeying a logic I had no control of and could not change, a logic in consequence of which I often refused to make final decisions and preferred to avoid them. They accused me of Hamletic cowardice and of inability to make decisions, when, in fact, I was a mere Cartesian who was afraid for his beloved, who continued to fall. Seconds or minutes or hours later—I don't know—she stopped falling, just before reaching the surface of the river. She bounced upward with the power of the rubber rope and began to swing like a human yo-yo, up and down, in that silvery blue space girded with fields and sun *rays, which now appeared to send their greetings of light in all directions. I was terrified to imagine myself in her place, hanging in space. I asked Colette to please help me untie my bonds. I was afraid Nadine would return to the bridge before I was set free and force me to jump. I was afraid of the day when Nadine would be transformed into a huge rook, to whose feathers I would cling in vain—to fly with her in fear.*

The mysterious lady continued to play the role of a matchmaker, embellishing the virtues of her bride-to-be. It would not surprise him if she had pulled the virtues out of her handbag like a snakecharmer. *The matchmaker role did not seem very strange to me after all. I lived in its atmosphere in Beirut in my childhood. The role was occasionally played around us, and some people made fun of it, but it did contribute to contracting a number of marriages. There was no illiterate, self-respecting woman in her fifties who, in those days, did not play the role of a matchmaker to any young man in his twenties. She would meet with him and bring out for him young women from under her cloak like a magician would bring out rabbits from his hat. I thought that this practice had ended with the war, or that the essence of that view of marriage had remained but with modernized ways and means to express it. However, it seems the skeletons have not been fully swept away from the garden of the house.*

He listened to her and tried to hide his feelings with an obscure secret glee as she stated and repeated, without boring him, "You are king of the house and master of all, and she is your bondwoman. When you walk, she will walk behind you at a distance of one step, no more and no less. She will not serve herself until she has first served you the plate with the biggest piece of meat. Your command is obeyed at once, you don't need to repeat it. Her voice will not rise above yours—except during labor pains. She does not understand politics, but she'll go out in any demonstration if you order her to. If you don't like anything she does, you can beat her, discipline her, and teach her how a cat should eat its supper in silence. She's a bride who is too shy to eat a banana in front of people."

The meeting seemed to him to be comical, sad, and enjoyable all at once. *Is it because she reminds me of old glories gone by, of distinctions I used to hold because of the mere fact that I was a male? Or is it because she awakens deep within me another person inhabit-*

ing my body who, I used to think, died and was buried in Paris? Am I happy about my strange meeting with this mysterious matchmaker because she reminds me of my value as a male in my country and in other countries where having certain male organs grants me non-negotiable distinctions and benefits? She reminds me of a time when I was spoiled, when it was enough for me to appear puzzled and maternal and paternal aunts would rush in to offer solutions and services. It was enjoyable to be a man in the Lebanon of yore, and it seems that I liked this lady's recalling of Andalusian masculinity or machismo. My family's old women used to sing popular obscene songs about the male organs of boys, rejoicing in them and taking pride in their future virility in front of the brokenhearted girls of the family.

He looked at his watch, lest he should be late for his appointment with Nadine, to pick her up at the door of her sports club. It was still five o'clock, as though his watch was not running or time had stopped. Yet the mysterious lady continued to finger the beads of her rosary.

It seemed to him that he had seen that amber rosary somewhere, with its rare stones and the age-old insects petrified within their honey-colored transparencies.

The mysterious lady continued, "'Abdul Razzaq, my son, a woman has broken wings. She is nothing without a man. Her worth is derived from that of a man. If she is widowed, she enters her first *'idda*, the legally prescribed period of months during which she may not see a man or remarry. After her *'idda* is terminated, she continues mourning her life in an open-ended *'idda* until God graciously grants her another husband. What is a woman worth if she is not some man's wife or aunt or mother? A woman has broken wings, my son."

She then began to repeat these last words with sorrow, beating her chest with her hands, which were bedecked with rings and old-fashioned Beirut jewelry, twisted bracelets and other trinkets. Tears almost flowed from her eyes like someone weeping for lost time. *A woman has broken wings? I wish she could see my own brokenness before the vigor of Nadine and her tyrannical human presence.*

She was skiing at Megève, and I was watching her, a modern mare from whose hooves snow sparked. Then she came to jest with me, "Didn't Hamlet ski on the snow mountains of Denmark?"

I replied, "I like to let my thoughts ski alone on the hills of memory."

She responded, "O Lebanese Hamlet, running away from action to poetry. Why don't you simply admit that, of physical activities, you only love the sports of the bed?"

I laughed, but inside, I did not. Her frankness and her piercing insight into things exhaust me. Perhaps that's why I love her. She is my opposite, in some sense. She hates illusions and likes to call things by their names, while I am an adherent of the language of allusion, insinuation, and Fayruz's song "Come and Don't Come."

I countered, "And you, aren't you Lebanese like me?"

She answered, "I'm a woman who is modern, realistic, free, independent, in love, and Lebanese. If I have the right to combine all these qualities with my Lebanese identity, then I am Lebanese. I see you clearly and I know your faults. I love you and know I'm riddled with faults. But I want you to love my reality and not an image you draw of me then attempt to force me to be."

"I love you too, to the point of reasonable madness."

"I love you and I'm ready to bind myself to you. But you have to make a decision. There's no escape from facing things. Let's jump together, my dear Hamlet. There's no escape from making decisions in life. This is what I am learning at the institute, the art of decisionmaking."

Trying to avoid a possible quarrel, I said, changing the subject, "Well, I don't like sports and I prefer poetry. This is my right."

She answered, "You hate sports when I practice them, because they mean freedom. Sports are a reflection of the freedom of my soul and my mind, a reflection of your inability to possess me in the Lebanese fashion as my father possesses my mother. At your home, you have a similar model of possession.

"Yes, I am Lebanese. But I am not another copy of my mother. As for you, it is suitable for you to be an image of your father in order to preserve your gains. You want to live your life as though the war did not happen and time did not go by. I came to Paris as a child, and I can't abolish what I saw and learned here. I am a woman different from your mother and mine."

I was brimming with anger but I controlled myself. I said to her, in affected calmness, "But you are Lebanese, too. Do you think that your French citizenship changes anything at all?"

She said, "I am Lebanese in the sense of freedom, in the sense that no male, Lebanese or non-Lebanese, can practice his tyranny over me by some inherited gains I had nothing to do with. The kitchen folklore at our home does not unite us enough to establish a family. I am a woman who will work, who will be free, who will choose whether to bind herself or not."

I thought to myself, "We've now arrived at the crux of the matter." I used the final weapon, saying to her, "You can't work after marrying any man. Who will bring up the children? Who will bear the responsibilities of the home?"

I did not use the words "after our marriage" because I feared getting married to her and I wished it, too, at the same time.

She pressed her luscious lips together and then said, "We will share responsibility. You will then find dozens of ways to run away from your share of it by employing maids, governesses, and the like. And I will follow your example."

She continued with unaffected calmness, "The fact that I keep the egg for nine months does not justify depriving me of my civil rights. I don't want to be an employee of my husband, that is, a home secretary. I too have my work, my world, my torments, my thoughts. You are part of my life, not the center of it. Marriage is no longer a part of a man's life and the end of a woman's. Love is part of their life together, not the center of it. I love you but . . . and the word 'but' is more important than the expression 'I love you.'"

I did not tell her that my tragedy was that love was the center of my life and that there were moments in which I felt I wanted to possess her, to burn her as the poet Dīk al-Jinn had done with his beloved, and to make from her ashes a vessel which I would continue to drink from until my final victory over her. That was not true, but it was not fully untrue, either. For, on the other hand, I loved her head and didn't want to cut it off on the wedding night or later on. I preferred to have an understanding with her.

Perhaps I was a Lebanese Hamlet. I knew all the possibilities and studied matters from all angles but knew nothing except that time was passing, the world was changing, and I was at a loss.

That evening she granted me her body in all simplicity, with spontaneity and innocence, like the sand on the beach stretching out under the warm body of the night. I remembered Dalal and my adolescence in Beirut; I remembered how she withdrew before her last castle fell, as though she was implementing a studied plan to show me what I would lose if I did not marry her. On that day, Dalal had offered me her apples, let me run in her orchards, touch her apples, smell them, kiss them, play with them as I wished, provided I did not bite one apple until the wedding night. Nadine did not know such cunning viciousness.

The mysterious lady prepared herself to leave. 'Abdul Razzaq did not know why he wanted to keep her a little longer to hear more about the qualities of the possible bride. She did not withhold further information from him: obedience, contentment, shy beauty on the very important wedding night. *Then I would play the role of actor as I dreamt in adolescence two decades ago— when I would sign my name in the blood of her wound on a white cloth, the cloth which, until recently, they would take around among relatives and close ones, while beating drums for seven days and seven nights, indicating that there was yet another virgin of the tribe who had been deflowered in accordance with ancestral tradition.*

The mysterious matchmaker asked him whether he wished for a blonde or a brunette, a tall or a medium height bride. Her voice faded away in his ears as if he was hypnotized . . . *On the beach at Juan-les-Pins, before Nadine took off her clothes, except for the fig leaf, in front of me, in order to stretch out on the warm sand and become an extension of it, she said to me, "I'm not a virgin."*

She was not baring herself to me alone, nor to the other beach goers, but to the sun and to herself as she said, laughing, "Why is it your right to enjoy the sunshine on your breast and it is not mine? Is it because I have breasts to suckle babies? How can your or my additional flesh be a source of regulations and social laws?"

I thought to myself, "She is beautiful and it pleases me to see her semi-naked, but it annoys me that others see her too, and it kills me to know she is not a virgin. I want her for myself alone. I want to tame that tigress, to possess her. My pleasure will be greater later, the more difficult the taming is."

She spoke calmly, "Does the fact that I am not a virgin annoy you?"

I answered in a similar but affected calm, "Yes, it annoys me. Who is the one who—"

She interrupted, "Do you mean you're virgin?"

I replied, "I'm a man."

She said, "And I'm a woman. Your being a man doesn't grant you any inherited gains, in my opinion."

I asked, "Who is he?"

She replied, "Who is she?"

I answered, "I'm not saying."

She responded, "Nor am I. Do you think I'll carve a memorial monument for every whim, adventure, or exploratory desire of mine? Remember what I tell you: I am exactly like you, with all your exalted-ness, your whims, your desires. You can't suppress me in France with the authority of society or the law, as is the case in our country. If this annoys you, it is better for you to find a matchmaker who will find you a bride whose mouth no one but her mother has ever kissed, who is quiet and obedient, as my mother says in her proverbial maxims. Here I am, a woman who does not feel guilty for merely having been born a woman, and who does not apologize even for her whims—like any man—and you can't possess her unless she loves you."

I almost said to her, "Then marry a Frenchman." But I remembered that some Frenchmen, too, would not accept her conditions. I spoke no more, for she is too beautiful for anyone to hurt her with words.

The mysterious lady rose up, saying, "I'm late. I can't stay any longer." She said goodbye to 'Abdul Razzaq without shaking hands with him. He asked her to leave her address so that his mother might get in touch with her when she returned. She said, "Getting in touch with me is difficult. I'll get in touch with her myself."

It seemed to 'Abdul Razzaq that her image was not reflected in the entrance hall mirror as she passed before it. He looked at her old-fashioned dress, similar to those in the family album, as she put on her long, black overcoat, resembling a cloak, then walked toward the door in her antiquated, out-of-fashion shoes. He did not know why he experienced an overwhelming desire to stop her. He did not want her to go.

He said to her. "Wait for my mother. She'll return soon."

She answered in a serious tone, "I no longer can, my son. I must go."

She hurried, stepping inattentively on the pane of glass which the carpenter had left on the floor. It did not break under her feet.

The elevator arrived. Its door opened. The next-door neighbor stepped out, and he greeted her. The mysterious matchmaker disappeared into the elevator.

He asked the neighbor about the weather as she took out her keys.

She answered, "It's fine. But why haven't you taken the elevator if you are going out?"

He answered, "I was saying goodbye to the lady."

She asked, "What lady? I didn't see anyone."

He returned to the apartment. The visit seemed to him to be unreal and real at the same time, as in a dream.

In the ashtray, he did not see any ash from the cigarette which she had smoked and which had attracted his attention by the strange name, Hanum, on the packet as well as by its dark red butt. It was a cigarette the like of which he had never seen. Nor did he see traces of her steps in the dust on the entrance hall floor, which was covered with traces of only his own steps, going back and forth. The pane of glass which he had seen her step on was even unscratched.

He rushed to the balcony and saw her. She was leaving the building and crossing the street heedlessly, turning to see nothing, inattentive even to the car that hit her.

He ran madly to the elevator, then to the door of the building, terrified at the scene he expected to see—the lady stretched out on the pavement, dying, while the porter of the building and the passers-by surrounded her. *Poor woman, had she come to die at our home?*

He reached the street. He did not see her and everything was going on normally.

He asked the porter of the building about the lady just hit by a car. The porter told him that nothing of the sort had happened.

'Abdul Razzaq insisted that from his balcony he had seen a car hit a lady. The porter told him he had seen and heard nothing.

'Abdul maintained that the lady hit by the car was a lady visiting him, and he described her to the porter. The latter assured him that he had not left his place in the glass cubicle opposite the door and had not opened the electrically controlled door to such a lady.

Confused, 'Abdul Razzaq returned to the apartment. *I am certainly imagining things. The neighbor did not see her in the elevator.*

The porter of the building did not see her enter or leave. The broken door bell did not ring. The pane of glass did not break under her feet. The sofa had no trace of her sitting on it. The ash of her cigarette disappeared, like her, because she simply did not come. My nerves are certainly exhausted as a result of my decision to marry Nadine, and perhaps I should reconsider the matter. However, the rosary was still on the table, where the guest had forgetfully left it. He dared not touch it. He was afraid it, too, might be an illusion like its owner.

He entered his parents' room, "the room of memories" as he liked to call it, as though he were someone searching for an answer. His memory became refreshed and began to send him vague signals.

He sat on the armchair, whose arms were decorated with his mother's crochet. The room was half-dark with the curtains always drawn, as his mother liked to keep them, perhaps in order to imagine that the sea was still just behind the window and the room was still in Beirut. Confused, 'Abdul Razzaq looked around at the paintings like one seeing them for the first time, paintings by Omar Onsi, Mustafa Farroukh, and George Dawud Corm. His parents had carried them with them from the "good old days," as everyone called the time before the war in Beirut.

He contemplated the lace bedcover which his mother had made, though her hands hurt with arthritis. He contemplated the mirror, framed in hammered silver, made in Lebanon, and slightly tarnished with attractive and venerable rust. He contemplated his father's whip hanging on the wall, suspended like a flag at half-staff that no longer had any strength to be erect.

He studied a table with a tablecloth of rich Lebanese brocade. On it were old family pictures he used to dislike and run away from. He wanted to belong to where he was with all his strength and leave his old parents to the past of memory.

In the weak light, he contemplated his own picture as a child, and those of his sisters and brothers, who were all older than he. Some of them had killed the others in the war, but in the pictures they were hugging one another. *These are the pictures of the family of Abel and Cain. The room is drowned in a gray light, between black and white, like dawn or sunset. And my heart is drowned in the same kind of light.*

This then is my picture as a child, when I was seven years old. On my face is a look of self-assurance that is not visible in the eyes of my sisters, perhaps because I was a boy in a family that loved boys or because I used to think I would remain the only boy after the death of the other "fighting" brothers, the youngest boy specially favored and spoiled by the maternal and paternal aunts and the other women of the family.

For the first time, 'Abd al-Razzaq wasted his time nostalgically staring at things in the room, as someone saying goodbye to a fleeting moment gradually disappearing in the dim light.

These pictures were always here and I did not see them. I was preoccupied with my life and distracted from them. It did not occur to me at all that they were part of me, with their mothballs, their dust, and their mysterious incense resembling the memory of a scent.

He contemplated the remaining pictures without dusting them off. His mother left them covered with dust, although she dusted everything else in the room.

He stared at the picture of his mother as a beautiful young woman, full of vitality. She stood under the wing of his slender and tender father, who had a smile full of contentment. He saw another picture of his mother surrounded by her sisters. Suddenly he froze, as though he was thunderstruck. *My God, this is my maternal aunt Badriyya standing beside my mother. I remember her. It is she, in all certainty.*

His eyes were fixed on her. He remembered she died of cancer when he was only eight. He was told that she had loved him as the son she never had because she never married. She was neither beautiful nor white, faults the matchmakers did not easily forgive.

His heart beat like a crazy drum. He was sure of a truth that there was no way to prove: the woman who visited him and asked for his mother was his maternal aunt Badriyya, or she resembled the woman in the picture, his aunt Badriyya, very much. *She even wore the same clothes as in the picture and had the same slanted scarf. I mean she resembles my aunt very much, for it is not reasonable that she is actually my aunt, since her bones became dust a long time ago.*

He felt at a loss. He heard a key unlocking the outer door and did not move. He heard his mother and father exchange congratulations for successfully obtaining gourds and endive from the stall opposite the Lutecia Hotel.

He did not move. His mother called him. He did not move. He heard her saying to his father, "What brought this rosary here? It is the rosary of my sister Badriyya, may God have mercy on her. She recited the Samadiyya prayer ten times with it when 'Abdul Razzaq was born."

He did not move.

She said in surprise, "Who brought it out from my suitcases in the basement?"

He did not move.

He heard his father say, "I don't remember it was in the basement suitcases. Perhaps we got it out from the bedroom closet when we arranged the closets a few days ago."

The telephone rang. 'Abdul Razzaq did not move. He was overwhelmed by confusion.

His mother entered the room. She found him sitting. Startled, she gulped, then she asked, "What are you doing here? Are you sick, sweetheart?"

He did not answer. He tried to tell her something about the guest who had come during her absence, but he fell silent as though the visit was his alone. His mother repeated her question. He said, "Nothing. I was only contemplating these pictures. This lady standing next to you in the picture, isn't she my aunt Badriyya?"

"Yes, she is. You were her favorite. and we used to joke about her enthusiasm for matchmaking, for she loved that role without being asked by anyone to play it. You were a child and yet she chose brides for you. If she were alive today, she would not have let you be what you are—an unmarried old man with a balding head."

She continued, redressing herself, "Pardon me. I didn't know you were here. Nadine called a minute ago and asked about you and I told her you were not here."

He looked at his watch. It was a quarter past five. *Time has then resumed its movement.*

As someone coming back to consciousness, he rose in a rush saying, "I have an appointment with her in fifteen minutes."

Before leaving home, he noticed the rosary of his aunt Badriyya on the table. He held it tenderly and thrust it in his pocket.

He drove out of the garage in his car, still exhausted, confused, and not knowing what was happening to him.

At the corner, he noticed his aunt Badriyya running in the streets of Paris, the cars were hitting her but she did not mind and continued to run before his eyes.

Now and then, he tenderly touched her rosary in his pocket and was amazed. *Who brought out this rosary from the boxes of time? Is it possible that I could have done it unconsciously?*

At the sports club entrance, Nadine was standing waiting for him. *How beautiful she is, how splendid with her healthy, youthful arms, her desirable, sportive thighs, and her full breasts ready for many things, among them suckling, as well as bungee jumping in empty space for adventure.*

She said to him, playfully, as usual, "Welcome, Lebanese Hamlet."

He pulled his hand out of his pocket, letting go of his aunt's rosary, in order to embrace Nadine with his arms, his heart, his body, and all the feelings he had. *Damn her, how I love her and hate her, how I miss her and fear her. But so long as I cannot behead the cat, nor even cut off its tail, I must think thoroughly. I wonder, can I jump with her from the bridge? To jump or not to jump, that is the question. Or rather, that is one of the many questions. No, I don't dare.*

As they drove off, he thought he saw his aunt Badriyya again, and the Paris cars hitting her. *I will not propose to her tonight, although I firmly decided this morning to do so. I should think it over again, for a long, long time. Here I am, my feet tied with a rubber rope, hanging over an abyss, merely another frightened human*

*yo-yo. My fate is toying with me, up and down. Yes. No. I'll marry
her. No, I don't dare. Yes, I will. No, I don't dare. Yes. No. Yes. No.*

He noticed his aunt Badriyya walking slowly in the middle
of the half-dark street as though she was lost. Lest he should hit
her, he stopped the car until she crossed. In her usual impetu-
ous way, Nadine said, "Why have you stopped, when the street
is empty and the signal is green?" He did not answer. He drove
on, but his hand groped for his aunt Badriyya's rosary in his
pocket and he grasped it in the dark.

The Metallic Crocodile

The chilly wind blew mercilessly on a long queue of human beings who seemed to be featureless in the darkness of the winter dawn. They stood in line like ghosts on the sidewalk, as though they were members of a secret organization for lamentation and self-torture.

Sulayman bent down and squatted. He withdrew within himself like one nursing a wound. He tried in vain to cover his face with the collar flaps of his overcoat. *What am I doing here?*

In the biting cold, my toothache is acting up again. If an astrologer had told me, when I was a young man immersed in the warmth of the Beirut beaches, that I would stand in front of a Paris police station a decade and a half later in 1985, immersed in humiliation at five o'clock, at dawn, waiting for the doors to open while the thermometer was at five degrees below zero, I would have scoffed at him, secure as I was in my Beirut empire.

In those days, I practiced amateur fishing from the beach rocks of Ras Beirut and felt my body to be part of the rock underneath it as it was firmly positioned on it. My father used to say, repeating the popular proverb against leaving one's birthplace, "A stone in place weighs a ton."

His tooth pulsated with pain radiating in all directions.

He almost regretted the fact that he was there. *I should have written a letter to the French police commissioner, complaining of this daily humiliation of foreigners in the cold—as Layla had done in*

protest, then carried her baby Firas and returned with him to Beirut—
saying that she would rather die under the shelling than undergo
this silent humiliation in the cold.

But what can I write to the police commissioner? Do my country-
men treat me any better than his men? Will I tell him that I am not
running away from the shelling but from what is worse and more
calamitous? Why will I blame him, when the corpse of my country hangs
around my neck, continuously reminding me of the tragedies of chaos?

We fought one another until blood ran all over our faces, corpses
accumulated on our carpets and in our cups of coffee, and everything
collapsed on our heads amid applause, ardent speeches, and political posters flying with shots fired in joy—and we ended up with this
inevitable humiliation. Returning to Beirut simply means I will be
killed by Abul-Mahawil.

I did not know that the lady who came to ask me that her husband's sexual organ be "bound" (in jinn language) to exclude any
other female human being—that is, that he be deprived of his sexual
powers (in modern language)—was the wife of the militia leader
Abul-Mahawil, in the shop next to mine.

At the beginning, Abul-Mahawil's clients were more numerous
than mine but, one by one, they began to come to me, and with them
came some of his own armed men, and they consulted me regarding
political matters. in addition to consulting me regarding their lifeline.

I was a fortuneteller, an astrologer, a magician. I did not really
mind what they called me as long as they continued to pay me more
and more. I had two wives, and seven children who needed school-
ing, food, medical care, and there were other expenses.

When she came to see me like any other unknown, rich client,
Abul-Mahawil's wife told me that her husband had betrayed her with
a beautiful woman, whose picture she showed me in the social pages
of a magazine. She told me that a friend of hers had whispered that
fact to her. She confronted her husband with it, but he explained that
what he was doing was "a national duty." He went to high-society
evening parties with "a tactical strategy" and was sometimes obliged
to cheat on her. She assured me, as she wept, that she understood
none of his pretexts but that she knew he was disloyal to her.

I was surprised at the story and wondered whether meanness could ever be a national duty. But I did what was necessary, knowing that it was neither beneficial nor harmful, and that it might increase her self-confidence and consequently help her regain her husband. I did not know that he was Abul-Mahawil.

He discovered the amulet that she had thrust in his bed. He interrogated her in his special ways which no one could resist, then came to me fuming, armed with a loaded gun.

I threatened him with demons and ghosts, and with a curse on him and his progeny. I was astonished when he was afraid of that and was content to ask me to undo the magic binding him and then emigrate.

Like everyone else, he feared the unknown powers. So did I, but I had none of them.

A long time ago, my poor father practiced sleight-of-hand tricks at nightclubs, cabarets, and evening parties, and he taught me many of the tricks. I decided to make more money than he did, and work less, so I put up a sign on my door: The Great Astrologer. I was surprised at the number of swarming clients, and I was getting rich quickly, like one scooping from a gold mine. All that fear of the unknown in their hearts was transformed into checks on my desk and gold ingots in my safe.

My father had said, "Sleight-of-hand tricks are an art, but magical charlatanry is imposture. There are rare people endowed by God with secret powers to move physical things with their spiritual will and to speak with the world beyond. But you are not among them, my son."

I had said, "What's the difference, so long as the clients are happy? You've retired, father, and my children are at school and are growing up. And I've become capable of marrying a third wife!"

The lady standing in the queue in front of Sulayman bent over, then squatted on the ground with her blonde companion, muttering an abuse in the Lebanese dialect, "D——— this biting cold."

She was Lebanese, then. He tried to speak to her and her companion, and seek shelter in the warmth of friendly togetherness. But he found out that his voice was frozen, and that his throat had become an ice cave and his tooth an ember exploding with burning pain.

He turned around and saw a black man behind him and a long line of people who had arrived after them.

Sulayman tried to turn his head forward. He could not, because the slim black man behind him, who had a towering height and resembled a skeleton with a huge skull, was staring at him with odd, fearful eyes, like two bulging balls, and looked like a creature from outer space. His eyes were fixed on Sulayman with a secret light that paralyzed him and perplexed him, despite his being in pain and feeling cold. Sulayman sensed something extraordinary. *My father said to me, "I'll take you to a man with really secret powers."*

In the presence of the fortuneteller who could really read thoughts and other things, I was overwhelmed by a paralyzing and perplexing sensation as I fell under the spell of black rays penetrating me like x-rays, almost fathoming the caves of my soul. On that day, I felt as though I was bare in front of him, and I was afraid.

It was the same feeling that overwhelmed him under the black man's looks, making him forget the biting cold and the fierce wind. *I love black people, perhaps because my skin is dark brown and I am almost half-black in a sense, and perhaps because they are—or I imagine they are—suffering like me, and we are unloved by the refined world of snow.*

The black man turned his eyes away from him and looked at a huge, terrifying dog that came out of the dark, barking at the line of ghosts standing in front of the door before dawn and seeking official papers which would permit them to reside in Paris. Anyone coming at nine, when the daily office hours began, would spend the rest of the day waiting, without having the opportunity of admission on account of the crowd.

The dog coming out of the cold barked as though to chase them away. It walked along the queue of frozen people, planting terror in their confused souls. Sulayman almost laughed in misery at this newcomer that added to his feeling of subjugation. The dog favored him with its bark, and one of the two Lebanese women clung to him in fear as they both rose up to their feet. The dog left them to favor the black man with its agitation. The black man did not appear to be afraid and did not move from his place. He stared at the dog with looks like invisible laser rays. The barking subsided and the dog withdrew, scared, and suddenly started whining in a way that was full of pain.

One day, I surreptitiously hit the dog belonging to the "heroes"
who owned the shop next to mine with a stone and it began to whine
in pain. I was ashamed and regretted it, because I had not dared hit
the dog's owner once.

The dog ran away, withdrawing backward, whining in pain
but not daring to turn its back to the black man.

Commenting on the black man's strength, Sulayman said in
Arabic to the Lebanese woman, "Don't fear, sister. In the queue,
there are men who will protect you!"

She answered in a sarcastic way he did not expect, "I'm in
no need of men to protect me. I'm here because I've run away
from their protection."

He did not want to pick a quarrel and said, "Forgive me, sister. I did not mean to hurt your feelings."

Her companion said in a loud, aggressive voice, "Some of our
country's males treated us as the dictator treated them. We'll
never forgive either of them."

Sulayman was alarmed at this aggressiveness. He was accustomed to treating brokenhearted women kindly but did not know
how to talk to this kind.

She went on, "We continue to accuse 'the conspiracy' and
ignore our responsibility for our own misery."

Sulayman could hardly believe his ears. Could anyone speak
in this way, at six o'clock in the morning when it was five degrees
below zero?

They both continued to spurt their worries in an explosion
resembling hysteria: "The males are the ones responsible. They
destroyed our country."

One said, "Naturally, because the men alone rule us. They
flee from one humiliation, we flee from two. We're all fleeing!"

The other said, "Oh, nothing unites the Arabs but their backward view of women."

Sulayman's toothache came back severely as he listened to
the two Lebanese women angrily pouring out their feelings of
suppression. He felt a certain apprehension because he thought
them to be unbalanced. *They are both crazy, it appears. But who*
is not, among us? What if they discover I am married to two women

and dream of marrying a third? They'll break my neck here and now,
on the sidewalk. No. The one with the long nails will dig her fingers
into my heart, like a knife. How I fear women, and love them.

Sulayman took refuge in silence, his show of chivalry having
been met only with scolding by the two women.

He turned to the black man, as if responding to a soft voice
he heard and did not hear. His toothache made him almost cry
again. He heard a soundless voice within his head clearly saying
to him, "Your tooth aches, doesn't it?"

His heart was filled with fear and amazement. Not since he
visited the man with secret powers in Beirut had anyone spoken to him thus, by telepathy.

The soundless voice repeated, "Your tooth aches, doesn't it?"

He answered, soundlessly, "Yes. Oh, how this cursed tooth
hurts me! But how did you know that?"

"You've deafened me with your continuous cry of pain since
my arrival."

Has my toothache pushed me into delirium and madness?

"No, you're fine, rest assured. I'll try to help you. Turn toward
me and stare deep into my eyes. Relax gradually, and let my cry
enter you."

He turned to the black man behind him, whose eyes were
like two remote bright lights at the end of a sad, dark street washed
by the rain, in the space between wonder, tenderness, and weeping. He almost relaxed, remembering what happened in sessions of hypnosis, then he shook in fear. *I don't hear a voice and*
yet I'm aware that something is being said to me, within my head.
What's happening to me? Perhaps my toothache, combined with this
humiliating wait in the cold has caused me to hallucinate and rave.

The soundless voice said to him, "I'm speaking to you without sound or language, so don't be afraid. Stare into my eyes.
You see nothing but them and hear nothing but my voice. Here
now is a warm wave that overwhelms you. You are no longer
standing on the cold sidewalk. You are wrapped in a wave of
warmth and your tooth is no longer part of you. You have separated it from yourself, you have secluded it. It hurts you no more.
It has no longer the ability to hurt you."

Sulayman surrendered to the voice talking to him in a friendly, quiet, and semi-commanding tone.

A policeman passed by them and yawned as he reviewed the queue.

Sulayman thought to himself, "I'm certainly raving because of the pain and the cold." At the same time, he was amazed that he no longer felt the cold or his toothache as much. *Pain becomes intense then it subsides. Perhaps the cold has begun to recede. It is almost seven o'clock. Half the suffering is gone.* He could not believe that this black man's staring at him was the cause of his relief from pain, as it had been a moment earlier the cause of the dog's terror, pain, and withdrawal. He could not be a real magician.

He heard the soundless voice answering his thoughts, "Yes. I am a real magician who comes from the jungles of secrecy. I am a descendant of a noble family of magicians from a famous African tribe and am not a strange charlatan like you."

Sulayman did not know whether he was a victim of his own imaginings. Did he think this black man was a magician simply because he had looks he imagined to be piercing, because his own toothache subsided as if by hypnotism, because the dog ran away in fear for an unknown reason, or was the man really talking to him by telepathy instead of speech, and did he really possess secret powers? *Is he the one who made the two Lebanese women standing in front of me hold their tongues completely? Or did they become tired and so hug the wall more closely in a semi-unconscious manner? I am exhausted and time is long.*

Sulayman heard the soundless voice saying to him, "Don't be afraid, time will pass quickly. You will sleep without sleeping, and you will not wake up until the doors open."

Again, Sulayman was wrapped up within himself on the sidewalk near the two women, thrusting his body against the stony womb of the wall. *Is this man a real magician? I've dreamt since childhood of seeing a magician. I always imagined him with a goatee, elegantly dressed in Ali Baba clothes, and with a King Solomon ring on his finger. It did not occur to me that he would be a black man, with a strange appearance and tattered clothes, whom I would meet on a certain miserable day at dawn in Paris.*

It was nine o'clock and the doors of hope in the walls of the police headquarters near Notre Dame Cathedral were opened. The sun was shining bright, but it was cold, metallic, mean, and sent icy rays full of black humor that made fun of warmth. Perhaps it was five degrees below zero, as the weather man promised the clients of sorrow at the city gates.

Sulayman felt that the cold sun electrified visible things with a secret, unseen threat.

The queue of tired people was ready. They entered, one cold body after another.

Sulayman stepped at last on the high threshold. The policewoman examined his papers. As he passed through the metal detector at the door, it whistled. He emptied his pockets of all metal pieces, overcome by fear. *How fearful I have become of policemen and of everyone wearing an official uniform, be it a militia man or a doctor in a white smock!*

After he passed through the metal detector again, he took back his metal things and walked on.

He followed the crowd moving toward a little square room of glass, on one side of which was a window with a policewoman sitting behind it.

Sulayman was about to be suffocated within the transparent sardine can of packed human beings. He turned around looking for the black man. He saw him in his place behind him and heard a soundless voice: "Don't be afraid. Your ribs won't break, I'll push back the glass a little."

Sulayman felt some relative calm as the human river swayed, and he finally reached the window and got a number that permitted him to move to the large waiting room.

The room resembled a theater with many policewomen, autocratic as he imagined them to be, judging from the confident way they sat and the haughty looks some of them had. Every autocratic policewoman sat at a high desk on a wooden platform behind a window. It was within their capacity to facilitate matters or make them difficult for unwanted foreigners.

Sulayman sat on a long wooden bench, waiting to hear his number called out. His heart trembled with fear. He tried to prepare persuasive answers to all the questions he imagined would be asked. Next to him sat the black man, as though he was his guardian angel or his companion demon.

Sulayman scrutinized the faces of the policewomen. His profession had taught him to try to discern people's inner worlds from their facial features. *This blonde seems to be arrogant and harsh. The black woman next to her will be kind with people, for she is black and is herself certainly subject to some discrimination. This third woman, oh, how beautiful she is! What is she doing here? And this fourth. . . and the fifth . . . and the ninth.*

He was bored. His eyes searched for the two Lebanese women who ardently supported women's liberation. He saw them standing. He thought of gallantly rising to give them his seat. But he decided to leave them alone, so long as they wanted equality. He was rather afraid that, if he offered them his seat, they would insult him and remind him that they, too, had legs.

He stayed sitting and fully attentive, lest he should miss hearing his number when a policewoman called it out.

He looked again at the black policewoman, hoping he would be lucky and she would be the one calling out his number. He heard the soundless voice talking to him in his head without language: "Don't let appearances deceive you. Try learning to penetrate to the essence. You are not as bad a charlatan as you imagine. You have some power, but you don't know how to use it well."

Sulayman turned to his neighbor, the black man, whose face was like one of those marble statues on the beach of a far-off island that he had seen in pictures. It was a face of lofty stone, flung on an eternal beach of secrets, as though it was that of the mariner of delirium.

The black policewoman's voice rose. She was scolding a North African, who as a consequence appeared to be shaking at the shock of humiliation and insult.

The soundless voice said to him, "Do you now understand what I mean? Logic prevents you from seeing reality. You imagine people are mere dolls. They are more complex than that. A humiliated and insulted person is not necessarily kind to people like him. He may rather become an executioner to them, like this black policewoman. In order to know people, you have to go under their skin and their teeth. By the way, does your tooth still ache, Sulayman?"

"No. Thanks. But how did you know my name?"

He could hardly believe that this was happening to him. He was terrified. *Have I begun to hear voices and go crazy?*

He stared at his neighbor, the black man, who turned to the other side. The scent of dark jungles full of mystery and wealth came from him, and Sulayman heard the soundless voice saying to him, "And I am called Dunga."

The black policewoman was railing at another foreigner. She appeared to Sulayman to be an example of that kind of person who would humiliate others unjustifiably and enjoy oppressing them publicly. Here she was, treating with extreme politeness another applicant for residence who was a Western man, to judge by his fair complexion and features, only to turn later to a poor man of the yellow race, who appeared to Sulayman to be a restaurant servant, and berate him.

He heard a voice within him saying, "She is always like that. She remedies her own oppression by oppressing others. I have known her for years, so has everyone who has visited this earthly hell."

Sulayman was afraid. This soundless voice within him was not his own, for he did not know any such information about the black policewoman and was coming here for the first time. Or was he imagining the story of her life oppressing people like him?

There was a nearby window that was ajar, from which the cold was coming in on Sulayman's tooth and reviving his pain. He felt humiliated because he did not dare rise and close it, lest he should anger one of the policewomen.

"I'll close it for you."

The black man stared at the window and it began to close very slowly as if an invisible wind was blowing it shut.

Nearby, a woman's baby started crying again. The black man, Dunga, stared at the baby, and he became quiet. *It is surely a coincidence. It is the wind that shut the window. As for the baby, well, I, too, was staring at him, and so were all those present. When a baby cries, one cannot help staring at him. But, no. I do know that the staring of my neighbor, Dunga, is different. I have no proof of that. On the other hand, how did my toothache cease spontaneously? How did time pass quickly and how did I feel no cold? Why did the dog run away scared? How do I know that his name is Dunga? I don't*

know how I know. But is his name really Dunga? He heard the soundless voice: "This is true knowledge. It gushes within you from secret inner fountains which join you to the First Fountain. Beware of setting up barriers of logic between you and the irrational, the metaphysical, and the secret."

The black policewoman called out a number, not Sulayman's. He sighed like someone who escaped a trap, but Dunga stood up and went toward her. Sulayman pitied him. *She will now flay him and hang his slim body at the entrance of her booth. She will cut off his huge skull and nail it on the trees of her jungle, next to those of thousands of foreigners she oppressed.*

The blonde policewoman called out Sulayman's number, but he hardly heard her because he was preoccupied with concern for his mysterious friend, Dunga. Despite his fear of his own policewoman, he wondered, "Will the black woman be merciful to Dunga, a fellow man from the same continent, jungles, and blood . . . from her own blood and roots?"

Questions rained down on Sulayman, politely and without aggressiveness. How much money do you have? Where will you work? Where do you live? Do you have the electricity bills to prove it? Do you have on you a copy of your work contract? The policewoman filled in a line he had missed in the application. *This blonde policewoman, who I thought, was arrogant, is very kind and quiet, and she's sympathetic to the Lebanese.* Everything went well with his interrogator. She asked politely and respectfully, and he poured out the details.

He said, "I am an astrologer, a fortuneteller. I know the future and play with people's destinies. I currently work at an Arab nightclub and entertain clients with my magic, until I can put my affairs in order."

She appeared to be very interested in his work and full of respect for his capabilities. He felt almost bewildered at her beauty, her kindness, and her hunger for the mysterious unknown.

He offered to read her palm.

She smiled, "Not here, I'm working."

He added, "Free."

She laughed sweetly.

Next to him, there was shouting. The black policewoman
was giving Dunga a dressing down. She properly called him Mr. Dunga. That was his name, then. Sulayman trembled, wondering, *"How did I know his name? Therefore, what happened did really happen. But if he is a capable magician, he would have prevented this policewoman from publicly humiliating him thus, he would have bewitched her with his looks and punished her for her evil deeds, she being the one who so badly insults her own black people.*

Sulayman turned to Dunga with some pity, his self-pride having been refreshed by the policewoman's interest and kindness. Like all fortunate people, he was now able to distribute his tenderness to those present.

Sulayman saw Dunga as a mass of black light shining with anger as the policewoman still harassed him. He did not know why he feared Dunga! *No gloating over what's happening to creatures of such dense spiritual presence as this kind, meek, mysterious, and fierce black man . . . If I were in her place, I would be really afraid of him.* Preparing himself to leave the hall, Sulayman saw the black policewoman collecting her things, then passing by him as she left. *It's time for her lunch break, then, after she practiced her harshness and devoured this poor black man and dozens of others like him and caused them pain by betraying her own blood.*

Sulayman left the hall from another door designated as an exit. He held the heavy door for Dunga and let him pass before him in a gesture of friendliness. He walked beside him with human sympathy that had no language, exchanging not a single word with him that had a sound. He heard the soundless voice without a language whispering in his head: "I'm angry now and can no longer calm your toothache, so excuse me. I'm very angry. I now have another concern. I'll focus my energy on another target."

Sulayman talked to himself, like any Lebanese who wanted no trouble. *Oh, when can I return to my furnished room, sleep for a few hours, and forget this delirious morning, which ended well with* *the acceptance of my application for temporary residence? When will the magician Dunga and the two angry Lebanese women become a passing nightmare to be forgotten? A glass of whiskey, a warm bath, a rich meal, a stroll on the Champs Elysées to look at the legs of beautiful women, and everything will be over . . . Tomorrow, I'll look for an apartment for my business. Rich female immigrants will come to me with their worries, their confounded wombs—girl or boy, pregnancy or no pregnancy—and also with their jewelry and wealth. When the shelling stops and the war ends—for every war must end— I'll return to Beirut and resume my former life. All the shops will fold up one day, and my shop alone will flourish. I alone will remain, because I am planted in the souls. I may be a swamp, but I feed on the sediments of the Fountain of Truth; mine will be the shop deriving the light from . . . Oh, my tooth aches again.* Sulayman's thoughts and dreams were torn as that soundless voice made its presence felt. "Beware of playing around with the truth to the benefit of a partial lie. The truth exists, even if you trade in it and don't believe it."*

He did not know whether it was his voice or Dunga's.

He turned to the black man, who was still walking near him, and he felt electrified by some magnetic, spiritual currents which almost smothered him as though the pressure of an exceptional explosion had emptied the street of air. *Why doesn't he leave me alone? Is he my companion demon?* He noticed that the harsh black policewoman was walking in front of them. *What prompted her to leave her workplace now? Is it her lunch hour or is there something I don't know and she doesn't know that took her out of her seat of authority? This matter does not concern me, at any rate.*

He continued walking to the Metro, while Dunga walked beside him with a dark current of energy gushing like a waterfall from his protuberant eyes, which were fixed on the black policewoman. Sulayman noticed that she walked quickly, as if hurrying to keep an appointment or a meeting she could not miss. The roar of the dark waterfall gushing in spiritual currents from Dunga's whole being was almost deafening to his ears.

He imagined he also heard the beating of angry drums, the tam-tam songs, and the primitive, clandestine incantations of the tribe, and he saw Dunga, with his awesome height, in the clothes of the tribe's magician. It was as though the black policewoman heard the same sounds as Sulayman, mixed with the roar of the dark waterfall of an invisible geography of a spiritual land in which the three of them moved. Bared of her position and authority, she looked back at Dunga as if she was seeing him well for the first time. Sulayman imagined he saw a real look of terror in her eyes. There was a car in the street, running toward her without a driver , and the black woman was like a half-hypnotized person, walking steadily to meet it. Sulayman and Dunga took a few steps back to avoid the car.

The car continued to move with increasing speed. Sulayman tried to warn the black policewoman by shouting, but an invisible hand held his mouth and paralyzed his throat. With true alarm sweeping through his limbs, he noticed that he was not imagining things. The car had no driver, but it was advancing toward the black woman as if an unknown power was moving it from a distance by remote control. He also noticed that the car was accelerating in an illogical manner, in silence, and without motor running—like a ghost. It finally swept away the black policewoman, hitting her with a fierce lightning blow which threw her into the air like a sacrificial animal cast in the primitive jungles to the god of punishment, and her handbag flew away. In an extraordinary moment, she appeared to rise in the air as though thrown by a giant force. After her swift flight, she landed on the sharp, spear-like, iron teeth of a backhoe that was being used for work on road repair next to the nearby flower market, which was never without flesh-eating equatorial roses.

Horrified and bewildered, Sulayman saw her body suspended from the backhoe's metallic teeth, her blood flowing and her eyes petrified in a look of terror.

All this happened in a wink of an eye, like the flash of a camera. That dark current of waterfalls and of unknown energies which moved things started now to gush aimlessly in all directions, overwhelming him, deafening him, and blinding him; then it slowly subsided and disappeared like water returning to its natural channels after a flood.

Overwhelmed and bewildered, Sulayman stopped not far from the corpse of the black woman suspended from the backhoe's teeth that looked like the metallic teeth of a remarkable crocodile.

A policeman ran, shouting, "I'll call an ambulance!"

Another policeman said, "I'll call for help from Saint Louis Hospital on the other side of the road."

The policeman guarding the entrance of the police head-quarters said, as he looked at the hand brake of the car involved in the accident, "How strange this accident is, for she has been hit by her own car. It is true that she forgot to put the hand brake on, when she parked her car this morning, but the car has been parked since morning. What made it roll now?"

Another policeman examined the car as onlookers began to gather, and he said, disbelieving what he was seeing, "Your analysis is correct. The hand brake is not on. But what made the car move now? Why didn't it move earlier? Why did it roll at this incredible speed when the ground here is almost level?"

A passer-by answered, "Perhaps the vibrations of the nearby underground Metro shook it, time and again, until it moved now, by coincidence."

It was an explanation that did not convince many. But the passers-by apparently had no other explanation that was better or more convincing.

Sulayman would have liked to tell them the truth as he saw it, which was that Dunga was a real magician who excelled in telepathy and in moving things with his looks. Perhaps his glance released the hand brake and pushed the car with excessive speed, which would explain its fast movement despite the relatively level ground. But he did not dare say this. He was afraid to be accused of madness and be deprived of the promised residence card.

Without being asked for his opinion, he said in French, with a Beirut accent, "Perhaps it is a coincidence and nothing more. Coincidence is the god of the world." He was surprised when he found that his explanation met with support and that others actually repeated it after him. What a strange coincidence.

Sulayman turned to his companion demon, Dunga, the black man, in order to talk to him for the first time with his voice and to ask for his opinion of what happened. He did not see him next to him but heard the soundless voice without language saying to him, "Yes, I killed her. She deserved it. This is the punishment of those like her in our country."

Sulayman caught a glimpse of him, with his great height, his tattered clothes, his huge skull, and his strange eyes bulging out of his eye sockets, as he disappeared around the turn of the street. He did not know why a shiver of fear crept through his body as though he had met a real magician.

The Plot against Badi'

—You know, Badi', you're in danger, and I've come to help you. Women. Always women. They're always your misfortune and curse, and the cause of your destruction.

—Give me a few moments, 'Idab. Let me finish these accounts now and we'll talk at length later.

—Do you think you can take refuge in work this way, burying your head in figures to this late hour, and be saved?

—This is not the first time I have stayed behind alone in order to work, after all the other employees have gone home. If I hadn't been doing so, I wouldn't have been kept by the company when it moved from Beirut to London.

—The important thing for you, Badi', is to keep your head before you keep your job.

—I'll see you later at the bar, 'Idab. I don't want anybody to hear us or see us together in the office. The cleaning woman heard us talking when you visited me last time but she didn't see you, so she told the other employees that I talked to myself when I stayed alone in the office in the evening.

—Don't worry, Badi'. I'll persuade her to remain silent and she'll disturb you no more.

—Perhaps it would be better to leave her alone. Gossip is all she can do. She has already harmed me, and that's the end of that, 'Idab.

—I'm your twin brother, Badi'. I may be absent for a long

while, but I am always present when you need help. You know, I've never abandoned you. Whenever you're in danger, I'm always ready to help you. I'll wait for you at the bar.

—Do you know its address?

—I know every place you go to. In your days of trouble, I follow you like your own shadow. I'm strong and can protect you in a world full of betrayal. Love is the first betrayal, and I mean Elizabeth.

—Please, don't mention this name. I am trying to avoid her as much as possible and hope to forget her.

—With regard to women, neglecting them doesn't work. They cling more to you and hate you more at the same time. She knows more about you than she should . . . We'll talk about her at the bar.

—Why don't we go home, where we can talk all night in peace without anybody seeing us together or hearing us?

—Because we should visit Elizabeth before we go home. We should persuade her to remain silent and to forget all she knows about you, which is a lot. You were weak and told her your secrets, and she's about to use them against you.

—Oh, how I have suffered because of her, because of others, and because of plots against me. I feel I've spent my life jumping from trap to trap, alone and wounded. Hardly do I have one wound healed when another starts bleeding. My heart and soul are broken, and I have no refuge. You alone feel my suffering and come to my aid.

—Goodbye, I'll see you again at the bar.

—I'll join you there.

Half an hour later, Badi' left the office after carefully collecting his papers and putting them where they belonged. He also dusted his desk for the tenth time that evening.

He saw the cleaning woman on his way out but did not greet her. He felt she watched him, and he was annoyed by her. In the empty elevator, he dusted off the mirror with his handkerchief, trying not to look at his image in it.

He left the building and walked to the bar. It was sunset, the moment he feared and felt suffocated in. *My mother feared sunset,* too. When I returned home from school at sunset, she used to hug me in a warm embrace as we looked at the sea. She did not rebuke me then, as she usually did, for dirtying my clothes while playing. And her clean, fair neck smelled of soap and Jeanne-Marie Farina cologne. I was happy in her embrace and no longer jealous of Uncle Abu-Ramzi, Uncle Abu-Marwan, Uncle Abu-Tanius, and other uncles I had never heard of and who, after my father's death, started to sleep at my mother's, to protect us, each in his turn. None of my real uncles came to see us. My mother explained that the war crushed everyone, and that each person had to earn his living by his own diligence, because no one helped anyone else in such bad times. The neighborhood children made fun of me at school and mocked my expensive clothes and hinted at things they falsely claimed my mother did.

Maher said to me: "Your mother is a ———. If I were you, I'd kill her."

I returned home and didn't find her there. It was sunset. I was suffocating and began to weep. Her little cat meowed ceaselessly, so I took it in my hands trying to silence it. 'Idab came and said he would do that for me, but I didn't know why he hid it in the refrigerator inside the pot of food my mother had prepared during the day for our uncle who was coming that night.

When my mother saw it, she was scared and screamed. It was Uncle Abu-Ra'ef's turn to sleep at our home that night, and he accused me, in front of my mother, of killing the cat. I was about to tell her that 'Idab was the one who did it, but I didn't find my voice. My mother was angry and defended me, shouting, "He's only a ten-year-old child. How can you accuse him of killing a cat?"

I said to her, weeping, that Uncle Abu-Ra'ef had fondled me in her absence and she flew into a rage like a tigress and kicked him out. I almost cried tears of joy upon his expulsion. But the next week she took me at sunset to a respectable boarding school, up on the mountain, and said I would be safe there from the war and from evil tongues telling lies about her. She also said that she did not do any wrong and that she only rented my father's room, furnished, in order to make money for my future education at the best university, my father having left nothing but debts.

As usual, she was speaking to me in a whisper in the taxi. The sun was setting, and it was suffocating me, and it finally plunged its head into the sea, and I pushed it further down into the water and felt a sharp knife tearing at my heart.

I began to cry. I was ashamed that I was crying. I hated feeling humiliated in the presence of the taxi driver, the sunset, the distant sea, the clouds, the cars, and the street cats. The more ashamed I was of my crying, the more I cried.

I wished I was alone with my mother on an island so that she could hold me in her kind and tender bosom smelling of perfume and protect me from people's harshness. But I pushed her away from me when she tried to embrace me, and I said to her soundlessly, "I wish you would die." When I said goodbye to her with a wave of my hand as she was returning to Beirut in the dark and I saw her sit next to the taxi driver, I repeated, "I wish you would die."

Whenever I remembered her and was about to weep because I missed her tenderness, I wished she would die and I imagined myself burying her naked in a pit and piling earth on her until she was covered up. Then I cried for a long time, yearning for the moonlight, which rained from her eyes into the depths of my soul.

When the school principal came to tell me that my mother had died when hit by a sniper's bullet, she embraced me, contrary to custom, but I shoved her and ran off weeping. I killed her. It's I who killed her when I sincerely wished she would die. Naturally I didn't believe the claim that one of her lovers had killed her. She had no lovers and I was her killer.

Badi' wiped away the tears in his eyes. He entered the bar and sat at a secluded table in a dark corner with dim light.

He ordered two glasses of cognac. The waiter was surprised that this man was alone but ordered cognac for two in two glasses.

He murmured to himself that he saw all kinds of people in the bar.

After the cognac arrived, 'Idab joined Badi'.

—You're crying, Badi'. The wound that is your mother was asleep in your heart, but cursed Elizabeth came and awakened it.

—Perhaps you're prejudiced against her, 'Idab. I loved her because of her beauty and innocence, and I took refuge from the desolate moments of sunset in the light of her blondness. Like a radiant butterfly, she moved about the office relaying instructions to me and making inquiries, like any serious administrative secretary.

—She was plotting against you, right from the beginning. Didn't you wonder why she chose you among all the handsome employees and favored you with her attention?

—She liked my Arab features and was attracted by the fact that I never made advances to her, which is contrary to what is commonly believed about Arab men in London. This is what she told me, at least.

—But you know well that she began to spy on you after you had trusted her. She listened to your telephone conversations with the help of her friend, the telephone operator. As the manager's secretary, she obtained your home address and even came to your home at night, unexpected, in order to uncover your secrets.

—True. That visit aroused my suspicion.

—Your life before her, Badi', was almost ordinary. Work, work, then rest in a secluded home. You had relations with beautiful prostitutes at long intervals under conditions of mutual silence that did not threaten your privacy. You had other relations with males from bars specializing in such matters, without meeting with any one of them twice, for fear of giving enemies an opportunity to infiltrate into your secrets.

Then the winds of Elizabeth threw you off when you got involved with her in a moment of passion and you told her you wanted to possess her only after marriage and wanted her to remain virgin. She explained to you that she was not a virgin and that she was a respectable lady by her society's standards, not a prostitute, and yet not a virgin.

—Yes, 'Idab. She laughed at my naiveté and made me understand that it was not easy in London to find a young woman of her age who was a virgin, unless she was sick or in need of therapy by a psychiatrist. She added proudly that she was neither, or else she would have sought therapy with her cousin, Edward, who was a psychiatrist.

—And when you declined to possess her, Badi', she began to behave as though she possessed your soul, and she spied on you and tried to uncover your secrets. Her curiosity was aroused by your refusal to possess her body, despite the fact that she knew you frequented women of ill repute. You know that she then began to besiege you and watch you.

—This is true, and it aroused fears in me. She tried to fathom my most secret depths and to spy even on you, 'Idab, after she felt your presence in my life—or that's what I thought. She began to thrust her nose into the curves of my soul, trying to open the locked, dark rooms in the corridors of my heart. I wanted my life to remain a secret within a marriage in which each of us did his or her duty: she would bear children and give herself to them, to cooking, to the female neighbors, and to the other womanly details, and I would lead a man's life under no supervision.

—That would be possible if you had married an Eastern woman who was tamed fully and brought up well by her conservative family. The mistake began when you tried to treat Elizabeth as though she was little, shy Fattuma, the Beirut neighbors' daughter.

—With her naive, innocent face, she looked like Fattuma to me. Perhaps I was happy with my great, platonic love for her and refused to understand anything else.

—Today, she is a danger to your safety, Badi', and you should get rid of her. She knows all your little habits and very soon you'll become the laughingstock of everyone at the office. You may lose your job because of that and be obliged to return to Beirut, even to the sanitarium, and your childhood friends will mock you again because of your mother. People in Beirut don't forget. They rather use memory as a tool to harm, when that suits their interests.

—But what can Elizabeth say about me?

—Well, it's true she doesn't know all the minutest details. She doesn't know, for example, that a big plot threatens you and forces you to be cautious. Nor does she know that you don't eat canned foods for fear they have been expressly poisoned to kill you. You buy your vegetables yourself, you sterilize them several times, and you wash them well. You don't eat at the same restaurant twice and don't have drinks more than once a month at the same bar lest your many enemies bribe the waiter to poison you. You are great, and they plot against you because of that and they persecute you. You even wash your new clothes lest they be poisoned by your enemies.

—. . .

—Perhaps she knows, for example, that you are afraid of ants and cockroaches, that you take great care to kill them at your home, that you store food and water as though you were under siege, that you hate having anyone take photographs of you or keep a picture of you, and that you are startled whenever the telephone rings. Perhaps she knows also that you are scrupulous about cleanliness, washing your hands dozens of times a day and keeping a bottle of alcohol in your office to sterilize them when there is an opportunity or whenever some creature shakes hands with you. You unconsciously dust your desk dozens of times a day, and hers, too, as you talk to her. She knows that you have no friends but the television set, and perhaps she finds you to be an ideal husband because of that.

But she does not know that you got rid of your car, not because it broke down and was almost more costly to repair than it was worth, as you claimed to her, but because your enemies sabotaged it, fearing your greatness.

— . . .

—They persecute you because you are better than they are and they know that glory awaits you. You do well to collect every paper in your handwriting or every paper that reaches you, for these will all be placed in a museum one day.

— . . .

—Elizabeth does not know all this, but she spied on you at home and went through your things while you were preparing coffee for her. She saw your little suitcase which you always keep near your bed and in which you put your passport, your money, your credit cards, and some clothes, so that you can escape quickly when the enemies surprise you and try to burn your home, or when you have an intuition that they are coming to assassinate you.

— . . .

—With infinite insolence, she opened the suitcase and asked whether you were about to make a trip. You were obliged to claim that you were going to spend the weekend in Brighton. She offered to accompany you and tightened her siege of you by claiming she loved you. You were annoyed and were about to suffocate. You felt you were getting a headache that split your head again in half, as you had never felt since you left the sanitarium in Lebanon.

But you did not say anything to her and continued to chat. She asked you about the secret of the tomb in the forbidden room. You felt a desire to strangle her so that she would be silent, but you did not dare. I had to be near you to help you get rid of her. I admit I was at a loss that night and did not know what to do in this difficult situation of yours. I did not kill her because I was afraid someone knew she was visiting you.

— . . .

—It was a mistake to accompany her to your castle, Badi', or to open the door for her when she surprised you and came without invitation.

—I couldn't tell her that I was sick and suffering from the same pains I used to have before coming to London. Those were pains I developed because I had then accepted the idea of marrying one of my relatives, in deference to the desire of my grandmother, who lived with me since my mother's death and your long absence on a trip. I regarded that forthcoming marriage as an ill omen and feared that my wife would spy on me within our marriage. When you visited me after a long absence and warned me about that engagement, saying my grandmother did not know that this relative had been drafted against me, I began to dream every night of strangling my fiancée, as you had strangled the cat.

When I was afflicted with that painful headache, I went to see our neighbor, Dr. Rajack. He was kind and good-hearted, and he said to me that I was sick and needed rest at the hospital. My grandmother advised me not to tell anyone that I was going to the sanitarium for a little rest, because people in our Beirut neighborhood were harsh and would say I was mad and would spread false rumors about me. In the sanitarium, the doctor let me take part in drawing pictures and planting flowers. I used to have nice therapeutic sessions with him after he gave me a special injection.

One time, he said to me, "You are fortunate, my son, because you told me frankly about your pains. Your psyche is split, and this is the meaning of the term 'schizophrenia.' You are not mad, but you can be violent. I don't advise you to marry now, wait until your treatment is over."

My pains went away and I was about to return to my job, as Dr. Rajack had promised, when the man died of heart failure. I believed my enemies killed him because he was my friend, and they made it appear as if it was a natural death. The treatment of the patients by the nurses became bad after that, and the war was all around the sanitarium, so they let us run away because the doctor's widow wanted to sell the building and leave the country. I ran away from the sanitarium and did not continue my therapy.

—You didn't want to run away, Badi'. I helped you to run away and dragged you out of your bed by force. Do you remember? I came and found you crying in sorrow for the doctor. You didn't know that he was part of the plot against your greatness, whereby he subjugated you by love and hypocrisy, just as Elizabeth has now done. Your enemies did kill Dr. Rajack, lest he should divulge the secret of the plot against you.

— . . .

—You weren't in need of any therapy.

— . . .

—You were in need of travel, freedom, and change of atmosphere. You needed to leave Lebanon and go to a city where people would not watch one another nor practice strangling under the cover of love. And that's what Elizabeth is doing to you now.

—She asked me about the secret of the tomb, 'Idab. I was taken aback and said to her that an artist who used to live in the house before me was the one who built it in his mother's room after her death, so that he could push the idea of the tomb out of his heart. I told her that that room used to be his studio. I did not tell her anything about the interior decorator who was surprised at my desire to sleep on a bed built in the form of a tomb.

—And you claimed that our mother's picture hanging on the wall was that of the artist's mother, and you said that you were moved by his loyalty to her and liked to leave everything in the room as it was, using it as a studio for yourself when you found time for drawing, and being inspired by that rare loyalty.

—I didn't know what else to tell her. But shutting her up as you suggested, by strangling her and hiding her in the refrigerator, as you once did with my mother's cat, was not possible.

They both laughed at the memory.

—Elizabeth did not believe you fully, Badi'. What you told her perplexed her, but her questions no longer annoyed you. She let you breathe. However, her polite abstention caused you suffering, and you almost admitted to the truth to her, including the fact that you had come to London with a suitcase half full of our mother's clothes.

Badi' burst out laughing.

—I wish you were with me, 'Idab, on that day when the customs officer searching my suitcase found half of its contents to be women's clothes. He thought they were mine and did not know they were our mother's, but he said nothing, for he sees many suitcases and there's nothing in British law which forbids a man to carry an old picture of a beautiful woman and women's old clothes with his own. I showed him my work contract and my other official documents, so he let me through.

—But his intuition was not wrong, for you do wear these clothes from time to time.

—They are still redolent of our mother's scent.

—And you buy more of the same.

—I buy them for our mother, not for myself.

Badi' called the waiter and asked for two more glasses of cognac.

—And, as usual, whenever you desired Elizabeth and did not have her, you went the next day to a prostitute. You risked exposing your secret, but I intervened at the right time and saved you.

—They usually take off their clothes in silence and, like me, they want to finish the whole thing as quickly as possible. I don't know why that wretched woman wanted to converse. She asked me about my love life and whether I was married or not. Then I realized that she was a spy, one of my enemies, and wanted to destroy me. When she asked me about our mother, I wanted only to shut her up. I stuffed my handkerchief into her mouth and beat her. I didn't want a woman like her to speak about our mother. I wanted to put on my clothes quickly, but she took the handkerchief out of her mouth and raised the telephone receiver to call the police . . .

—Had I not intervened, Badi', you would have found yourself in trouble. But I always arrive at the right time. I let you enter the bathroom to take a shower and, this time, I tightly wound your tie around her neck and did not let go of her until she no longer could say another word about our mother . . . or our secrets.

—I was stunned, on leaving the bathroom, to find her strangled. Strangely enough, when I was taking the shower, I was dreaming that someone was strangling her as though I was with them and saw the minutest details of the event. I laughed the next day when I read in the papers about the investigator's astonishment at the fact that the murderer took a shower after killing the prostitute, according to the evidence he gathered of the event. It did not occur to him that we were two persons.

Badi' fell silent when the waiter put down the two glasses of cognac, stared at him with bewilderment, then went away as though nothing astonished him any longer.

Badi' felt the danger he was in and the need to end the matter decisively and leave the bar.

—What do you want me to do now, 'Idab?

—I believe Elizabeth must necessarily be silenced.

Badi' thought deeply.

—The important thing is that Dr. Edward, her cousin, with whom she was able to embroil me, must be silenced first.

—Both of them must be silenced together, Badi'. We'll begin with Elizabeth before Edward has the chance to get in touch with her and warn her against you under the pretext of seeking information about you.

—Yes. I myself heard him say that he would do that. But it's not Elizabeth's fault. The mistake started when you, 'Idab, strangled that prostitute on the day after Elizabeth had surprised me by coming unexpectedly to my home. After you killed her, I was afflicted with a terrible headache that was splitting my head in half. I began hearing voices wrangling within it, almost tearing me in two. Unconsciousness. Dizziness. Nausea. Exhaustion. Sudden weeping in the underground train. This was despite the fact that I lived next to the office because I feared means of transportation and assassination.

The first doctor said I had no organic disease and referred me to a nerve specialist, who referred me to a third, a psychiatrist.

I admitted this to Elizabeth in a happy, merry moment. I had invited her to dinner at Turner's Restaurant. After she paid the bill and I paid her my share of it, I revealed to her the fact that I had pains. I did so in order to justify our earlier lukewarm relation and its ebb and flow. She suggested that I should go to see her cousin, the psychiatrist, who would take care of me and would not charge me a lot because I was sent to him by her.

That tempted me, for you know my extreme care with money, and how I befriend no one lest I spend a pound on someone other than myself. So I went.

After long, strange, and enigmatic tests which I had not been subjected to by Dr. Rajack, including drawings—I had to tell him what they suggested to me without direct questions—and therapeutic injections after which I joyfully spoke about myself, even without being asked anything, the doctor said goodbye to me and told me he would get in touch with me again. He declined to charge me a fee, and I was so happy I forgot to take my handkerchief and left it on the table, which I had dusted off from time to time as we spoke.

In the elevator, I remembered it. I returned to him in order to take my handkerchief. And I was horrified at what I heard.

Badi' interrupted his conversation, called the waiter, and ordered two double glasses of cognac. He then continued in a slightly louder voice.

—When I returned I found the rascal speaking to a colleague about me.

—Lower your voice, Badi'.

—'Idab, the rascal did not expect me to return or his secretary to be out—perhaps in the bathroom. But I overheard him saying to his colleague about me, "This patient suffers from split personality and can be very violent. If it were not for professional ethics, I would now contact my cousin, Elizabeth, to warn her against him, for she is in danger. The fool said she was sending me her fiancé-to-be, but he might well be her murderer-to-be. He needs treatment."

His colleague answered, "You can do nothing. The law does not permit you to commit anyone to a sanitarium against his will. Nor can you divulge professional secrets, even to your own cousin."

The waiter put down the two glasses of cognac and asked Badi' to pay the bill. Without any hesitation, Badi' paid it and left a big tip, contrary to his custom. He wanted to get rid of the waiter and continue his important conversation with 'Idab. He wanted to tell him everything he overheard that cursed Dr. Edward say about him, but 'Idab interrupted.

—I know what happened. I was next to you and I prevented you from weeping on the stairs. Do you remember? You weep a lot. You weep in front of women, and they imagine that to be weakness, so they tighten their grip on your heart and dig in their nails like knives. Come on, let's get out of here. The waiter is hovering around us more than he should, and he may be another spy. We must be cautious.

—But I'm tired. I can no longer stand up. My head is splitting in half. There's someone hitting me with an axe, mercilessly, to split me into two parts.

—Don't worry, Badi'. Together, we'll reform the world and save it from the evils of women. But from now on, don't let your weakness lead us into perdition. We must become one united whole. Don't renounce me, from now on, and don't run away. Our fate is that we should be one.

—I'll try. But I'm in pain, and I'm weak and tired.

—Everything betrays a person, even his own body. Come on, drag it behind you and let's leave this place.

After Badi' left the bar, the waiter said to his colleague, "He's been here for one hour, gulping cognac and talking to himself."

The colleague replied, "Is this the first time you've seen a person talking to himself, man? Don't you do that, too, many times?

Badi' walked, heading toward Elizabeth's home. He collapsed on a public bench opposite her window, in a little square in the middle of the street.

—You must go upstairs to her, Badi', and silence her once and for all.

—I can't. I'm tired and sick. The world has been plotting against me, humiliating me, insulting me since the time I was crammed into a child's body.

—Fine. Let me take over. You trust me, don't you?

—Certainly.

—Sleep here on the bench and let me persuade her on your behalf to maintain silence.

Badi' lay down on the public bench in the little square in the middle of the street as sunset was mercilessly falling on his chest. He remembered his mother and the taxi taking him to the boarding school. He remembered many obscure, painful, and disturbing things. He then closed his eyes and slept.

He dreamt 'Idab rose from the bench, saying he would do what he must, and walked to the telephone booth in the street. He called Elizabeth and she sweetly replied, 'You're welcome, I'll open the door for you. My cousin, Dr. Edward, will also come after a while. He said he wanted to speak with me about you. He wanted to ask me about things concerning you. Why don't you yourself answer him?"

"I'll do that, sweetheart. I'll ask him for your hand. It's our tradition that the males of the family be asked permission by a suitor before he sleeps with his beloved and possesses her."

She emphasized, laughing, "You'll sleep with me, but you'll never possess me. Things here are different. Come on upstairs. I'll open the door for you."

Badi' woke up in his bed at home, overwhelmed by happiness.

—'Idab, all that was a bad dream, then?

—No, it was all real. Elizabeth opened the door for me. She thought I was you. That did not surprise me, for I'm your twin brother and a spitting image of you as you know from the mirror.

I gave her a long, long kiss with some vehemence and strength, not a tender one as you give her when she makes you do it.

Her desire was in flames. She undid my necktie and began forcing me to take off my shirt and gloves. I refused to possess her. We scuffled and laughed, then I heard the door bell and the voice of her cousin, the doctor, on the intercom.

I let her answer that she would open the door for him, then I quickly did what I had to, and I silenced her well, as I once did with the cat. After strangling her, I took back my necktie from her neck and dragged her to the kitchen. I didn't have enough time to put her in the refrigerator, for her cousin Edward knocked on the door.

I left her where she was. I opened the door for him. He entered. My presence and her absence surprised him. He was afraid. He tried to distract me with unnatural conversation, meanwhile edging toward the door, intending to run away.

I began to come closer to him. He trembled but continued to speak to me in a calm voice, saying that he wanted to help me and that I could get rid of 'Idab, who was annoying me. It seems that, under the influence of his injections, you said things to him you did not mean—he used this method to steal the secrets of your soul then make you say what you did not really mean.

I told him that I did not want to get rid of 'Idab because I was 'Idab. He gave me a file he was carrying in his hand and said it was my medical file, which I could take and forget everything.

It angered me that he had joined our enemies, and I was surprised to see a gun in his hand. In a quick move, I turned its muzzle away from me and stuck it to his head, and the gun went off. He fell dead on the floor. I quickly undid his necktie before it could be smeared with his blood, and I wound it around Elizabeth's neck as though she had been strangled by it. I laughed as I was leaving the place, imagining what the police might conclude. They might think he killed her and then committed suicide. He strangled her with his necktie and then shot himself in the head. Why not?

I left no fingerprints behind, thanks to the gloves I was wearing, which you had specially bought for me. The important thing was that I quickly left, taking the fire escape stairwell in the building so that I would not be seen by anyone in the elevator. You now have to go to your office and receive condolences on the death of your fiancée, Elizabeth.

Didn't she claim to everyone that you were her fiancé, as a means to control you and keep other lovely women away from you? Be calm. After a suitable period of time, you will move to another city.

Badi' did not respond. He did not hear very well what 'Idab was telling him, because he was running inside dusky gray corridors, from which emanated the fragrance of a bygone perfume.

Badi' put on his black suit most favored for mourning by 'Idab; then he changed his mind and put on a gray one. It was important for him to play the role of one surprised by the sad news.

On the way to the office, he bought the morning newspaper but did not see Elizabeth's picture on the crime page. He became angry.

A colleague at the office approached him, offering her sympathies as she called him by his name, Badi'. He almost told her he was 'Idab and not Badi', but he would never abandon his twin brother, who was trembling in bed with fear and sorrow. He heard whispers about a relationship between Elizabeth and her cousin, the doctor, and how the police found their bodies together. Others offered their condolences. Even the manager's only daughter, to whom he had paid no attention earlier, offered her sympathies, flashing all her beauty and diamond rings.

'Idab whispered to himself, "How charming she is! The enemies are attempting to bring a new agent into Badi''s life, but I will not let her harm him. She will not succeed in getting under his skin and weakening him, even if he agrees to marry her in order to take control of the company after her father's death. The enemies are plotting against Badi', but I will always plot against them and defeat their persecuting schemes with my greatness."

When 'Idab left the office, he passed by the flower shop and ordered that a wreath be sent to Elizabeth's funeral in Badi''s name. He then passed by another flower shop and ordered another wreath for the funeral in 'Idab's name. He smiled maliciously and thought, "No one will notice, not even the police, that the Arabic name 'Idab is the name of Badi' reversed. In English, it is written differently." A great cheerful feeling took hold of him because the investigator would be unable to solve the puzzle. He was more intelligent than all of them, those he knew and those he did not!

Register: I'm Not an Arab Woman

The insistent ringing of the door bell woke me up. I turned on the light. It was 3:20 A.M.

Nobody would ever visit me at this ungodly hour of the night. I got up, terrified, for I lived alone. I looked through the peephole of the door. I saw Gloria. She appeared to be frightened. She knocked on my iron-plated door with one hand while still pressing the door bell with her other hand.

I unlocked the door, one lock after another. She entered, terrified. She flung herself on the seat nearest to the door and asked, "Do you believe in ghosts, Madam?"

It was a real surprise to be awakened by my maid, who came twice a week to clean the apartment, and to be asked at 3:20, before dawn, whether I believed in ghosts or not. I didn't know what to tell her after she sat on a seat, exhausted and without waiting for anyone to permit her to do so, in a city in which discarding formality is not customary.

I frowned and tried, by my silence, to express my extreme resentment. Apparently, she did not see me, for she repeated her question in a feverish tone, with tears beginning to flow on her cheeks: "Please tell me, Madam. Do you believe in ghosts?"

"You woke me up at this hour to speak about ghosts with me?"

"Forgive me, Madam. I'm afraid."

She trembled and trembled.

I suggested that we discuss the matter in the morning and

that she return to her studio apartment on the floor designated for servants who worked in the skyscraper in which I lived and she slept. She wept, begging me for permission to spend that night on the wooden floor of the entrance hall, for she was terrified and did not dare return to her apartment that was haunted by a ghost.

She wondered how there could be a ghost in a studio apartment and said she thought ghosts only haunted ancient palaces and came to important people. I did not tell her that literature and American movies and television had spread such lies about racist ghosts with class discrimination, as though only the wealthy, the princesses, and the nobles had ghosts, but not the simple folk. But I thought the time was not suitable for a lecture on ghosts, who definitely haunted tents, too.

I asked her, almost sarcastically, "Are you talking about a ghost who comes out of an ancient box, for example, who arrives only in the dark and wears white sheets, who conceals himself or moans in the corridor and tries to kill you, sometimes revealing a skeleton with a speaking skull that bursts out in thunderous laughter, and who escapes at the crow of the cock?"

She answered, weeping, "I'm talking about a ghost whose voice I hear within me, a ghost who was frenzied tonight and frightened me."

I listened to her, my interest in her ghost growing all of a sudden. If she had said the ghost was of the kind that wears white sheets, I would have laughed at her. But she was apparently talking about a real, familiar ghost she knew, since she heard his voice within her.

Here I was, paying the cost of being a writer. I usually led people to speak about themselves, and I listened to them with interest, in the hope of stealing their very soul for a story or a novel. But they thought my interest in their tales gave them acquired rights on my life, so they treated me as they would a village sorcerer or a psychiatrist. Later I had to listen to their worries whenever they chose, even if that was at 3:20 A.M., and I had to find them solutions, even if they were related to ghosts.

It is true that I have never published a single line in newspapers or in books and that nobody but myself knows I am a writer. But my curious listening to Gloria's tales over the years granted her an acquired right, in her opinion. *The French concierge of the skyscraper in which my husband and I rented an apartment said, "I'll send you Gloria to clean the apartment for you. She works in the building, cleaning stairs and elevators, and lives on the fourth floor designated for the workers."*

Gloria came. She was a beautiful young woman of eighteen. Her fair complexion was radiant with beauty and vitality and the sun danced on her blond hair. She was meek, gentle, and full of friendly cheer. She was not reserved like most French women in the first meeting but rather glowing with hearty warmth. She almost reminded me of my daughter's warmth. In the beginning, she liked my empty apartment and she was struck by the breathtaking view of Paris from on high, as though she was seeing it for the first time, with the Eiffel Tower in the center of my windows which were so large that my walls appeared to be all glass. When it rained, my apartment was transformed into a transparent, aerial submarine floating in the watery airspace of Paris, and the city below lay quietly, bathed in the pale wintry light.

Gloria later befriended my furniture, celebrating each new piece that arrived. She spoke with the pieces she liked as though they were alive and able to hear her, and as though they were joyful or sorrowful like the plants, which she also pampered very much. She dissipated the desolateness of the pieces of furniture and brought joy into their inner, secret life—which could exist, so Gloria thought. Likewise, she dissipated some of my own desolateness in a foreign country, and, while working, she often laughed at my mistakes when I spoke French, using the feminine gender instead of the masculine, such as when I said to her, "Clean this [cette] mirror." She would correct me, saying, "Say this [ce] mirror, because mirror in French is masculine." And I would ask, "But why?" She would only shrug her shoulders in wonder and perplexity. And so our relationship became stronger, year after year, and we sympathized with each other. I gave her many of my fine clothes and listened to her a lot, but I often kept silent when she tried to lead me to speak about myself.

Her voice still pleaded, "Please, Madam. Let me stay here tonight." *Well, I can't chase her out. I don't have the heart to do that.*

I answered, "I'll give you a blanket. Sleep on the sofa in the sitting room and tomorrow we'll talk about all that." *She doesn't know yet that we carry our ghosts with us, wherever we go, and that she isn't really safe, wherever she goes and whoever is the one she seeks protection from.*

I avoided further conversation with her and gave her a warm blanket.

I returned to my room, turned off the light, and tried in vain to go back to sleep.

I almost started laughing in the dark. Couldn't this poor woman, escaping from a ghost, find any other place to take refuge besides this "ghost house" I lived in? *The telephone rang on our first New Year's Eve, a few weeks after our arrival in Paris from Beirut. On the line, my close friend Antoinette said, "What are you and your husband doing at home? Come, let's spend the evening together at our place."*

We had left Beirut together. Her voice sounded happy and excited. I felt both alienated from her and happy for her at the same time.

My husband and I were sad to the point of death, not because we were in Paris, the most beautiful exile in the world, but because of what had happened in Lebanon. Our story of the war there is long, for my husband spent the war years in one prison or another, visiting his friends, on whom he spent part of his wealth due to his belief in the freedom of thought, even during the civil war. We did not leave Beirut until the war had ended and we were finished, too. My husband was fortunate because no one had killed him and they were content with torturing him. But our only daughter was killed by a stray bullet which someone shot in joyful celebration of the end of the war.

I did not tell Antoinette that my husband and I were going to spend the evening with the ghost of our daughter and the ghosts of the past, which we did not know yet how to uproot from our hearts.

I claimed we had been invited to spend the evening at one of the grand hotels, since the proper bourgeois ethic I grew up with was never complain to anyone, never grumble, never explain!

I heard Gloria moaning in her sleep. Her voice came through the door, groaning intermittently like one having an endless nightmare. She was still at the beginning of the path to becoming acquainted with ghosts.

In the first days that we discover the ghosts' existence around us, we reject them, because we are overcome by the inherited view that hates them and consequently fears them and desires to deny their presence. This is a view we never get rid of. Thus, we rebel against the first moment of acquaintance with them and are frightened by any friendly relations between them and us.

In time, however, we begin to recognize many facts which have, at first, seemed irrational and uncomfortable, such as the fact that they share our lives.

Our relation with them resembles the one we maintain with inhabitants of other planets: a relation full of contradictory feelings such as fear, enmity, curiosity, and jealousy, because we are not alone in the arena of the universe, and perhaps also a desire for acquaintance and friendship.

It is a relation with the unknown, and we all have our own style of maintaining it, if we wish to recognize the other.

Gloria continued to moan in the next room. She would suffer a long time before she befriended her ghosts or rejected them.

I wished to convey to her my long experience in this arena, but I knew that transplanting experience or transferring it to others was impossible.

Perhaps a long time would pass before she would discover, like me, that ghosts fill our lives year after year until a time comes when the number of ghosts we live with exceeds the number of living beings around us.

When my husband died a few months ago, I was not very sad. I knew that he would remain with me after becoming a ghost. Nothing much would change, for we had begun to be transformed into ghosts since we left Beirut, perhaps even before that. For when my daughter was killed by a celebratory bullet, my home was killed, too, and her ghost remained in it. We imagined that leaving the country would liberate her and us. But Paris is an ideal place for two gentle ghosts like us, who do not desire to hurt anyone and want to live in peace with our daughter's ghost and the rest of the ghosts.

We were surprised that beautiful Paris was haunted by other ghosts who had suffered like us before they died. Some of them, great lovers of freedom, had left their homelands to seek consolation and liberty in Paris.

And thus, we often visited the homes in which outstanding artists exiled or self-exiled in Paris had lived; these artists then loved Paris as much as their original homelands. We also visited their tombs to keep them company.

And we listened to the music of Chopin, the exile, as though it was the music of the sorrows of the foreigners in the city.

Since our arrival in Paris, we had said we were on a vacation for rest, and we were not lying. We stayed for years, the vacation was prolonged, but we did not rest. We continued, however, to visit the houses in which the departed great artists had lived, and we liked to sit at the cafés they had frequented and be in the neighborhoods they had moved in.

Their ghosts continued to live there in stone inscriptions, on bridges, in statues. We befriended them and, in time, our capability for love as two ghosts was enlarged. We therefore began to regularly visit all the homes of these creative artists, who had certainly suffered and made those around them suffer, and their ghosts acquired a rare spiritual density of presence . . . similar to our daughter's.

Yet our favorite place of recreation was the garden of Père Lachaise, I mean the beautiful Cemetery of Père Lachaise, with its trees, its splendid statues, and its inhabitants, the ghosts of artists. We sat for long hours at Chopin's tomb, listening to him play especially for us on an invisible piano and then tell us stories about his relation with George Sand and express his annoyance at curious tourists.

I became aware that my husband's good financial situation facilitated our quick transformation into two ghosts.

I was afraid of that, and I decided to find a job. That was not difficult, for—like my husband—I was a graduate of one of the universities of Beirut, where we had met and lived our most splendid dreams. Those dreams have all been dissipated by a war we all dissociated ourselves from by being unwilling to repent and make peace with ourselves and with friends, though most of them had died or become fugitives.

Furthermore, it was not difficult for one to find a job if one did not demand a salary. And that was my case.

Returning from my job as a volunteer teacher of Arabic at a school for immigrant children, I used to find my husband continuing his transformation into a ghost at a rate faster than mine. And so he abandoned his material body one day, and I buried it for him in the garden of Père Lachaise after having paid a small fortune for a grave site owned by others.

I did not feel very desolate upon his death, for he remained with me like our daughter, so much so that I continued to knock on his office door before entering, as I did when he was alive. He also continued to accompany me on our customary walks with our daughter, and I talked to him and he talked to me. He even jested with me sometimes and surprised me with Chopin's music playing automatically on the recording machine, or he replaced the anchorman on the television screen and related clever jokes that made me laugh a long time before I switched channels. On my return from work, he received me with his Aramis perfume diffused spontaneously in my bedroom, or he picked a little blossom of yellow genista and left it for me on my desk, where I would find it and almost accuse the wind of carrying it to me, but I knew it was from him. He also encouraged me to write and publish, perhaps because he knew my inner life and was aware that story writing was in essence living with ghosts we summoned or invented or knew.

In my opinion, the difference is not really big between story writing and ghost summoning. But I never felt the desire to publish and I continued to write stories silently within my head, stories like ghosts, and I have become the first Arab woman to be a ghost writer. Those to whom I write read me even if my books are not published. They simply read by telepathy all that I don't write on paper.

Before going to work, I used to leave my own ghost behind to keep my husband and our daughter company.

Don't I have a ghost, too, who, perhaps at this very moment, is chasing someone on another continent, causing pleasure and pain simultaneously, just as the ghosts of many whom I loved or hated (or whom I loved and hated simultaneously) cause me to suffer and rejoice? I no longer know whether they died in their exiles or are still alive.

Being alive does not deprive me of my right to have a ghost. Don't the living have ghosts? Isn't my life haunted by my own ghost (who lives within me, talks to me, and quarrels with my body) and by other ghosts, some of whom died and some of whom are still alive but enveloped by time and kept in my memory? Aren't my depths a museum of ghosts, who roam cities in which time stopped long ago?

Ghosts of towns, of streets, of fleeting moments. A lifetime spent with ghosts. *Nawwaf said to me, "What about having dinner with me tonight? Enough of your mourning and sorrow over your daughter, then over your husband. Why don't you think of life again?"*

I said to him, "I don't want to have dinner with you because you're not bald and you have no ghost. I can't love a man unless he is bald and has a ghost."

I meant what I said, but he did not believe me. He thought I was being coy.

He was rich and a friend from younger days when he did not have the opportunity to possess my body. Perhaps he wanted now to kill my ghost, in his lifetime, by possessing me in order to satisfy the pain of his ego.

Perhaps he really loved me as he claimed. For love is a mad and stupid boy who has no logic. There was nothing in Paris, which abounded with beautiful young women, that prevented a rich, middle-aged man like him from loving an elegant woman in her forties like me who did not look like a ghost on the outside.

Because he knew I had no children, he offered me financial help, since I had a right to inherit only part of my rich husband's wealth according to the religious laws of my community. I set his mind to rest and told him that my husband was a peerless man who practiced what he believed in. (That was the cause of his misfortunes and his moving from one friend's prison to another's.) I also told him that my husband had given me in his lifetime all the wealth he possessed (so that the temple ravens would not descend upon me after his death to eat my flesh alive because I was merely a woman who did not give birth to a boy who would inherit all the wealth of his father; otherwise, most of the wealth we jointly worked hard to amass would have gone to my husband's brother).

I said, "Keep your money, Nawwaf, and let me keep my body, and let's remain just friends."

He said, "How can I be transformed into a bald ghost so that we may be more than just friends?"

I said, "It's not easy for a person to become bald if he is not fortunate to be so, for there is no treatment yet for thick hair. And there's no one who is trying to invent a drug that will make a person bald, despite the beauty of that. That's why, my dear friend, there is no treatment for your thick hair! Regarding how you can become a ghost, I am now writing a book entitled 'How to Become a Gentle Ghost.'"

He laughed and said I was charming—though I wasn't. I meant what I said, but when we tell the absolute truth, no one wants to believe us.

I try in vain to go back to sleep.

Gloria screams in terror like one hurt in a nightmare. I rise and go to see her. I turn on the light in the next room. *Perhaps like all people, she thinks that the dark is the cause of her fear and she does not know that her own dark, inner corridors are the abode of her ghosts. Perhaps she is now being introduced to them, one by one. She can never befriend them unless she comes to know them. Know your ghost and you'll know yourself. In my opinion, this is the golden rule completing the other that says, "Know thyself."*

She moans again without opening her eyes.

I contemplate her in the dim light. Tears are flowing down her cheeks; she looks like one walking on the planet of sorrows with closed eyes in order to see well in the dark with the eyes of the soul, while her body lies like a rag on our wretched planet, the planet of ephemeral earthly appearance.

I approach her on tiptoe. She opens her eyes, startled. I bend over her and give her a handkerchief to wipe her tears from her face, and I murmur a few words to calm her and help her to visit, though briefly, the island of oblivion and quietude.

I contemplate her face, which looks almost old, as she closes her eyes and tries to go back to sleep. How her face has changed! It's no longer radiant with youth, hope, and joy. *She had returned that day from her vacation in North Africa, her beauty blooming as never before. She said to me in simple Arabic, "I got married to Safi!" I was stunned, not because she got married, for this happened everyday, but because she spoke Arabic and I had thought she was French by ancestry.*

I was also surprised that her hair, which had grown, was pitch black at the roots, like Arab women's hair, and I had thought she was a blonde.

She did not wait for me to ask, and she hastened to explain, "I am of Arab origin. I was born in France. My mother is French. My real name is Zakiyya. My mother calls me Gloria and my father calls me Zakiyya. He is a miner in the north of France. My name as recorded at birth is Zakiyya-Gloria.

"My mother speaks French to me, and my father speaks Arabic to me and my brothers. My father retired when the mine closed, but my mother refused to accompany him back to his village in North Africa— as strongly as he had always refused to apply for French citizenship."

I remembered that I had once seen her mother with her at the entrance of the building, and she was still beautiful and elegant. And on that day I saw with them an old, time-worn man of dark color, whom life had chewed like a mouthful of tobacco and spat out as withered, decrepit, slim human garbage wearing tattered clothes. He was smoking and coughing with a whistle, as though his lungs were perforated. He appeared to have been mummified ages ago, but his eyes shone with a dark light.

That day, Gloria seemed to be proud of her mother. When I asked her about the old man, she ignored my question and continued introducing her mother to me.

I asked her, "Was that worn-out man I once saw with you and your mother your father?"

She nodded affirmatively and said, "His work at the mine since childhood burnt his lungs. He is very sick and extremely obstinate. His refusal to apply for French citizenship made me and my seven brothers suffer as immigrants. If he had consented to become a French citizen a long time ago, he would have saved us many difficulties. I have personally applied for French citizenship for myself, and also so that Safi may obtain it, for he wants that, too. He came with me to Paris and now lives with me in my apartment. He has many contacts and friends in France and he will easily find a job. And he is well-to-do, so he told me."

"And how did you meet him?"

"At the wedding. Safi was playing the drum at the beautiful village celebration on the warm beach. Around me were faces with kohl and henna tattoos, smiles, colors, kisses, and warm hearts. I fell in love with them at once, nothing of the sort has ever happened to me. What a village! Look how it tanned my skin."

"What village? What beach?"

"My mother had said to me, 'Come with me, Gloria, to see your maternal aunts at Deauville and spend your vacation on the beach.' My father had said to me, 'Come with me, Zakiyya, to my village to spend your vacation on the warm beach.'

"I decided to accompany my father, for he tempted me with the warmth and the sun. We stayed at my paternal aunt's home, and I went with her to the wedding.

"I've never felt so happy. I was overwhelmed by the rapture of music, and my aunt enticed me to take part in the Arab dance with the other girls. I had earlier seen it only on television, in the movie The One Thousand and One Nights.

"Everyone spoiled me. They clapped for me, and I felt I was an important person in my father's village, and not merely an auxiliary maid with a number in Paris."

She was panting with happiness and spoke with exceeding speed and in a colloquial Arabic dialect different from the Lebanese dialect. It was difficult for me to understand what she was saying.

She added, "Safi pursued me, thinking at first that I was French. We withdrew to the beach for a few moments away from all eyes, and I almost gave myself to him, as I do in Paris when I fall in love with no complications. But my aunt had followed us and was on the lookout.

"My father learned of the episode and he called a shaykh who married us. And here I am now: in love, married, and happy. My father is even happier than I am, and this gladdens me. It seems I love my father more than I thought I did."

"What do you know about Safi?"

"Nothing, except that I love him. He is looking for a job. He also sings and has a beautiful voice. He continuously repeats the song 'Register: I'm an Arab,' and I have learned it from him."

Before I could tell her that the song "Register: I'm an Arab" was a beautiful poem by a poet living in Paris, she interrupted me, overflowing with happiness like a stream, and she began to sing, "Register: I'm an Arab woman . . . Register: I'm an Arab woman . . . And my name is not Gloria but Zakiyya . . . Please, call me Zakiyya from now on."

"Done, O Zakiyya, O Arab woman!"

She wiped the bathroom tiles while singing, "Register: I'm an Arab woman."

I rise to go back to sleep. Zakiyya-Gloria returns to her moaning. What hurts her? What ghost does she in vain try to satisfy or get rid of? Is he the ghost of Safi, since their love story quickly came to nought like the fall of a shooting star? *She came that winter evening to work and looked exhausted. I said to her, "What's the matter, Zakiyya?"*

She answered in French, "My name is Gloria."

I realized that a disaster had befallen her.

I said to her that the apartment was clean, and I invited her to a cup of coffee. She sat down in a hostile manner, as though every Arab, including myself, was an indirect ally of Safi, just as her love for me had increased without logical justification when she was passionately in love with him.

I led her into conversation with unaffected kindness, but she refused to answer me in Arabic to explain what had happened to her. She said in French, "I'm pregnant. Safi beats me. I obtained my French citizenship. They refused to give him a residence permit for more than one year, because many Arab men marry French women with the sole aim of becoming residents. He is still without a job and spends his time squandering my salary, drinking wine and smoking hashish in my apartment, and acting like a raging bull. He curses Paris and yet does his best to stay here. Contrary to what he claimed, he has no friends here, nor is he well-to-do. He is escaping from poverty, but he does not have mercy on me or himself. He beats me, then he gets drunk and sings, 'Register: I'm an Arab.' I regret this marriage that was imposed on me by my father and the tribe. I want a divorce. I wish I had not disobeyed my mother."

"But you loved him."

"Yes. But I did not have to get married. My father wished me to get married."

She spoke and sobbed. On her beautiful face and on her arms I could see black-and-blue spots. I could also see fresh, hardly dried blood in her nostrils. I did not dare tell her that some men continue to beat their wives everywhere and that this is not limited to Arab men.

I let her unburden her pain.

"He takes possession of my salary and yet he goes a step ahead of me when we walk together. He insults me because I'm French and yet he dies for the right to stay here. After he beat me, I chased him out of my apartment. He contradicts himself: he's autocratic with me and obsequious with those who don't like him. He refused to leave my apartment when I chased him out, and he said that I no longer had control over my affairs and that the man alone in our country decided when to divorce his wife and when to leave her. For me, this marriage has turned into insults, humiliation, daily beatings, and an obligation to work in as many homes as possible in order to bring him money. Meanwhile, he smokes hashish, humiliates me, and sings 'Register: I'm an Arab.' How I hate this song now. I'm French and I don't want to be an Arab woman, nor do I ever want to be married by a shaykh. Whenever he insults me, I sing to vex him, 'Register: I'm not an Arab woman.'"

I looked at her hands. The traces of henna had disappeared. How happy the poor woman was with the henna on the day she returned from there and proudly related to me that the young women of the village had decorated her feet and hands with henna, dot by dot, like someone painting a picture. They sprinkled rose water on her, clothed her in silk, and sang in her wedding procession with joyful and warm hearts, "like those dancing in a funeral," as she put it.

She continued, "He now wants me to wear the Islamic scarf on my head. I want a divorce, I want to get rid of him."

I thought to myself in silence, not wanting to add to her pain: The henna of joy has gone, as well as Safi's dreams of having French citizenship, money, and glory. The outer shell of the kind artist has fallen off, and the swamps of his contradictions and implicit scorn of women have appeared. The summer of good wishes has passed and the autumn of realities and desolation has come.

She took out a telephone bill from her handbag and showed it to me. She was being asked to pay an amount three times her monthly salary for long-distance telephone calls Safi had made to his family because he missed them!

I asked her, "And your father?"

She said, "The poor man is very sick. As usual, he is obstinate and wants this miserable marriage to continue. He asked me to be patient. The wife's duty, in his view, is to tolerate her husband in everything. It's a marriage until the grave!"

She then asked, accusing me as though I were the representative of the Arab nation, "Why do you treat women like this?"

I knew that she loved her father and was ashamed of him at the same time. Her relationship with him was real but also contradictory. I let her chatter by herself. We spoke in French in that session of ours; she resented any question I posed in Arabic and pretended she did not understand it, forcing me to repeat it in French.

She seemed to be in pain and was really suffering.

After she left, I had to clean the apartment myself, with the help of my husband's kind ghost, who had not yet abandoned his earthly shell at the time. He did not forget to blame me because I paid her her wages, when she did not do any work at all and I should have rather given her a bill and charged her a fee as a psychiatrist!

Calm reigns over my home. Zakiyya-Gloria has gone into deep sleep.

It is half past four. I try to sleep like her until morning, when she can tell me about her ghost. Is it Safi or her mother or another person I don't know? Do her ghosts like classical music or do they respond to beating on the drum?

Despite my living with ghosts, I find that I know little about them. Some people claim that ghosts love the dark of night, fog, and corridors. This is not certain. Perhaps these things sensitize us to them. Perhaps we notice their existence at night only, because we are alone with our hells and are thus more capable of noticing their presence.

I claim that some ghosts love music. When I listen to Chopin, for example, I know that his ghost is present in the room, watching the effect of his music on my face and the faces of dozens of other ghosts attracted by his melodies.

I claim also that ghosts love children, but we frighten children with ghosts. I think that ghosts have temperaments like human beings and that every ghost has certain things it likes and is attracted by.

My beloved husband, for example, is attracted by the electrons of my sorrow, and I now feel his presence in my bedroom. His Aramis perfume is diffused in the air. If I turn the light on at this very moment, I will find on his pillow a blossom of genista or a violet or a pansy or a very small rose as gentle as he is, great and humble at the same time.

Perhaps the dividing line between the dead and the living in our hearts is not final to the extent that some people would like to imagine.

There are living people in our hearts who died a long time ago, and there are also dead people within us who are still moving around us like a sad memory of what they were one day before their death that was not announced in our depths.

Since my husband left his clay shell (I don't say, since his death), I have become aware that the dividing line between the dead and the living is imaginary, like all that we like to claim to be decisive in our lives.

I have come to wonder, when I go to teach and when I leave the Georges Cinq metro station and walk in the Champs Elysées, How can I distinguish people from ghosts, as of today?

Those I see in the streets, behind windows at home, in the airports, and in the trains, are they all ghosts or human beings?

This old lady sitting at the café and dressed up in the fashion of the fifties, is she living or dead?

I escape to teach, and I work all day. When I get rid of Nawwaf and return to my nest, I listen to music and write within my head a new novel to my ghosts about my ghosts.

I wonder: Doesn't writing transform me into a summoner of spirits as ghosts take over my throat and say their words? Isn't the writer in this sense merely a spiritual medium between the hero of the story and the reader?

My God, how can I sleep tonight? Did Zakiyya-Gloria have to choose me from among all people and take refuge in my "ghost house" with her own ghost, awakening my sufferings all at once?

In vain I try to sleep, but Zakiyya-Gloria has apparently fallen into a deep sleep. She is now entering into moving swamps that are more obscure, namely, dreams and nightmares haunted by the ghosts of those she knows or those she does not know. Perhaps she does not know yet that all those she sees in her dreams and does not know are ghosts of real people.

She moans as though some secret, spiritual electrons wrap her up like a cloud, as she simultaneously quarrels with herself and the ghosts within her.

Moaning is a language that suffices her for dialogue. She is in no need of familiar speech to say what she wants to the spirits surrounding her and tormenting her. *We gradually sink in silence like a stone that sinks to the bottom of the sea. Sometimes I speak with my sweet, tender, and bald husband's ghost, not so that he may hear me but so that I may hear my voice, which alone ties me to the world of the living or those who think of themselves as such.*

Here I am, gradually gliding into the bottom of the well. I see rats as large as human beings walking in the streets, gnawing both the old and the new buildings.

I see a cat giving birth to a mouse, a tiger, a squirrel, a snake, and a kitten—all from the same womb.

I wake up terrified: How are they going to live together? But then, why should they live together? Why should anything be? What is the use of anything? What is the use of interpreting the dream to myself? How difficult it is to interpret anything, even to myself.

Zakiyya-Gloria's loud moaning is certainly what awakened me. Apparently, there is no sleeping tonight. *Gloria came weeping to me, "I went and had an abortion. I don't want to go there with him, where he orders me around and humiliates me continually. Whenever he is kicked out of an official department, he returns home to beat me savagely. Humiliating me has become his enjoyment. If I gave birth, I am afraid he would kidnap the child and go back to the homeland where he is protected by everything because of the mere fact that he is a male. When I married, I had no idea of all this. I dreamt of my country as conceived in my father's stories, and I fell* in love with the warmth, the sea, the good people, the folklore, and I did not know that my obligations as a woman exceeded my rights.

"If I go there with him and finally carry my father's citizenship, my husband will be able to prevent me from traveling. He will make me live with him by court-enforced obedience, and he will marry other wives beside me. My mother explained my legal situation to me and made me understand that my interest as a woman makes it incumbent on me to hold fast to my French identity and escape the abasement of becoming an Arab woman, humiliated by Safi.

"I returned home from the abortion clinic and found that he had torn to shreds all my colorful, beautiful clothes, which you and the other ladies whom I serve in the building had given me. He had smashed the telephone and all the souvenirs we both had brought from our country. He had torn up my French identity card and my photographs, he had broken the television set and the furniture, he had wreaked all the havoc he could in my apartment—to punish me because I complained to the police that he beat me, and I resorted to French law to evict him from the apartment, the rent agreement being in my name and I being, here, a female citizen with rights like those of any male.

"My lawyer submitted my divorce case to court and an injunction was issued ordering my husband to leave my apartment, so he wrecked everything before leaving."

In an attempt to remind her of his other traits, I said to her, "But he is usually gentle and polite. Whenever I asked him to do anything for me, he did it willingly, such as moving furniture or going on an errand for me."

She replied with hurt feelings, "He is just like that with strangers. He wrecked my furniture as a punishment for me because I asked for a divorce and resorted to the police to evict him. If you could only have seen his face when he learned that, a few hours earlier, I had an abortion and that his claim, called a baby, was burned!

"He flew into a rage when I explained to him that everything had ended between us and that he no longer could humiliate me merely because I was an Arab like him. May I stay here for a while until he leaves the building?"

Her stories run within my head. I grow tired. I glide gradually into a certain well.

Zakiyya-Gloria awakens me: "Your coffee, Madam."

Perhaps I fell sound asleep. How dark it is this morning. My God, it's only 5:30. What does she want now?

She says, trembling, "The ghost is now in my apartment." *She therefore feels, even here, the electrons of his presence and his psychic currents overflowing like waterfalls.* She continues, "While sleeping, I saw him going about in the apartment with anger."

"Whose ghost is it?"

"I don't know. He is an angry ghost. That's all I know."

"Let's first drink our coffee in peace. I promise I'll accompany you to your apartment to prove to you that there's nobody there."

I wonder: Is it Safi's ghost? Is he the first of her life's ghosts? And one's love is always for the first ghost.

She insists that I accompany her to her room to see what is happening. The stupid woman wants to have witnesses to her ghost's existence in order to believe that she is not losing her mind. She does not know that meeting ghosts is the beginning of waking up.

She will be terrified of the most beautiful thing that is happening to her, until she becomes familiar with her ghosts, like every beginner. Apparently, this is how things happen to us all!

We sip our coffee together, and I can hardly open my eyes.

Zakiyya-Gloria looks at her face in the mirror in terror and says, "My God! Serge will see me tonight in this bad shape. I look like a corpse."

"And who is Serge?"

"He is my new love, but I'll not marry him. I'll never get married to an Arab. I'm still paying the lawyer's fees and the court expenses of my divorce from Safi in monthly installments out of my salary, in addition to the telephone bills and the cost of the furniture he wrecked. He did not agree to divorce me until I gave him all the money I had saved. This is unfair and I regret having accepted my father's opinion regarding marriage to Safi instead of having a free relationship with him during which I would have come to know him."

"And is Serge an Arab?"

"Yes. His original name is Salah al-Din, but he changed it to Serge when he obtained French citizenship a few weeks ago. His father is from my father's village and was a colleague of his in the mine and also rejected French citizenship. His brother has been married to my eldest sister for the last ten years. His family still lives in the north, in the same village in which he and I were both born and in which our two families continued to live even after the mine was closed. He is two years younger than I am."

"You have, then, loved an Arab for the second time?"

"I never thought I would love an Arab again. But we don't choose those we love, do we? I don't know what attracts me to him. The important thing is that I have learned my lesson and I'll never get married.

"I'll have children without marriage and thus preserve my right to the children's custody in case of separation."

I don't want to interfere in your affairs, but I'm not comfortable with the idea of having children without marriage. Children are both a responsibility and a sacrifice. We women must find a solution to being persecuted by some males. But the solution is not having children out of wedlock. I feel the need to tell her so, but I will post-pone that until another occasion.

I am not a racist, but the fact that she is a perplexed and suffering Arab woman brings her nearer to my heart. We have both gone through common agonies, in a certain sense.

She continues, "Serge was supposed to come tonight to take up residence at my apartment. We didn't dare do such things when my father was alive. When he knew what was happening, he got angry because of my relationship with Serge. He insulted and cursed me before his death two months ago, because I have been living with Serge 'in sin.' When he learned that we intended to live together in the Western way and to have children with-out getting married, he was enraged and we were obliged to keep our relationship secret. But he knew what was happening between us."

"And what did your mother say?"

"She tried to persuade my father that it was my right to live like any other French woman of my age, refraining from marriage, and that I was not better than Princess Stéphanie of Monaco, who gave birth to two babies from her consort, like hundreds of thousands of women of my age. My father was not convinced that marriage was a men's invention that was becoming extinct in France."

"And did it not occur to you that you could marry Salah al-Din on condition you retain your *'isma?*"

"What does that mean?"

"It means that you retain the right to divorce him whenever you wish, just as he does exactly."

"Nobody told me that, neither my father nor the shaykh."

"I am saying it to you."

"I don't even want to think of marriage to an Arab. I have not forgotten my suffering with Safi. One day, he came to my apartment with a beautiful woman and said that he wanted to marry her and that he would force me to live with her, because that was his right. He said that I would be one of four wives. That night, I contacted the police and they came and kicked her out. The police in his country would never do anything of the sort, if we were there. I can't accept this humiliation and I'm not obliged to. I have a job, and there are modern laws here to protect me. I shall not enter legal labyrinths of the past that I don't understand. I will never allow anyone to destroy my life from now on. Register: I'm not an Arab woman!"

"And why didn't you and Serge live together earlier, after your father's death?"

"I don't know."

"Is the ghost in your apartment the reason?"

"Perhaps. I didn't dare tell Serge about him. I was afraid he would think I was crazy. There's someone playing around with my things . . . He writes to me in French on the mirror with lipstick the word 'Prostitute.' He opens the perfume bottle which Serge gave me and spills it. He uses my toothpaste and smears the whole place with it. He sprinkles red wine on my white walls and stains them as though with blood. When Serge sleeps over at my place on the weekend, several unpleasant little things happen to his belongings, such as more than one button of his overcoat is cut, holes grow in his new socks, and his keys are lost, or he cuts himself more than usual while shaving, the shower water becomes suddenly hot and scalds him . . . and other similar phenomena."

I listen to her calmly. *I wonder, must I advise her to go and see*
a psychiatrist? Is she sick and committing all these acts herself in obscure spells which she does not remember when she comes to? Perhaps she suffers from a guilt complex . . . Perhaps she is being torn for a reason I don't know, which only a doctor can uncover.

She says to me, "I swear I'm not lying to you. Please, believe me. All this happens in my apartment and much more. The night-gown I bought to celebrate Serge's coming tonight to reside with me—I found it torn to bits yesterday evening.

"The ghost's presence in the room was dense. The glass shade, which is supposed to protect me from the bright halogen lamp, exploded all of a sudden, the glass flying in the apartment as though a mysterious power had pulverized it into fine crushed bits."

"Such accidents do happen to that kind of lamp. Haven't you heard of the caution in this regard? This is a scientific phenom-enon, not a mysterious one."

"Yes, but it happened when the lamp was off. It happened at a moment in which I felt there was a dark, angry presence run-ning furiously in my apartment. I don't know how to describe that to you. I only know that he is there, and that's it. Please, believe what I'm telling you. There is a ghost in my apartment, and he does all that on purpose. I don't know why."

"Have you seen his face?"

"No. I am conscious of his presence and don't know who he or she is. It is a presence without gender, like a soul. Or this is what I claim to myself. There are moments in which he seems to be Safi, but I'm not sure of anything."

"What was the cause, in your opinion, of his great fury last night when you returned home?"

"I don't know."

"Do you know that he will not leave the apartment until you become aware of the cause of his presence and attempt to under-stand what he wants?"

"You, then, believe that he exists? Please, believe me."

"I don't believe or deny anything, and I have no final explanation for anything. All I know is that no one knows why and how such things happen. God has endowed us with many senses which we know nothing about, and we don't understand why they sometimes become active, more sensitive and more able to see what can't be seen and to feel the presence of the invisible.

"I know that telepathy is a fact. I know also that moving things from a distance by an inner power, which some people can use, is a fact, too. Science has confirmed the existence of many extraordinary natural phenomena and continues to search for rational explanations for them, within our limited mental capability of understanding this vast universe full of mysteries. Metempsychosis, or the transmigration of the soul, is one of the disturbing phenomena, and science has confirmed the existence of certain cases that cannot be logically explained. Likewise—"

She interrupts me, terrified: "This ghost started to infiltrate my life when I began my relationship with Serge. I think it is Safi's ghost. But do the living have ghosts? Did he die and I didn't know? All I know is that Serge is like me and is not enthusiastic about getting married. We're like most of the men and women of our generation. I'll never give up this position of ours out of fear of a ghost. Besides, I don't want to get married to him. Concubinage grants me many more rights than those legal rights my father wants for me. Why should I abandon it because of a ghost?"

I said, "Why don't you ask for the right of *'isma* for yourself, and then marry him?"

"What's the use of something written on a piece of paper if we can't implement it? You have not suffered what I have before I arrived at divorce in Paris. And God alone knows what I would have suffered, if I had been in his country and had a baby by him. Nobody ever told me that, but their alliance against me is powerful. Even if I write everything I wish on the piece of paper, nobody will take heed of it there. No, Madam. Register: I'm not an Arab woman."

Zakiyya-Gloria pleads with me to accompany her to her apartment, to see for myself that she is not lying. An unpleasant thought crosses my mind: What if she is hallucinating and I find that there is nothing in her apartment of which she spoke, and that I wasted my night with a young woman, unaware that she was making fun of me?

In the elevator, she says to me, "You can't accuse me of making all that mischief myself in my apartment. The ghost sometimes dirties my belongings with things that aren't here, such as black coal dust on my white refrigerator door."

She opens the door of her studio apartment. We enter. She hesitates at the threshold, then says, "He's here."

I share her feeling. I feel a mysterious presence attracting me to the place.

I walk like a hypnotized person. I step on the smashed glass from the halogen lamp, strewn on the floor. I hear it being crushed under my shoes, but I don't care. A certain power draws me further inside, to the little balcony. I don't go to the bathroom in the narrow corridor near the door to ascertain the truth of what she related. The power leads me to the balcony in particular, to the light and not to the darkness of the kitchen which has no windows.

On the balcony, I think I see a man sitting on the floor, suspended between the rays of light and the dawn's shadows. I distinguish in him the features of the decrepit old man whom I once saw at the entrance of the building: Zakiyya-Gloria's father!

I stare at him. He glares at me with eyes gleaming darkly, commanding, not without a certain entreaty.

I hear Zakiyya-Gloria's voice saying inside the room. "I don't know why I don't wish Serge to come tonight to take up residence with me. Perhaps I ought to postpone that for a while."

The man still glares at me with tired eyes, full of pleading. His slim body in his loose clothes appears to be lost under his ample Arabian cloak, over which hangs his skull with his eyes bathed in sorrowful anger. I whisper as I ask, "Are you the one who sent her to me? Why have you chosen me?"

His tight lips are like two sharp razors glimmering in the cold air of dawn.

Zakiyya-Gloria comes out and stands by me, saying as she stares in his direction without apparently seeing him, "I feel that the ghost is here in the apartment, but I don't see him."

I am surprised that she stares at him and does not see him.

I say to her, without sound, "As for me, I see him."

She returns inside to make a telephone call to Serge, saying, "He is a construction worker and goes to work early. I hope he has not yet left his room. I'll tell him what I have decided."

I whisper to the old man, "I promise I'll try to help her . . . on condition she sees you!"

Visitors of a
Dying Person

The Rolls-Royce carrying Ra'if stops at the traffic light on the Champs Elysées in Paris. The passers-by eye Ra'if with great envy but, for the first time, he is not filled with pride and does not feel like showing off in this moment he dreamt of a long time ago in his distant village on another continent, when he did not have as much as the bus fare to go to the capital.

He sits up in the soft, velvet back seat to answer a call on the car's cellular telephone. In his other hand, he holds a crystal glass containing aged whiskey. His chauffeur, with a formal driver's cap and white gloves, waits in the front seat.

A beautiful female tourist admires him with a silent call in her eyes. He withdraws into the corner of the car like a living oyster on which lemon drops have been squeezed. *On that hot morning, my mother said to me as I looked at her clean, exhausted face framed by a white scarf that covered her hair even at home, "I have no more jewelry left but this gold bracelet. I'll go tomorrow and sell it in order to get you money for the university tuition fees."*

My poor father had died early in his life. He was stricken by fever after a night which, it was said, he spent working in the field because he did not have money to pay a helper's wages. It was also said that his illness was called worry. My mother had sold everything she owned, including her cheaper jewelry, and had nothing left but that last bracelet.

I said to her, "Give me the bracelet. I won't sell it, I'll pawn it, and I'll manage from now on."

She said, terrified, "Don't get yourself in trouble with bad company. Don't break the law, son."

I said, "Don't worry. I won't break any laws, but there will come a day when I'll make laws serve my interest.

She did not understand and asked, "What do you mean?"

"Nothing . . . and everything."

The Rolls-Royce crossed the Place de l'Etoile in the direction of Avenue Foch, the wealthiest and grandest of Parisian avenues, where millionaires live in secure mansions. *"Oh, what wonderful objets d'art," sighed Caroline, my last divorcée, when she saw my Parisian mansion for the first time before our marriage.*

She was a young woman from an old, respectable family. She knew how to appreciate my paintings, my objets d'art, and my antique furniture perhaps more than she ought to. That is why I had a prenuptial agreement that, in case of divorce, she would get nothing of them, only a meager alimony. In spite of all that, she abandoned me instead of enjoying it all with me. Oh, women. I have always loved them and have given them everything, even my mother's bracelet, but I have never understood the secret of how to deal with them.

In our last meeting as two friends on the French Riviera, I tried in vain to persuade her to return my mother's bracelet to me against payment of whatever amount of money she would demand. But she refused and left in anger and her convertible crashed into the sea. Neither her body nor the bracelet could be recovered.

"Stop here," Ra'if commands his chauffeur. "I'll walk home for a while."

The driver protests, murmuring words about "security measures" in a muffled sentence as he opens the car door with his cap off. *Those who don't want to kill me desire to kidnap me in order to exact a ransom. It is not easy for one to rise to Avenue Foch from the Shahhar alley in the village of Milhiyya, paved as it is with mud and smoothed by bare feet and buzzing with flies, without accumulating a large number of enemies and former envious friends who see their failure in the mirror of my success. Yet no one expects me to return home on foot like all other human beings, and so my walk is safe and home is only a few steps away.*

He walks on the autumn leaves covering the sidewalk. *This is one more autumn whose leaves I tread on, but there will come an autumn that will tread on my leaves . . . If I had a son . . . If only I had a son.* He walks slowly, seeking the heaps of golden leaves, and finding pleasure in the sound of their crisp crumbling under his expensive shoes. *I have been forced to walk like this on the lives of persons I hated and others I loved, persons I knew and others I did not know, as well as on women whom I perhaps loved and scorned and feared at the same time . . . beautiful women who cried with tears as black as kohl . . . I was always the killed and the killer at the same time . . . Perhaps I was the killer most of the time. There was no other means to defend myself and not sell my mother's bracelet. I was poor and weak, and everyone was ready to harm me or use me. All I did was that I traded roles with them. My mother had knelt down for a long time to clean the floor tiles of the wealthy, and in turn I did not. I have never forgotten that.*

The evening seems friendly and calm. A man in green clothes passes by him, cleaning the sidewalk energetically with a green broom. *Is he a professional hit man in disguise? Is his broom a machine gun under another form? I sold so many arms and explosives disguised as dolls, radios, and other things that I have come to think every passer-by is a killer and every broom, a machine gun. As I advance in age, I go back over my past and sometimes feel the pricks of con-science resembling repentance. But I have never known for certain when I was the one killed and when, the one killing.*

He looks back, contemplating the Arc de Triomphe in the middle of the Place de l'Etoile. *A long time ago, I used to believe this arch was built for me, even before I was born. Tonight, I feel I am nearer to the autumn leaves than to monuments. It is comfort-able to know that no one reads my thoughts, otherwise I would be laughed at. No one knows my real value other than myself or my mother, but this evening I feel I am mere dust.*

A bevy of female tourists passes by him and among them there are some beauties. *Here I am before them, denuded of my Rolls-Royce. They will not linger to look at my potbelly, which has become even more flabby, nor at my balding head, nor at my big nose, which I inherited from my mother and which is growing as days go by. I often wished to believe women's lies about my distinguished and extremely* handsome looks, and about my exceptionally attractive bald head, as they always assured me. At any rate, a curse on them all —except my mother, who finds me (I know) the most handsome of men and will, alone among women, put a rose on my tomb when I die.

He contemplates the trees with sweet melancholy. The autumn has attacked early. *I no longer like the changing seasons; I used to celebrate them in my youth. They now remind me of fugitive time and of my own life span which is not long enough any more for me to enjoy all that I have worked hard to collect and did not pause a moment to relish. I have grown old and have begun to think of death. The thoughts that assail me are thus: When and how will I die? What happens to a person when he is dying? Does he hear voices or see ghosts that others don't?* He continues to contemplate the familiar picture of that Parisian evening, a sharp, happy, and yet fleeting picture, in the middle of which is a beautiful lady who appears to have been nursed in the lap of luxury. He unclothes the woman with his eyes. *It is a habit that has never left me since my adolescence in my village. Perhaps that is why I hate strip-tease dancers in the refined Parisian cabarets. I like to possess my women in their clothes so that I may myself undress them with my own hands, and repeat the process again.* He notices that the lady of luxury is holding her child's hand. His looks are fixed on the spoiled little boy as invisible pins dig into his own heart. *We did not have enough money for my treatment when I had mumps in my adolescence. And when I was finally able to see a doctor, he only said, "Your virility will not suffer but you will not be able to have children."*

The gate guards whom the chauffeur has joined receive him with excessive respect, for which he pays exorbitant salaries. *I pay them salaries for this histrionic reception. What a fool I am!*

He sighs with satisfaction when he finally finds himself alone in his museum-like, secure mansion, where not a fly can enter without first passing by his guards or setting off alarm bells. He has rid himself of his servant and his old cook by giving them a few days' holiday, during which he will be alone with himself and his objets d'art. *After divorcing Caroline, I gradually got rid of her servants, one by one. In the past, I used to boast of my servants. I used to group them around me in the background of a picture when*

*female journalists photographed me in front of the swimming pool
of my palace in Marbella. For some time now, I have desired to be
alone, and this is my first night in my private museum without a
servant or an observer. I will be alone with my treasures, taking pleas-*

*ure in touching them, embracing them, and having sex with them
with my eyes until I fall asleep. I will play for a long time, as I wish,
without a wife or a sweetheart or a servant watching. I have become
tired of being crowded. Tomorrow is my fifty-fifth birthday. I have
reserved all the tables at the famous La Serre Restaurant for my guests,
so that I may enjoy seeing envy in their eyes. States have fallen all
around me, and I have been able through finesse to adjust to difficult
times. Whenever one of my benefactors is forsaken by fortune, I forsake
him in turn, and I expose him, for we all make mistakes. Exposing
someone is not difficult, only timing is the important thing. I may
still make more deals tomorrow. I may also seduce some beautiful
women, for I have a weakness for female beauty. I love it, I am power-
less before it, but I am incapable of being faithful to one woman for a
long time, and I resort to lies with women. I have recently lost interest in them, relatively speaking. But I am afraid of being accused of
getting old if I refrain from flirting with them and appearing in public with them. However, tonight I will rest from them, from my medi-
cines, from everything, in order "to be myself." I have often heard
this phrase said by refined, charming men at evening parties, but I
do not exactly know what it means, nor who is my self. All I know is
my own strong desire tonight to dally with my objets d'art imprisoned in armored, dark rooms. It is a desire which grows whenever my
interest in women languishes.*

Ra'if takes off his clothes and roams naked around the house.
He takes a bath and enjoys the hot massage of fragrant bubbles
in his marble tub. *I will not heed my doctor's advice. No one can
deprive me of enjoying hot water, after I have taken cold water baths
most of my childhood.*

He devours a rich, cold dinner in the kitchen, while standing next to the refrigerator most of the time, and not using any
fork, knife, or spoon, as he prefers; he eats caviar with his fingers as though it were bulgur, then he eats dozens of smoked
salmon slices without bread, and he drinks a whole bottle of rare

champagne, emitting animal sounds that please him as he further crunches chicken meat and sucks it off the bones and does other things which etiquette forbids but which have appealed to him since the time he was poor, alone, and in good health. How he enjoys rich food without servants watching and without a wife representing his doctor!

Without washing his hands, Ra'if makes the tour of his rooms of treasures, unlocking with his keys one cupboard after another. He even unlocks the transparent, bullet-proof window of the table exhibiting his rare jewels, like one who takes his kidnapped, beautiful sweetheart out in the open air for a short while. He roams among his various objets d'art with exceeding happiness, holding a glass full of cognac in his hand. *My doctor has forbidden me to eat delicious fatty foods, to drink more than one glass of alcohol a day, and to have sex more than once a week. But those stupid doctors don't understand anything about great men like me. I am different.*

He puts aside his glass of cognac from time to time in order to run his hand over his rare collection of archaeological figures, some of which have been stolen from museums in response to his offer to pay a high price for them. He contemplates his walls decked with rare paintings by great artists and is as excited as a child entering a toy store for the first time. He fingers the valuable Sèvres porcelain and the bare Galet vessels, trembling like one touching the body of a woman of whom he has dreamt since adolescence and who is still as beautiful as her legend. He almost cries. He has a talent for fake crying in front of his women in emergencies, but he now cries in joy as he returns to caress his private collection of crowns and jewelry. He puts a crown on his head, contemplating himself with rapture in an antique mirror, but his joy is vitiated by a lump in his throat. *I only wish my mother's gold bracelet were in the middle of my jewelry, although its price was no more than a tip I now give the bellboy at the Eden Rock Hotel or the Cap d'Antibes Hotel. Caroline insisted on keeping it after I gave it to her as a present. The cursed woman was drowned in the sea and took the bracelet with her to the deep along with her car. It is no longer within my power to negotiate with her to return it. Oh women. They always know how to hurt me. I love them and grant* them the most precious thing I have: my mother's bracelet. But love always goes, while regret and agonies abide. I always had to try to save myself from those women I loved. There is a chronic misunder-standing between them and me. I move about, terrified of their traps. Every step I take with them leads to some trouble. Only with my mother do I feel at ease. How have I forgotten to pass by her this evening to visit her as usual in the villa next door? She will no doubt forgive me. She forgives me everything. She alone forgives everything and continues to overwhelm me with love. Because of her bad health, I have transformed one wing of her nearby home into a small private hospital for her, with oxygen tubes, an electrocardiogram machine, an operating room, and a resident doctor for emergencies. I was accused of having done that to show off, not out of love for her, and it was said that leaving her back in the village would have been better for her. This is absolutely not true! Only with her was my relationship unlike going through a crossword puzzle or a mine field.

He wipes the tears from his eyes. He feels something like sudden fatigue. He goes to the library after pouring himself another glass of cognac. He relaxes on his luxurious, leather sofa. His eyes wander about the books surrounding him on the shelves. *I used to dream of reading them one day, but I've had no opportunity to do that. My wealth increases and my lifetime decreases.* There is a pain that is beginning to run in his left arm and shoulder, extend-ing to his chest. He thinks of making a telephone call to his mother to ask her to send him her resident doctor. *But no. It is only a passing weariness. Perhaps I have overeaten. Cognac helps digestion.*

He takes a big gulp of it and refills his glass as if it were a glass of beer. *This is how I used to drink when I was poor and found some-one to invite me . . . in those days of moonlight, poetry, dreams, the distant village, and good health . . . when I used to drink all I could from the bottle, from its mouth, without ice in the shape of hearts or dollar signs, without canapés of bread topped with first-rate caviar. Tonight I have a desire to return to the beginning, to food and drink, as in the good old days.*

The pain in his chest grows stronger, running like unseen ants crawling in his veins to their nest in his heart.

The door bell rings. This surprises him because no one can

reach him without first passing through his guards and the plated, locked doors at the entrance of his mansion. He looks at one of the monitor screens on which he observes the entrance of his mansion and the rooms of his home. He sees nobody. But the door bell still rings and the monitor screen is completely empty. It is as though an invisible finger is continuing to press the button of his musical bell.

He decides that there is something wrong with it, so it is ringing by itself. He gets up with difficulty to open the door and try to pull the button outward to silence it. On his way to the door, he regrets that he did not instead get in touch with the guard to ask him to do that for him. *I am still a young man and am able to do that.* His eyes catch a glimpse of his face in the mirror. For the first time, he sees it clearly and he is stunned. *Who is this old man reflected in the mirror? I am still in the prime of my life. My God! What happened to me?*

He casts a last look at the monitor screen next to the door, showing the stairs, the entrance, the hallway, the closed elevator door, and the room door with no one in front of it.

He opens the door to repair the slightly defective bell. He is surprised to see a woman ringing the bell, wearing black gloves, clothes, and hat, as though she is in mourning. She raises her black lace veil from her face, hangs it backward on her hat, and puts forward the radiant face of a young woman in her twenties. He is stunned on seeing her. He whispers weakly, "Tracy?" But that's not possible. He is overcome by sudden terror. Unable to believe his eyes, he thinks of calling his guards, of chasing her away. *What will I tell my guards? Will I ask them to come upstairs and kick my former wife out on the street, and will I scold them because they permitted her to come upstairs and because the monitoring cameras are not working?* He is paralyzed by surprise. *It can't be Tracy. It has been three decades since we divorced. How could she remain a blend of radiance and youth while I have grown old?* He feels unable to hold his body up. His legs are sinking. He lies down on the soft seat in the wide entrance hall, his chest pains having returned. Tracy sits opposite him on one of the seats. In the light coming from behind her, her transparent black dress appears to him to be without her body, as though it is empty and suspended in the space of the room over two black stockings and a pair of shoes with spike-like high heels.

He contemplates her face and he is again amazed at her radiance. It does not stand to reason that she could remain so young after thirty years of separation. Is this her daughter? It must certainly be, but what does she want of him? She answers him as though she is reading his thoughts, "I've come to say goodbye to you." *How did she know I intended to travel to New York in two days on a business and love trip?* "I've come to say goodbye not because you're going to New York but to another place. You have an intuition about that but you don't want to believe it. I've come to tell you what I always wanted to tell you: You're a little scoundrel, not a knight and a poet as you always liked to convince yourself and those around you. I knew you when you came to Beirut from a distant village in Qam'istan (Repressionland) in search of freedom and a livelihood, and you were my colleague at the newspaper, but did not share in my wealth. You overwhelmed me with your poems and romantic acts, and I was much older than you, and so I loved you back. And despite my family's rejection of our marriage, my father later took you under his wing and surrounded you with prestige and wealth, and Beirut granted you position and prominence, although you were a stranger. But you divorced me a few days after you got Lebanese citizenship, by virtue of a special decree obtained through my father's influence, and you claimed I was trying to humiliate you and dominate you with my wealth."

Ra'if opens his mouth to answer her. But she continues, "You betrayed me several times but my love for you was greater than everything. Your ability to lie was astonishing. Your tears. Your repentance. Your regret. Lies about the demands of your business. Your absence away from me. I used to rejoice on believing all your lies because, if I did not believe them, I would lose my mind—I being the one who changed my religion in order to marry you!" *It is not reasonable that she is Tracy. Tracy was several years older than I was; she was a university graduate doing her training in one of her father's newspapers. There must be a logical*

explanation to what is happening. The guards were not attentive
when she entered and the monitoring cameras were not functioning.
This is not Tracy. Perhaps it is her daughter or granddaughter.

She says to him as though reading his thoughts, "You always
knew that I was able to bear children, that I was not barren as
you made me believe, claiming one time that you kept me despite
the fact that I was unable to give birth to children, because you
loved me, and another time threatening to marry a second wife
to bear you a child or perhaps three women to be co-wives with
me, as your religious law permits.

"After you divorced me, I continued to cry for you and for
the loss of your mother's bracelet that you gave me as a present
one day to show me in what great esteem you held me although I
bore no children. I always continued to love you somehow. And
when I used to get drunk, I would find that my car took me to
the repair garage at our old home in the Hamilton Building, and
I continued that painful habit until the garage was transformed
into a commercial agency for selling vacuum cleaners! But I did
not vacuum you out of my life until I discovered that I was pregnant after I married Pierre, who loved me and wanted to tie his
life to mine although I had frankly told him I was barren. You
were therefore lying when you claimed that you underwent medical tests and that your friend Dr. Bassam confirmed that you were
in the best of health. Nothing equaled my joy in being pregnant
and my sad disappointment in you. I said to myself, Your great
love, then, was that of a rascal and a liar."

"I was no rascal. I only feared that my manliness would be
insulted if people knew I was infertile. I was afraid of your family,
who watched me while I ate at your home as though I was the
cook's son who was able to sit with you and be part of your family
only in a blind moment of fate, and they counted every one of
my mistakes. I had to be doubly polite in order to be accepted in
your harsh and derisive family. I had to play the role of the clown
at evening parties so that it would be whispered, 'It is true he is
from a backward village and mean lineage, but he is intelligent
and pleasant.' Pierre, whom you married, could remain silent all
through an evening party, and he could even say stupid things,

but no one would say he was backward, for he was one of you. But I had to exert double effort to become accepted. I felt I was a Negro, my white skin secretly lined with black, and I did not dare to tell my secret to anyone."

"But your being suppressed did not make you sympathize with one like me, who was suppressed because those around pitied me and perhaps scorned me because I was unable to bear children."

"But you did. You succeeded and became pregnant. Why then do you blame me?"

"I became pregnant but my joy was not complete. Lying in my bed, I hemorrhaged for a long time, and I struggled to keep my baby, but my advanced age caused the pregnancy to end in miscarriage. After several unsuccessful attempts, the doctor said I could no longer keep a baby to full term. You kept me as a wife until you feathered your nest and arranged your financial affairs, then you divorced me. In the meantime, it was too late for me, and thus you deprived me of motherhood. You did not really love me ever. I was the wooden log you clung to for safety from drowning until you reached the first island."

"But I loved you. It was you who changed. You became fat and flabby. You got drunk. You used obscene words. You had no job but watching me and spying on me."

"And you, too, imprisoned me by your jealousy, which increased in ferocity after every time you betrayed me. Do you think I did not know about Myrna? You stole your mother's bracelet from me and gave it to her, then continued to upbraid me for months for having lost it."

"We loved each other one day, then we fought and separated. But you will always remain my beloved first wife, who taught me how to eat lobster with the fork and knife and other complicated kitchen tools, and how to distinguish between lentils and caviar, and between sardines and smoked salmon, and at what temperature I should drink my wine, and how to dress elegantly, and how to distinguish an earthen jar from Sèvres and Galet vessels, and how to have a taste for art and objets d'art. I am indebted to you for all that as you are indebted to me for extraordinary moments of love in which I rode you like a pony and ran off with you to beaches of pleasure and to far dunes of endless ecstatic thrills and shining light. Don't you remember?

"We met, we exchanged love and interests—yes, interests because there is no pure love—and we lived days which were not without bitter moments and hurts, then we separated. I admit I went beyond what was acceptable when I claimed that you were barren and did not confess to my own defect. But I was obliged to defend myself against your universe, which was ready to trample on me. Yet, you will always remain my beloved first wife."

It seems to him from Tracy's face that she is touched.

The door bell rings.

He stares at the monitor screen. No one.

He tries to stretch out his hand to press one of the buttons on a panel on the nearby table, to call a guard to repair the bell or the monitor screen and to rebuke him because people are knocking at his door without being observed. He cannot. His hand stays pressing his chest, which is undergoing some distress resembling pain.

Tracy goes to the door and opens it. A beautiful woman dressed in black mourning clothes enters. Her long hair covers her shoulders and thick powder covers her beautiful country features. He tries to remember where he saw her, but at the same time he feels he does not want to remember.

She strides toward him like a projectile, thundering, "You scoundrel . . . I am your first wife, not she. Stop lying. Have you forgotten Tahiyyat?"

As she says this, she sways her hips in her special way that he once knew and liked.

Ra'if is astonished. Tahiyyat, too, is still a youngish woman in her forties, as she was when he married her. *I saw her dancing at the night club and I lost my mind. She appeared luscious when she moved to the rhythm of drums. I thought her to be the perfect woman, who was difficult to obtain without marriage. That is what she made me think. I was then a university student who did not have money to buy food and pay tuition fees. I married her, I was nineteen years old, and I divorced her a few months after that. Is there no one to forgive the rashness of youth?*

Tahiyyat sits next to Tracy in an atmosphere of harmony, as though their common hatred for him united them more than any love!

As soon as Tahiyyat sits down, she says to him as though she has read his thoughts, "It was not the rashness of youth but rather the ruse of a mature man. You took possession of all my earnings to pay your tuition fees and claim back your mother's pawned bracelet and provide her with some money. I ignored everything until you began to beat me. You protected me jealously and wanted my money at the same time."

Hardly does he open his mouth to defend himself when the door bell rings again. He does not see anyone on the monitor screen. Tracy opens the door. Myrna enters. He sees her as one sees things in a dream. *I am certainly drunk and perhaps I am asleep and having a nightmare, of which I will wake up in a short while. If it wasn't for the pain that tears at my chest, I would jump up off this soft seat by willpower, as I do when I have a nightmare and decide to leave it and succeed.*

Myrna approaches him, and he clearly sees her fair features and golden hair and her ever-shining, honey-colored eyes.

She says, "When you gave me an ordinary gold bracelet and said it was your dead mother's, I really believed I was your great love, although I was married. It did not occur to me that you befriended me and my husband in order to become acquainted with his friend at the university who was an Arab ruler's son. And when I read in the newspapers about your visit to him and your readiness to publish a magazine that supported him and his father, I was greatly astonished and said to my husband, 'The man supported Nasser. Why has he changed loyalties? What happened to him?' He answered, 'The king died, long live the king. The head of state who pays journal publishers sits on the verbal throne of people like him.'"

Tracy asks her without rancor, "You are then the lady with whom he spent New Year's Eve, when we were still married, claiming that he was working to establish his magazine?

Myrna answered, "No. He visited me in the afternoon, claiming he was obliged to spend the evening with you. It seems he spent it with a third woman. The bracelet disappeared that day, and I did not know whether the nanny or the cook stole it or whether he regretted having given it away and decided to take it back!"

The bell door rings. Ra'if looks at the screen and sees the entrance empty. He gulps the last drop of his cognac and lets the glass drop to the floor. The door opens by itself. A lady of moderate beauty and elegance enters. He does not remember her face. She approaches and he sees her clearly. *No. It's not possible for anyone to forget that black hair and those blue eyes. She is certainly Hana, and I am certainly drunk.* Without greeting, she addresses him as though reading his thoughts, "As is your habit, true and false at the same time. Yes, I am Hana, and you are not only drunk, you are in worse condition. If Myrna, Tahiyyat, and Tracy knew your face as that of a poet and an educated journalist, you presented to me the well-wrought face of a freedom fighter. You made much money playing the part and strengthened your financial relations thus, while I did not know. I worked night and day, risking my life under heavy shelling, to write the best reportages for your magazine, *Freedoms*. And when you did not pay me my salary, I would thank you because you were an honorable freedom fighter, just like that, and because the magazine continued to appear even during the war. Every evening I came from my divorced mother's home to the magazine's office, not heeding shells and bombs and full of great ideas and high ideals, not knowing that you had started your march toward lavish wealth.

"Rivers of wealth flowed from here and there. Your only problem was to weigh which of the factions paid you more, so that we might bark in support of that one. My problem was that I had not discovered then how independent my thinking was from my body, which was enslaved by you, until I discovered in the basement of the building of *Freedoms* dozens of those who refused to acquiesce in serving your interests, and so had been imprisoned by you. I was stunned that day: *Freedoms* magazine transformed into a prison, and revolutionary Lebanon into a nightmare, while you, who claimed to defend freedoms, were defending those who paid you more! For the first time, I understood how sudden departures from fixed aims happened and I understood the practical meaning of vague words like opportunism, unscrupulous drive, militia depravity, and Mafia-like rottenness. I shall never forget

the night in which I discovered your reality. That night, I succeeded in sneaking into the building of the magazine. I had imagined you would be sitting in your office under the shelling, but
I did not know that your projects had grown, when I and people
like me were not paying attention, nor that you had moved those
projects to London with you. As for the magazine building, it
was abandoned even by the guard, who was terrified by the shelling. There were many tales of terror for me to hear from the
lips of your forgotten prisoners, locked up in the basement after
the guards had stopped coming because they were afraid of the
shelling. I released all the prisoners, being thunderstruck by the
irony: the building of *Freedoms* becoming a prison!

"Only one young man could not escape and breathed his last
in my arms. He was twenty years old. You certainly remember
him. He was your driver, Anis. As he lay dying, he said he knew
more about you than he should have. He saw you ally yourself
to both the Klashnikov Embassy and its enemies at the same time
and receive money from both. When he refused to be paid and
silenced, you imprisoned him and forgot all about him. You also
forgot to tell your henchmen, before you left, that he was innocent. So they tortured him until he admitted all that they wanted
him to admit. When you returned from your trip with new funds,
new instructions, and new positions, 'in the service of the cause,'
required by the 'necessities of the present stage,' poor Anis had
died in my arms.

"He breathed his last in front of me; he had been dying under
torture for a long time before that, in the basement of *Freedoms*.

"I did not say anything when I saw his picture in one of your
posters saying that he had been kidnapped and his whereabouts
were unknown, and that it was thought likely he was martyred.
I realized that you and your men had gotten rid of his corpse. I
began to plan so that you would have a painful death, before
which you would suffer for a long time. But I did not have the
opportunity to implement it, because you did not return from
London but instead moved to Paris and closed the publishing
business, revealing your true nature as a businessman dealing in
arms, real estate, drugs, and women."

Ra'if tries to bear the pain in his chest and responds in a weak voice, "This is not true. I did not abandon the cause. It abandoned itself. I did not escape until I was aware that I was no more than a pawn in a chess game between big players who ordered small players to move and sacrificed the bishop, the rook, and the queen, to say nothing of the knight and the pawns. I always tried to escape and persist. My only crime was that I was more intelligent than those who died as victims, thinking they were heroes, and that I realized what was coming before the others. As for Anis's death, I am really sorry for that. But in war, nobody can guarantee that a bullet will reach its target. Revolution means victims also, and when it goes wrong, everyone becomes a victim . . . and you are the victim of yourself."

She opens her mouth to answer him, but he interrupts her, continuing, "You were in love with my body, and you covered up our relationship, which was shameful in your view, with an 'ideological' crust by adopting my thought. Then you exaggerated my faults to yourself to justify abandoning me intellectually after I had abandoned you! I confess to you that I prefer a real prostitute to an 'ideological' thinking woman who cannot distinguish between her orgasm and her intellectual delight."

He hears the door bell ringing. He sees the door opening by itself. A young woman enters, dressed in black like all his other visitors. He does not remember where he saw her. She is plumpish and has a beautiful face with two dimples. She sits next to the other women without asking permission. He sees them sitting around him as if he is in a strange, nightmarish trial in which he is the accused. But who is this newcomer and why is she in mourning? She says, "I am Nahid, your secretary. I never failed to distinguish between my orgasm and my intellectual delight, because matters of the intellect did not interest me, and that was what appealed to you immensely. And yet, you were perfidious toward me, too. Between encouraging invitation and veiled threat, between one shell and the next, you took possession of me on the dirty floor of the office."

He hears his own voice like a death rattle in his throat as he defends himself, "What is my crime if you yourself wanted that?

Your mouth says no and your body shouts yes. When a woman thrusts her body in my overcoat, I don't know how to tell her: Excuse me, lady. I will never marry you. Take your virginity elsewhere."

"Then you abandoned me and did not heed my pleas."

"We lived together and exchanged pleasures, joys, and individual whims. Life is so, and we are so."

The door bell does not cease ringing. He feels unable to press the red button to call his guards. The pain in his chest tears at him. Dozens of women enter in black mourning clothes. Their faces approach his face and recede from it, as in a nightmare. They yell as their angry features come close to his eyes, but he cannot move because of his chest pains.

"I am the one who committed suicide because of you, and you pretended to be sorry but were really proud."

"You did not commit suicide because of me. You were a nervous wreck and needed a peg on which to hang the responsibility of your death."

"I am the one whom you hit with your car, and I am still crippled."

"The light was green and I did not see you. You did not pay attention when the passers-by cautioned you."

"I am the one you chased for years, and when you got me you tried to humiliate me."

"In love, there are no guarantees . . . I am a man in whose depths abides a hunter . . . I love the road, not the arrival."

"And I am the one to whom you gave a diamond necklace, then you stole it and blamed me for losing it."

"Despite my wealth, I suffered from fits of avarice following spells of generosity. I am a human being, lady, not a model lover."

"And I am the one you desired madly and could not obtain, so you intentionally aimed to tarnish my reputation."

"I am not proud of that. I only wished that it would make you surrender to me."

"I am the one with whom you had fun one evening during the war. When you were taking me back home, the telephone rang in your car, so you let me out into the terrifying street, because you were called to an important meeting, and you lied, saying that I would find a taxi to take me home. Then one of your 'guerrillas' raped me."

"I acknowledge that I am not an extremely gallant knight. I could not permit myself to lose the deal, for I would have lost it, if I had not gone to the meeting . . . It is unfortunate that that happened to you, but in wartime, when we leave our homes, we take risks wherever we go . . . This is not my fault."

"I am the dancer who loved you, but you abandoned me and left me as a gift to one of your clients."

"This caused me pain that night. But I knew that you would abandon me anyhow."

"As for me, I abandoned you for another man before you abandoned me for another woman, so you took revenge by kicking me out of my job."

"Like all men, I love to be a womanizer. It was difficult for me when you took away my role and acted like a 'manizer.' You had to be punished!"

How numerous they are around him! He painfully remembers that all his objets d'art cupboards are open, and he is afraid of robbery.

He tries to rise in order to close and firmly lock them. But he is unable to move. He wonders: Have they come to rob him?

He stares at them, sitting around him in a black circle. *Yes, indeed, I am in a trial like the one witches hold for a person they imagine to be their executioner in some burning at the stake. How can I explain to them that a man is both killer and killed at every moment, that his fate plays havoc with him, and that he is neither white nor black but merely another gray man? How can I explain this to this gathering of the women of my lifetime? They are now closing circle around me to take me to account, along with others who will certainly join them, for I have known many women. I am almost happy at their presence, coming thus all at one time and holding a dialogue with me with bare knuckles. What worries me is this invisible dagger which slowly sinks more deeply into my chest and hurts me. Were it not for this, I would laugh at this nightmare.*

The ringing of the door bell does not cease in his ears. He sees

Caroline entering. His mother's gold bracelet around her wrist shines in his eyes and he is overcome by amazement. Caroline is dead, how did she come? Are more of these women present dead also?

He feels terrified as Caroline's voice reaches him, "Yes, I am dead. But I loved you once, before I died. You were dozens of years older than I was, but I really loved you. You had an astonishing power to act like an adolescent, you had childlike impetuosity, and you lied as if you spoke the truth. After you possessed me, you wanted me no more. I was transformed into an extinguished light in my bed. You jilted me to go to another victory. No longer did anything occupy you except being unfaithful to me, and no longer did you try to possess me with warmth except after cheating on me, when you would again come alive as a lover. I was too young to understand your tricks, but after our divorce I learned a lot. I would have proved this to you, had we not had a quarrel, which led to my driving the car when I was drunk and crashing into the sea, dying and remaining at the bottom unseen by the divers searching for my corpse."

The bell ringing continues. Ra'if tries to stare at the monitor screen, hoping the person will be one of his guards who might have finally become aware of the noisy women at his place, as they all spoke together at once, as if in a hallucinatory trial.

A woman with a decrepit body and tattered clothes enters. All the women sitting fall silent at her presence. He tries to stare at her, almost overcome by terror. She is wearing black as though she has never known anything else in all her life. She is an old woman with a slight body, and he can swear that he never knew her in all his life. Her eyes are red. Her eyelids, weary of chronic crying, are like the walls of a cave corroded by salt over the centuries. Despite all this, her face looks familiar. She says with a dignity that makes the women sitting put down their legs, previously crossed, and sit up like pupils in a school of sorrow, "I am Anis's mother. It is a name that certainly means nothing to you. Anis, my son, was your driver who was tortured to death. And I committed suicide in sorrow for him. Do you have anything to say to me before you die?"

He feels real terror. *Will I wake up from my nightmare before they sentence me? Will I get up before I die? Help . . . Where is my voice to shout for help?* The sorrowful mother repeats her question: "Do you have anything to say to me before you die?"

A miserable, bitter feeling takes possession of him. Its bitterness has a sound like moaning.

He has nothing to say to her. Furthermore, she appears to have a great resemblance to his mother. He wonders: Is she his own mother or his driver's mother? At exactly that moment, he sees her take out a dagger with a thin blade that shines before his eyes. He does not move. He does not yell. He does not know why he surrenders. The blade penetrates his heart and transfixes him in a moment of extreme pain. He sees her pull it out with his blood dripping from it, and she throws it on the floor.

His arm, extended to the bell to call for help and summon his guards, falls on the red button on the panel and all the bells ring.

His first wife, the dancer Tahiyyat, gets up calmly. As he is almost passing away, she gives him a farewell kiss on the lips and leaves. The other women bend over him and follow suit. He sees them with difficulty as he sighs with pain, unable to breathe.

They leave the house, one by one. Caroline takes off his mother's bracelet and places it on his chest. They all go. As for Anis's mother, she appears to him to resemble his mother more and more. She approaches him as in a dream, her face drawing up to his, and she seems to him to be his mother in person. He calls her, asking for help, "Mother." She spits in his eyes, so he closes them as he falls down into a well, passing away, vanishing into the void.

The guards and the driver rush in, terrified at the ringing of the special bell for help. They are surprised to find the outside door open and Ra'if fallen on the entrance seat. He appears to be dead and has an antique gold bracelet on his chest. On the floor, there is a dagger that appears to be very ancient.

The police close the cupboards of the objets d'art. The guards assure them that they saw no one enter the mansion, well-guarded as it is by dozens of electronic alarms. They did not hear the ringing of the door bell and have no explanation why the door was open.

The investigator agrees: "It appears that nothing has been stolen. Perhaps he died of a heart attack."

The doctor confirms that.

The investigator is perplexed by that old dagger they found near the corpse.

Ra'if's mother assures them she never saw it before, but she thinks it probably belongs to her son's archaeological collection.

The investigator's perplexity increases when the fingerprint specialist tells him the dagger has no fingerprints, not even Ra'if's.

Ra'if's mother laments weakly. Despite the tragedy of the sudden death of her son, caused by a heart attack, she cannot help wondering: Where has my bracelet come from? Ra'if told me that Caroline was wearing it when she drove her car and crashed into the sea before his eyes, and her body was not found. Where then did my bracelet come from? And that dagger . . .

The Swan Genie

Fog. My beloved river is wrapped today in a cloak of fog, and humidity flows from its feet.

Like one stealing a look at her lover, I stare at it from my window as is my custom every morning while drinking my coffee before I go to work.

My husband is jealous of it. He says to me, "If it were a man, I would have challenged him to a duel in the Bois de Boulogne like old-time knights. But what can I do with a wife who betrays me with a river called the Seine?"

I contemplate the river as it changes faces and colors every moment. It runs in front of me lined with greenery, exhibiting a beauty that is impossible to contain and pushing my heart to the brink of tears. A mad artist poured silvery gray paints into it, which the genie of Swan Isle[1] hardly touched with its brush to transform the water into a river of mercury.

I sip my coffee and celebrate all that splendor as well as Swan Isle, as I like to call the island I can see in the river.

Behind the Seine stands the Eiffel Tower with its exquisite metallic lace, looking like a *mécano* toy of a crazy genius. The modern Radio-France Building is at my right. And at my left is the admirable Chaillot Palace with its garden, whose statues dance secretly at night and have veiny complexions in the summer.

The gardens and parks sway in green raiment up to the Ecole

1. Allée des Cygnes is an island resembling a path of greenery in the middle of the Seine River near the Eiffel Tower.

Militaire, the Tour Montparnasse, and the many houses proud of their unique character and long history, and up to the Sacré-Coeur Basilica, which the Montmartre fog enfolds.

I no longer feel I am a stranger in Paris. I am sometimes ashamed of myself because I no longer feel I am a stranger in Paris; I feel like one who has betrayed an old lover named Beirut.

No one likes to confess to having two lovers at the same time. I was raised on the song that says, "You alone are my sweetheart," and on the belief that there is no pluralism in anything, and yet I love both cities. I sigh with relief and freedom whenever I land at the Orly Airport in Paris, coming back from a visit to Beirut! And I close my eyes in a silent, heavy feeling of guilt toward my native city, Beirut. Today I have to choose and I am unable to choose. When I am here, I feel I have betrayed Beirut; and when I go there, I feel Beirut has betrayed me!

Furthermore, matters are more complicated than that. *Last night my husband said to me before we went to bed, "You have to resolve the issue and make a decision—either you stay alone in Paris or return with me to Beirut."*

In plain Lebanese, this means divorce. It is not acceptable for a woman to live alone in Paris while her husband is in Beirut and she does not have his approval.

I remained silent.

He asked, "Is there another man?"

I remained silent.

How can I explain to him that there is another city, another life, which I no longer wish to abandon.

He said, "I can't understand how you could prefer a life of work, misery, and relative poverty here and alone in Paris to a life of wealth there in Beirut."

I remained silent because I, too, did not understand. There is a black spot within me, wrapped in fog. My inner depths are fog. The "yes" is fog and the "no" is fog, alternative paths are fog and the conjugal bed is deep in fog.

We have already said all that can be said in the last two months, since our daughter got married to her university friend who hap-

pened to be Lebanese like us and she returned with him to Beirut.
Our second daughter followed her brother to the United States to
continue her higher education in one of its universities.

After sharing life with the same husband for a quarter of a cen-
tury, I am able to hear what he does not say but means in his heart:
I want a wife who is comfortable and lives in luxury, who is elegant
in high heels and wears contact lenses, who waits for me at home,
supervises the cook, and is able to accompany me to evening parties
and throw better parties in return. I want a home that is open to
people. I want you to be at home, as we used to be before the war. In
short, I want your university diploma hung in the proper place for
it, namely, on the kitchen wall of the conjugal villa.

I know that a wrangle at the end of the night with a man I love
(despite this being so and despite it being my husband) is painful and
may last until dawn, because of our deep disagreement that resembles
an abyss.

It sometimes happens that we love "the wrong person," and per-
haps we do really love only "the wrong people."

I could not discuss all that again with him or have the leisure of
an altercation because I had to be at work on time, early in the
morning as usual.

He repeated, "You can no more take the children's education in
Paris as a pretext for staying here, and I can no longer stay here and
wait. You must make up your mind and decide. I am obliged to return
to my office in Beirut to administer my estate and care for my sisters
as I did before the war."

I almost answered, "You have been able to petrify your life from
the moment the war began, and now you want to resume it from that
very moment in the past when it stopped, as though it were a statue
brought back to life. As for me, my real life started with the war,
which set me free . . . I have been alive, working all those years, and
I have changed."

But I remained silent, for I had often told him that in the past.

I quickly drink the remainder of my coffee. I put on my
clothes and my make-up. I am forty-five, but my mirror harshly
says I look older, with eyes whose swollen, black circles my

make-up cannot successfully conceal. Around my mouth there are wrinkles, and night creams have failed to remove from my forehead the testimony to my hard work, my worries, and my efforts for the past nine years to earn my family's bread. But when peace returned to Lebanon a few months ago, war started in my personal life.

I rush to the metro. *I have become accustomed to the suffocating daily crowds; the sweat of those who are unable to pay the price of perfume and find themselves too tired in the evening to enjoy a shower; the little daily battle to occupy a metro seat that would spare me from standing at a door or in the aisles of the train, exposed to shoulder shoves—becoming part of a human block whose waves go to and fro, carry me, and hurl me against the metal walls, a human block throbbing with exhaustion, vitality, and stench—the feet that step on other feet, with or without apologizing; the river of humanity that almost sweeps me off as it gushes down through automatic metal doors that open with a slight circular pressure on the handle, which appears like the last thing distinguishing the relation between what is mechanical and what is human, and perhaps is the last communication between them.*

When I don't succeed in occupying a seat, the human river getting off the metro at the stations almost sweeps me off, with my slim figure and obstinately weak body. So I hold on to one of the metal posts until the tributary that was waiting on the station platform gets on the train. Then, its new waves hurl me away from my safety post in the middle of the train and to the other door of the metro carriage, which continues to roar and run in dark tunnels, while a small fear takes possession of me: What if the door bursts open under the pressure of the thundering river of human beings?

Every morning I thank God that in the metro I am not surrounded by a jammed human block in a city of sexually repressed beings. Otherwise, I would be exposed as a woman to the humiliation of being pressed by feverish bodies and burning fingers.

It is true that it never happened that a man gave up his seat for me here. In return, it never happened that any man insulted me by thrusting himself upon me in the crowded rush for my livelihood.

Every woman out of her home here is not, as she is in my country, "a project for a seduction" or "a prostitute" until she proves to be otherwise.

I once asked a female friend of mine why she took to wearing the veil, and she answered, "In order to rest from being harassed and in order to be free!"

A few little things draw me to this city as a woman. I would like to tell my husband about them, but I know he will never understand. One of them is that, here, I am not in need of his permission to obtain a passport. I am an independent person here, bound to a family, yes, but a person having an individual existence, a person accepted for herself, like any man in my country. Many things attract me strongly to Paris, and he will never understand them. Or rather, he will understand them, for his intelligence exceeds mine; but he will say that I give them more importance than they deserve and that I am no longer obliged to undergo daily contact with their harsh realities.

The stars are happy with me today. I have been able to find a seat in the metro. I relax a little. I take out my book and my reading glasses. This is also one of the things I will miss if I return to Beirut. *Our chivalrous driver opens the door for me. I get into the Mercedes in order to be taken to perform some showoff charitable acts as an atonement for our luxurious living, meanwhile chattering with my female friends laden with gold earrings and bracelets and other ornaments and wearing expensive clothes—all in a continuous battle to earn the title of being the woman most able to expressively demonstrate the wealth of her living or dead husband . . . as if we were moving advertisements for exuberant vanity.*

I now wear simple clothes. I walk about in low-heel shoes in the streets and the metro corridors. I read books in the trains of the poor class, of which I was a part before my marriage, and I like the liveliness of all that.

In the beginning, reading in public transportation seemed to me to be a strange habit. Instead, I read the faces of those around me.

Day after day, I discovered I could read faces better after every book I finished reading. And so I became like them. I put on my reading glasses in the metro without being ashamed of my short-sightedness, for things are different here. *My mother* rebuked me: "Stop reading. You will lose the beauty of your eyes. And take off those horrible glasses. What will people say if they see you like this, and what bridegroom will want to come near you?"

My four brothers could wear glasses in peace. But the alliance of my mother and my maternal and paternal aunts made me feel ashamed of my glasses and my weak vision. So I took them off in the streets and did not recognize some friends as they passed by; and I later had to listen to their criticism because I ignored them. I remained silent, not daring to tell them the shameful truth of my physical weakness.

Since childhood, at the cinema, I had to put on my glasses secretly after the lights were turned off and the movie began, otherwise I would be scolded by my mother. Before the lights were turned on at the end, I took my glasses off. I continued to do that even as an adult in the cinema, unaccompanied by my mother.

I said to her, "But tomorrow is examination day. How do you want me to review my lessons and study without glasses? I would like to obtain a diploma in interior decorating."

She said bluntly, "Why? To hang it in your husband's kitchen?"

My father said, "Be thankful that it was she who chose this worthless subject to study, not her brother who is a medical student or her brother who is a law student or the others. Imagine our misfortune if our two boys had not chosen to study medicine and law; and their two brothers will follow suit."

My brothers smiled proudly, for they are continuously praised, merely because they are males, but in addition they study medicine or law or civil engineering. All other modern studies besides these are nonsense in the sight of my mother and father.

As for me, I can study any nonsense that suits me until the bridegroom comes. The fact that I study anything is an imitation of a tradition that came from the West. The bridegroom will put an end to this comedy at the appropriate time.

The bridegroom came. He was wealthy, thirty-three years old, from a respected Beirut family and, above all, handsome. I was nineteen years old, of moderate beauty, quarrelsome, anxious to be free from my brothers' oppression and their interference with the details of my clothing and my times of going out, as though they were a higher class of human beings. There was no dialogue between us but rather repression!

My father said "yes" to the bridegroom, and I said "no" until I finished my studies.

They all tolerated what they considered to be coquettish, spoiled behavior on my part. For we were close to poverty and my family considered me to be fortunate. I pitied the bridegroom for having to go through a long engagement period of two years, during which I did not succeed in hating him, as I had hoped.

I wished to rebel against this continuous planning of my life by poverty and by them, too. But Wafiq did not kindle in me any hatred for him, and so I got married and gave birth to a boy and two girls, meanwhile not knowing whether I loved my husband or not.

And amidst wedding ululations, my mother hung my diploma in the kitchen, and I was eventually tamed by three children and much luxury. And thus I fell into a cobweb-like net made of gold and silk threads.

The metro stops at one of the stations. I take a deep breath. It is less crowded than usual and relatively comfortable in the month of August, when I receive a double salary because I do not go on vacation like the rest of the people of Paris.

Around me are tourists who laugh and chatter aloud, excited because they are in Paris. But they don't really know Paris, for Paris conceals within it another secret, magical city with which I have fallen in love. It is a love sharpened by the hundreds of books I have read in the metro over the years and nurtured weekly by visiting art exhibits, attending literary and intellectual debates in public panels and watching them on television, going to the theater and the opera whenever I could economize on household expenses enough to go to their enchanting world—otherwise an almost free visit to one of the museums would satisfy me . . . This is in addition to dozens of rich historical exhibits of articles traveling from everywhere and meeting in a collection in Paris.

I leave the metro at the Etoile station and transfer to another metro line that will take me to the Franklin Roosevelt station on the Champs Elysées. This is repeated every morning and evening. *Nadia gasped gloatingly in 1986 when she learned that I had often not attended our women's circle to drink tea at the grand hall of the*

Plaza-Athénée Hotel because I worked at a large fashion house as a saleswoman and was the one responsible for the layout of the shop window.

She said in gloating pity, "Have you then become a saleswoman at the very place from which you used to buy your clothes? And do you go there by metro every day? How terrible! I am sorry for you!"

I knew the impact the news would make on members of our circle, we who often skied together on winter holidays at Gstaad and St. Moritz in Switzerland, swam together in Monte-Carlo, had dinner at Eze and Antibes, and went on cruises on the yachts of friends between St. Tropez and Cannes. Not one of my friends ever tried once to use the metro. They preferred to use their own Rolls-Royce, Mercedes, or Jaguar.

In time, something in Paris made me unashamed of being poor and practicing an honorable profession. Something in the pride of the garbage collectors, the restaurant waitresses, and all the other women workers here made me return to my own reality as a daughter of a poor family and take pride in that, after having tried to conceal it. I decided: A human being is a human being, and professions are similar whatever they may be. If that feeling which Paris instills in me and teaches me is all that remains after the horrors of the French Revolution, it is sufficient.

That is why I told Nadia simply and without bitterness "You know the war. My husband did not take precautionary measures and did not smuggle any of his money to Swiss banks. All his wealth is in the form of real estate in Beirut, lands and properties. Sales are now at a standstill because of the war."

Our bank account here was opened originally for the expenses of summer tours. But we bought our home here with the amount, and that was the end of that. We no longer possess anything.

Though I did not tell her, I felt I had a lump in my throat, or rather several lumps. One of them is that my husband was ashamed of our poverty, so he withdrew within himself and boycotted his friends. Another is that he discovered we were poor suddenly, when we had no more money to buy furniture after we had bought our grand home in the very prestigious Sixteenth District of Paris, where the wealthy Lebanese live and continue their showoff rituals and traditional style of living. Instead of wisely spending what remained, he made decisions and implemented them without consulting me or taking into consideration the advice I volunteered, which had no effect but making him angry at me.

The blow broke him down, and he collapsed without words and indulged himself in drinking arak in a process of slow suicide. I had to look for a job. I began as a junior saleswoman at Galérie Printemps, in a small branch of this large fashion house. I was promoted gradually, my salary was raised, and then the manager transferred me to the main sales center on Avenue Montaigne, where the wealthy of all nationalities shop.

On the day after the women met for tea, I was surprised to see my former friends, the wives of wealthy Lebanese and Arab men in Paris among our acquaintances, come to the store under the pretext of shopping but really to take pleasure in looking at my poverty and defeat, and to celebrate the fact that this did not happen to them.

That did not bother me too much after I had successfully sold them dozens of articles all at once and asked them to come again and bring their friends. I earned a commission from their visit to my defeat, and it was enough to pay for the tuition fees of my children and our humble vacation for two years.

Arab female clients followed in large numbers. I chose for them what suited them, and, in overtime hours, I also took care of dressing the store windows.

I began to be responsible for home expenses.

My husband suffered in silence as he saw me act as "the man of the house." Meanwhile, he was unable to accept working for any one of the friends from our former evening parties during the good old days of dignity and wealth.

He suffered and was unable to do anything other than follow news of the homeland and be ashamed of my condition. My children became more respectful toward me. My opinion came to have importance for them. I was obeyed at home because I was the one who paid the expenses.

I felt that this bothered my husband, despite his love for me. To put it simply, I had been sick and tired of hanging my diploma in my husband's kitchen and performing the duties of director of spousal receptions and public relations when the war had liberated me!

O my God! I have inadvertently missed getting off at my daily station, Franklin Roosevelt, near Avenue Montaigne. The metro stops now at the Chatelet station!

I get off, having missed several stations because I was distracted! *I will not blame myself profusely as usual for a most trifling mistake I have made. It is my right to be distracted once in a while, for the decision I have to make is difficult. Perhaps it would have been better for me if I had not left for work today as though hypnotized.*

I go down to the riverbank and walk on the foggy embankment.

The sky is suffocated with hot, dark summer clouds, much like the corridors of my soul . . .

I go up the stairs to the sidewalk on the street. I walk along the stalls, which I like and find to be part of the secret Paris, as are its statues, birds, old cafés, alleys of forgotten time, and homes of artists and creative beings.

I like the stalls of the *bouquinistes* along the Seine, where rare and specialized books, paintings, and souvenirs are sold. Most of the stalls are locked up today, probably because of fear of the rain or respect for August, the month of vacations.

I stop for a long time at one stall that carries old magazines for collectors of old memories. I contemplate them. Here is a copy of *Paris Match*, published on the first week of my arrival in Paris. On its cover is Romi Schneider lamenting the death of her son.

I remember this cover very well, for I read the magazine at that time on board the airplane which flew us from Larnaca to Paris, and I sympathized very much with that woman, for I had suffered a lot from my own worries for my children. I had feared they would die at school or in a car or in our burning house. It seemed to me that it was stupid to speak of having lost many of our possessions and much of our wealth, after the tenants stopped paying the rents and after the value of the Lebanese pound collapsed. *In the summer of 1984, my husband was still spending from the funds we had in the banks of Switzerland and Paris. We even left Paris to spend the summer in Lucerne, then London, Corsica, and the Riviera, while still keeping our luxurious furnished villa near the Champs Elysées Drugstore.*

The telephone rang. The voice of the landlady of the villa came across the wires, requesting that we leave it because she wanted to live in it.

My husband answered in the Lebanese way, "We are comfortable in it and I will buy it from you."

Her asking price was fifteen million francs for the villa.

He was tongue-tied, unable to continue the conversation. He began to tremble and sweat flowed from his forehead.

I took the telephone receiver from him and calmly said to her, "We'll think about it and we'll call you, Madam."

Like a terrified child, he became suddenly aware of a truth that had not occurred to him: he had no more than four million francs, which is an insufficient amount and, in his view, not good for buying anything better than a moderate house in Paris. He was unable to sell any real estate because the market in Lebanon was at a standstill and tenants were unable to pay rents, let alone buy property.

He did not voice this truth aloud until I calmed him down and prepared a dish of tabbouleh *salad and a glass of arak for him. For the first time, I began to look at him denuded of his wealth and power. He is almost bald and short. He has a pleasant potbelly as round as his face and narrow eyes above a wide nose and big mouth.*

My heart brimmed with compassion for him, and when I held him close to my bosom, like a child frightened in the dark, it seemed to me that for the first time I was on the path of loving him.

He was frightened as I have always been at bottom for just being a woman. I felt that his fear brought us closer together in a way his wealth never did.

I continue to contemplate the covers of the old magazines. Here is a supplement of *Le Figaro* going back to 1989. The date is in small print. *I said to my husband on New Year's Eve of 1989, "I really love you."*

For the previous five years, we could not afford to spend the evening out as we used to in Beirut every night. Poverty made us closer to each other and our inner life was enriched by our children. On that night, our son decorated the big house plant with Kleenex tissue paper, and it looked like a surrealistic Christmas tree. Our older daughter drew eyes and lips on the computer screen and our younger one put a dusting broom on top of the monitor to look like hair, and they said the computer was the guest of honor at our evening party. My children and my husband cooperated in preparing dinner and buying all the needs in my absence, for I worked double hours at Christmas and New Year. My husband revealed much tenderness and an ability for compassion and sweet behavior toward me; he sympathized with me when I was tired, helped me in half the kitchen chores, and, when I was exhausted, he took them all over by himself. He withered silently but did not withhold his pleasantries from me or from the children, in whose concerns he took interest without the Eastern despotic attitude. Perhaps his care for them made him abstain from finding an escape in the bottle of arak.

That evening, I announced to my family the news of my new appointment as supervisor of decors at the fashion house, one of the most magnificent in all the European capitals. This meant my salary was quadrupled, and it was therefore possible for us for the first time to go on summer holidays for a whole month after five years of poverty.

My children applauded, but my husband was a little miffed. However, our mutual compassion for our own middle-age and ill health overcame most of the negative feelings. Yes, some remained; whenever I scored a success at my job, his internal cockiness went into a crisis and was dwarfed further. He was forced to remain silent, having no other choice in what was happening because we had no other source of income for our livelihood.

He was proud. I don't think he ever tried to borrow money or mortgage a thing. And who would lend him any money even if, as collateral, he mortgages a palace he owns in an area of war, fire, and earthquake? There was no choice. The children had adjusted quickly to our penniless state and made friends who were in similar conditions. My husband, however, escaped from time to time to the bottle of arak. I will never forget how angry he became when I bought a lithograph by Dali. I was putting a nail in the wall to hang it when he yelled, "Don't put any nails in this wall. We are not going to stay here in exile!"

I wander listlessly. I cross a bridge. I walk and walk on the riverbank toward the Quai d'Orsay.

I am unable to escape today by going to my job. There is no way out of having to make a decision. Procrastination is no longer useful.

I have faced poverty with greater courage than I now have to face our return to wealth!

On that day, a letter arrived which my husband had awaited for six years. I knew it would arrive as soon as the Lebanese war stopped. My husband's face beamed, and he began to speak with enthusiasm of going back to Beirut.

Since then, I have rejoiced at his happiness, but I have been uneasy about the idea of return!

I said to him, "We can't return before our children graduate from the university."

My daughter graduated and, a week later, sent us a telegram from Beirut saying, "I got married to Nabil, whom, I know, you both like. We eloped to save all the wedding expenses, and we returned to his home here."

Our other daughter joined our young son at his American university. But nothing much changed until the day that letter arrived, for which he had waited for a long time.

On that day, I knew that something extraordinary had happened: His feminine-like tenderness, which had brought me closer to him in our days of poverty, left him, and the old sheen of his eyes returned, the sheen of the victorious wealthy, and he said to me, "This letter is for you." I opened it. I found that it was a notice from the bank for an amount of a quarter million dollars credited to my account, which I thought did not exceed three thousand French francs (that is, less than a thousand dollars). I was stunned. A quarter of a million dollars credited to my account?

I said, "There must certainly be an error. Furthermore, I don't like your custom of opening my letters, even if they are from the bank."

He ignored my "European" remark, he who had formerly mocked my lack of Parisian flamboyance. He said, "There is no error. This amount is a gift to you from me. I sold a little piece of land in Beirut and I wanted to give you the money I got for it as a present. And there is another present for you."

He handed me a bunch of papers. I looked at them and found they were executed at the office of the notary public who had legally helped us purchase our home. He said, "And this Parisian house is also a present to you from me for all that you suffered in the past years, for your loyalty and your effort. You have made us all proud of you. The time has now come for us to return to our home in Beirut and to our former life. This house will be our Parisian home when we are on holidays."

I felt like a warrior being pensioned off, the time having come to decorate me with medals in preparation for my burial!

He continued, "Come on. Put your clothes on, and let's go out for dinner at a fancy restaurant. Remember we're no longer poor. Tomorrow I'll accompany you to the place of your job, where you'll submit your resignation. I'll buy you some costumes and evening dresses there. The time when you were a saleswoman has gone and you'll become a client again . . . We're no more in need of buying clothes from Tati[2], and we're no more in need of your work!"

I put on my humble clothes while choking, for I felt he did not really want to give me all that wealth as a present but wanted to restore his power over me, to buy me, and to make sure that I knew he was master and that he had regained his throne.

Stunned by the impact of the surprise, I nevertheless went out with him to spend the evening at Le Doyen Restaurant. I had to know that, since the war had ended, my husband had become rich again and that many things would change.

I danced with him for the remainder of the evening at Régine. He greeted friends proudly, the big cigar having returned to his lips. And they in turn greeted us with warmth again and reproved us for our absence, as etiquette would require.

When we were back at home, he made love to me with a virility I had forgotten since our honeymoon, although he had not touched me for several long years since we had become poor, and I did not complain or grumble . . . Compassion had replaced sexual desire in my heart, which was in sympathy with his sorrow, and I had forgotten my body in my deep concern for earning a living and in my great anxiety about the future of my children.

2. A store that carries clothes for the poor class in France.

When he took off, in his deep exploration of my body that night, awakening long-abandoned, sleeping demons and nymph songs, I felt that he was no closer to me than we had been when he fed the pigeons, the birds, and the seagulls on Swan Isle on Sundays during the years of our poverty.

All night long, he continued running with me on warm, forgotten shores, whinnying with ecstasy, then being transformed into an enchanted horse flying with me from peak to peak. At dawn, he fell asleep, exhausted. But I did not sleep.

I sneaked away from bed. I don't know why.

I washed off the remains of my facial make-up of the previous evening.

I drank my coffee in front of the window. I put on my simple work clothes as usual and took with me the novel I had been reading in the metro in the last few days, along with my reading glasses. I did not forget to take my French identity card, in case the police should ask for it. For the police have lately focused their raids on the metro passengers; my children and I had obtained ID cards a few months earlier, but my husband had refused to apply for one when we did.

I sneaked out of the house quietly and was on my way to work, taking the underground train as I did every morning. He had woken up and, still half asleep, had said to me as I was leaving, "It appears you do not understand what has happened to us."

I had answered him, "I'll be late for work."

And I had rushed out. When I returned in the evening, my husband had brought home a cook to prepare the food, after he had shared kitchen chores and housekeeping with me and the children all through the years of poverty and hard work.

There is no way; I must make a decision. I know that his patience has run out. From now on, nothing can oblige him to live in Paris.

I will not go home yet, lest we quarrel. I have not decided anything anyhow, but I am exhausted. I will sit in this tearoom until the appointed time comes for our meeting on Swan Isle at exactly 2 P.M. It is the place Wafiq has chosen for this decisive meeting, when we will have our "last lunch" on a free, blue, city bench. It is a good choice, because the seagulls, the birds, the trees, and the river will all be the allies of his love in my heart and will remind me of our days of poverty when Wafiq discovered the tenderness of nature, our mother that we take for granted, and I discovered that I loved him and that there are thousands of common things that tie us together other than money.

The tearoom waitress comes. I choose what I want, without going through calculations in order to economize as before. Wealth is comfortable! *I am comfortable in this city, which does not insult me as a woman, sitting alone at a café and drinking tea quietly. On a beautiful, ceramic statuette in the nearby shop window, I read the following: "Four things a woman must do: to appear as a young woman, to behave as a lady, to think as a man, and to work as a dog." Perhaps I had implemented all these old teachings for ages in Beirut. On the other hand, nothing is required of the man there but to be born a man!*

I am tired and no longer able to adjust again to a society that daily humiliates and insults me, directly and indirectly, in all matters of life, large and small. Here I have rested from all the small details which used to offend me in my homeland and which I did not know how to respond to, because they appeared to be part of the prevailing customs that no one paused to protest. I no longer feel it is normal or acceptable to be insulted merely because I am a woman and to have no right to travel unless a male permits me, when I have been the one who, like a cat carrying its kittens with its teeth, carried all the males of my family in our misery away from our homeland. I am no longer willing to hear stories or read them in newspapers about a man who killed his sister because her behaviour did not please him, or about another who required his wife to return to the home out of obedience to a court order sought by him and took one more wife for himself in order to spite her, or about women being mocked; nor am I willing to read the popular sayings, related to such matters, that newspapers vie with one another to publish. When they wish to praise a woman, they say she is "a sister of men," but of what kind of men is she the sister? Now, I own my house; I have a quarter of a million dollars in the bank; I have a job that keeps me from the humiliation of begging;, I am a citizen of a state which will take care of me in my old age and pay my health expenses and my pen-

sion. *I can say I am a free woman and, for the first time, I can freely choose my husband; for when I married him, I did not really choose him, and I was not really free to have a will. I don't want to be separate from him, but I also don't want to return to Beirut. It is not possible for him to stay here, and my children will not accept that I stay here and leave their father. I don't know how to solve this problem. The truth of the matter is that I don't choose him alone. Either I choose him along with the homeland or I lose them both. What shall I do?*

It is 1 P.M. Lunch customers flood the tearoom, and I am being chased away in a subtle, French way: "Is there anything else you need, Madam? Would you like to have lunch?"

"No, thanks. Give me the bill, please."

I remember Beirut with a nostalgic feeling—at Dbebo's on the seashore, the tables that we occupied at noon to drink a cup of coffee and smoke a water pipe without ordering lunch and without being chased away by anyone.

I remember the cities of myths, of the irrational, and of curiosity—not only those of harshness.

I remember that I was part of what was going on, not merely an onlooker waiting for the homeland to become a place that was good for life before it was loved.

What happened? Something that is at the same time simple and extraordinary happened: I no longer believe in miracles or in the stories of The One Thousand and One Nights.

I call the first taxi available. I ask the driver to take me to the middle of Bir Hakeim Bridge, where there is an entrance to Swan Isle. The sky is getting cloudier. In a corridor of greenery along which we have walked, the trees being our witnesses, my husband wants to dare me to tell him, in view of the geese, the pigeons, the seagulls, and the birds that we have often fed together, that I will remain alone here, that I will not return with him, and that I will not leave my job. But how will I say that to him on Swan Isle? My love for him flared up on this enchanted, beautiful island. He knows that I did not really love him until I knew him well and lived with him in our days of poverty. I discovered many things that are common to both of us, among which is the love of birds and trees. We had our children and lived together for years, while each of us knew nothing of the other except the erogenous regions of the body, times of vacation in Europe, and telephone numbers of our private chalet at Tabarja Beach, the Brummana apartment, and the Cedars Snow chalet. On Swan Isle we really got to know each other well. We can see it from our window at home, long like a path in the middle of the Seine River, not wider than a city street, shaded by trees on both sides. *He said to me in that past summer, as we prepared our humble lunch in the kitchen and looked out at the Seine River and an island in its middle resembling a path covered with trees, when our children were away on holiday with their friends at the Colonie des Vacances, "Do you remember how we used to have lunch every Sunday at the Grande Cascade, Napoleon's resthouse at the Bois de Boulogne, or at the Pré Catelan?"*

By that time, we had begun to record every franc we spent in order to learn how to economize, and we had not visited a restaurant for several years. As a one-time poor woman, I had not found that to be difficult. That was why I said to him, "Nothing prevents us from taking our food as is, going down to one of the blue benches girding Swan Isle, and eating there next to the water and the greenery."

This city is not hostile to the poor. One can enjoy all its pleasures as a person of average means—except for the pleasure of showing off.

And so we began preparing our food for our first picnic in Paris.

We were surprised at the many things one had to remember to take: salt, water, beer, tomatoes, bread, cheese, napkins, a bottle opener, pepper, and so on. He said with some vexation, "God bless the days of yore when we had servants. Do you remember how Zaynab used to get up from bed when we returned home from an evening party at 3 A.M., and she would come down from the servants' wing to ask us whether we wanted her to prepare some food for us?"

I said, "Yes. But I also remember that we later began to sneak out on tiptoe in order to escape her watchful vigilance. And we once thought we did, but when we returned to our bedroom, I found my clothes that I had thrown on the floor with my jewelry were now

hung up properly, and my jewelry was in its box. How pleasantly we
laughed that day because under her vigilance we were spoiled to the
point of suffocation."

He added. with a lump in his throat, "Gone are the blessed days
of Zaynab, the good old days, and all the other blessed days we now
mourn that have brought tears of joy to our eyes!"

Where is Zaynab today, I wonder? When the war was about to break,
I accompanied her to the Egyptian consulate, after she had committed
some petty legal infractions, and asked a friend there to set her pass-
port in order. I saw her off at the airport, and she said, "May you never
fall in the jaws of poverty and may you always land on your feet."

Had it been Zaynab's prayers that opened closed doors before me?

Who knows. Perhaps such things do happen in this world full of
mysteries.

The taxi driver stops. "Here you are, Madam."

I descend the stone stairway leading to Swan Isle. There is some
magic here. One is suddenly separated from the somehow familiar city and enters the invisible, enchanted Paris. Perhaps that
is what made the people of the city raise the metro rail on a high
bridge so that its noise may not impair the metaphysical calm
of this place. Perhaps they could have otherwise thrust it in a
tunnel under the river, for they are known to have dug a tunnel
under the sea.

Here I am, trying to think of Zaynab, the metro, the bridge,
the tunnel under the English Channel, and anything to run away
from making a simple, though complex, decision: Will I return
to Beirut with my husband or will I stay and work here, laying
myself open to the certainty of divorce, sooner or later; for people
will gossip about my disobedience and my husband will be obliged
to divorce me in order to keep his dignity and reputation.

We preserved the unity of our home in poverty. Will wealth
now break it up?

Since my husband regained his wealth, he lost that tender
feminine quality in his face and conduct. His virility, his passion
for possession, and his cockiness returned to him. But I know
he is the two men at the same time.

One thing has not changed in him since his return to wealth, taking pleasure in folk tradition and memories. He tries to recall local expressions and enjoys speaking about shops and cafés of Beirut of the past that exist no more, having been destroyed, along with their popular customs, by the war. When I sympathetically try to share his joy, he always goes beyond me. If I regretfully mention the old La Ronda Café that stood in the middle of ruined Beirut, he shows greater regret by mentioning the building that stood there before La Ronda! And if I say how much I miss the Express Café, he laughs at me and reminds me of what stood there before the building of the Sabbagh Edifice, where the Express Café was!

He still lives in the Beirut of his childhood, the Beirut of half a century ago.

I know his face engrossed in tradition, his face enveloped by tenderness, his face fired by desire, and his face broken by poverty—but I don't claim to know all his faces. I sometimes imagine I know him, but I am aware as years pass that there are passages leading to other passages in his depths, as is the case with me. No one really knows another person, even if bonds of marriage tie them together.

I certainly know this beautiful island, resembling an enchanted path, more than I know my husband! I know it tree by tree, bird by bird, cloud by cloud, and tramp by tramp.

How easy it is to know an island and how difficult to know a human being, even if we live with one for many long years.

On my left are several steps leading to the river. They are like a harbor for invisible ships carrying wandering souls of crazy people like me, lost in time and place, no longer knowing where they belong.

This blue bench is occupied daily by a tramp wearing a general's uniform; his chest is decorated with medals. He drinks wine, day and night, whenever he is awake. When I was a tourist in Paris, I used to think the *clochards*[3] were lazy vagabonds, but no

3. Plural of *clochard*, which is the name given by the French to homeless vagabonds who sleep in public parks and streets.

more. Now I know that tramps are the gypsies of cities, some of whom have chosen to move in the invisible, secret Paris as a cry of protest and spend their nights conversing with statues, pigeons, birds, and seagulls, like all free people. The second bench is occupied by an old woman, a tramp who always wears children's clothes. She appears as though she does not know what suddenly happened, for she is still a child although she is an old woman on the outside. She does not understand why her body is worn out when her soul is still that of a young girl. A third tramp does not refuse charity, but he refuses to give up anything for it, and he will never tell me about his life for my charity. Nor will he thank me either, for it is sufficient for me to have the honor of having my charity accepted by him.

This, at least, is the scenario that my husband and I have had of these tramps and others since we came to like Swan Isle and it became the place we frequent every Sunday. *Look how arrogant the birds are, how strange, and how quick to fly away. This is what my husband said to me on our second picnic, when I fed the pigeons and birds the remnants of our food.*

He claimed he felt a desire to kick a pigeon, but he was satisfied with kicking the tin plate of food I left for it.

In the times following that, he began to feed them himself and did not forget to feed the seagulls on the surface of the river. He threw pieces of bread to them, and I was surprised to see them come close to him.

I used to think seagulls were wild creatures like me—or this is what was suggested to me by the writer Richard Bach in his novel Jonathan Livingston Seagull, *which I read in the metro. But no, they are like human beings, hungry for love and ready to bend down to pick up their sustenance, ready to descend from their soaring heights to any dirty hands which hold pieces of bread and love.*

Love. I loved my penniless, unemployed, sick, and heartbroken husband on Swan Isle as I had never loved him before. It is comical that one may love another person for his faults before his virtues. But that is what happened to me as I embraced my husband's tragic loss of country and his sorrow at what came to be its condition in an age that scorned individual destinies, and I tenderly met his hidden, feminine qualities, his great compassion toward our children, his excessive goodness in facing his tragedy to the extent he was able to understand it, and his sensitive gratitude for my efforts to fight my fate, our common fate. He was like a lost person on a boat lashed by fierce tempests. I kissed his beautiful bald head and pitied his rock-like, sad face as we drank beer, sitting on the beautiful bench in nature's wealth on our poor weekly outings to Swan Isle. We became acquainted with its creatures. Its first half, from Bir Hakeim Bridge, is given up to permanent "apartments"; that is, its dirty blue benches are inhabited by permanent tramps. The other half, toward the Radio Building, is dedicated to Sunday guests like us. We chose a bench in the middle of the island, before the bridge crossed by the suburban train. We always rejoice on finding our bench unoccupied; it sweetly overlooks the Fifteenth District of Paris with the skyscrapers of the Front du Seine neighborhood.

Before he would sit down, Wafiq would take out the beer bottles. On the bench whose back is turned to ours, overlooking the Sixteenth District of Paris on the other bank, there always sits a tramp looking like the Wandering Jew, with a long beard and a hat, and he talks aloud to the seagulls and the birds, greets the passers-by, and treats their children fondly.

Thus, we used to sit, back to back, the Wandering Jew on one side and the Wandering Lebanese on the other, while the pigeons, the seagulls, and the birds ran to and fro after their sustenance.

There, during our days of poverty, I discovered the pleasure of the weekend after the week's hard work that I lived through outside the comical, social game of the bourgeoisie. Wafiq no longer missed with regret the good old grand restaurants, like the Grande Cascade, on Sundays.

When the summer passed and the trees became bare, we continued to visit Swan Isle in the bitter cold, only to feed the birds and the pigeons. That constituted an acknowledgment of the binding relations between us. We always wondered: Why was the island called Swan Isle when there was not a single swan on its shores? When we brought the food, the pigeons flocked first to eat. Then came that pleasant, slender bird which had strange white feathers that looked like a crown on its head and distinguished it from others, in addition to its extraordinary ability to flee. It would pick up a piece of bread from the midst of dozens of pigeons and fly away with it in order to eat it calmly in another place, but other birds would flock around and fight over it. I used to think it was an exceptional bird and wonder why its strange ways reminded me of Beirut and made me distinguish it from all other birds. My husband laughed at me and used to say to me that it was a different bird every time. But I did not believe that.

We are always in need of distinguishing some bird in order to invent love. And so, I gave it a creative name from my grandmother's mythical tales: Clever Hasan.

It is a quarter to two. The clouds have gathered in the sky in an angry, gray readiness to roar. This is our familiar bench.

I sit down on it. I have to make a decision! I think of everything and of anything, the birds, the tramps, memories, the name of Swan Isle where I never saw a single swan—but I do not make a decision. Here comes the bird with the white crown on its head, approaching me with its pleasant gait, one hop after another, and my heart overflows with love for it, and I ask, "How are you, Clever Hasan?"

The rain suddenly pours down in a thunderstorm brightened by lightning, and the bird flies off.

I call out to it, "Don't go, Clever Hasan. I will hide you from the storm in my raincoat." Lightning flashes and its zigzag light branches out into the heights of heaven's dome, from which comes down a huge, long-necked white swan that says to me, as in the Arabian myths and in my grandmother's tales, "Here I am, at your service. Command, I'm your obedient slave!" She says so without sound, but I hear her as though her voice is as loud as thunder. I disregard the rain that has begun to soak me. I tremble with fear as I contemplate her huge body that looks like that of the legendary rook, her white feathers iridescent with rainbow colors as if she has just come out of the tales of *The One Thousand and One Nights*.

She says to me, "I'm the swan genie. I'll grant you two wishes. What would you wish?"

Astonishment and fear combine to choke me. When I finally find my voice, I hear it saying, "I'm decidedly dreaming . . ."

The swan genie says, "What's the difference between dream and reality? I'll give you two wishes. What would you wish?"

"Before I tell you what I wish, tell me who you are. What's your story? Do such things still happen these days?"

"Nothing really changes. But I can't tell you my story because I'll die if I divulge my secret."

"Tell me that part of it which is permissible."

"I once loved a bird and thus broke the traditions of the swans. So the king of the genies punished me by making me have a bird instead of a swan as my progeny. And it is that lost, unbalanced bird which you have so often treated tenderly and called Clever Hasan and fed, thus saving its life several times, for it refused to eat from my beak, perhaps as part of my punishment. That's why I'm offering you two wishes."

I say, "But why two wishes, not three as in all myths?" *I am certainly dreaming and everything is permissible in dreams, even being greedy with the swan genie.*

The swan answers, "Two instead of three wishes because you human beings are stupid. We grant you three opportunities and the third is always the cause of your death. You don't really know what you want! Therefore, we decided one thousand and one years ago that two opportunities were sufficient. Now, what would you wish?"

"I want three wishes!"

"Fine. Let that be."

"I want to see what my future will be if I stay here alone."

With her golden beak, the swan points to an old woman sitting on one of the benches under her umbrella and feeding the pigeons despite the downpour. The woman turns into a stone statue, and the swan says, "This is your future if you stay here alone."

The statue appears to me to be a monument of desolation and melancholy.

I say to the swan, "I want you to help me make a decision that is not wrong. Should I return with my husband to our homeland or should I stay here alone? For "here" has become the homeland of my convictions, not "there," which is the homeland of my emotions. How can I make a decision which is not wrong? Help me. I don't want miracles."

She answers, "Everything is wrong. It's within my power to give you the impossible, not the possible. Making a decision is a task you should do yourself. As for what is easier, that is the impossible, and it's my duty to realize it. The realization of miracles is easier than making a decision that is not wrong."

I say, "I love my husband and don't want to be separated from him, but I want that to be within my own conditions: I want to stay here with him forever . . . Yes, that's what I wish."

My husband is coming toward me as the giant clock behind him on the top of the Radio-France Building points to two o'clock.

The swan genie says, "I'll transform you both into two statues that will stay here forever!"

Before I can discuss this idea, the wish comes true. Hardly does Wafiq arrive, smiling in the rain, and we are about to spontaneously embrace each other, when the swan genie casts her magic spell and we turn into statues. No one notices what happens because the path is almost empty of people in such rainy weather.

The rain pours.

Here I am, a statue like all the statues I always liked. And here is Wafiq at my side forever and no longer able to leave me or return . . . We've become a single stone statue. I stare at his petrified face, which is no longer able to abandon me or force me to do anything.

I finally understand the secret of the statues—those no one knows who sculptured. They are alive like me! I wonder about most of the statues in the museums whose sculptors are unknown: Are they human beings like Wafiq and me, who don't know how to say no or yes, and that's why they say nothing?

The rain and lightning cease. The sun shines. The swan genie disappears as though she can only come down on the zigzag flash of lightning. The transient summer storm passes, leaving us petrified in a moment of welcome about to become an embrace.

I stare at his face. He is a happy statue. He does not know what has happened and does not want to know. He is now as he has always been during the years of exile until he woke up from his nightmare and was again a wealthy man. All these years I have been as conscious as I am now—I have lived, suffered, wondered, changed. And yet he wants me to abolish all those years lived in Paris—as he has.

He did nothing but wait during those years. As for me, I lived and worked like any unimpaired human being.

They were enriching years, and I discovered myself, my capabilities, and my love for work and for facing challenges.

It is not acceptable that work be permissible for others when they need it while I am deprived of it when I need it to fulfill myself as a human being.

I am tired of constantly feeling that I am an impaired, incomplete thing, a spare tire at best. I don't want to return to a homeland that I love, but that loves me only when I'm tame. I can no longer bear the little daily humiliations there that are meant to tame me.

I am no longer an Arab woman, and I am not yet a Western woman. Who am I?

Will I accept becoming once more a gossipy woman living in luxury, covered with gold, immersed in a meaningless life, whose horizon does not exceed the size of a postage stamp? Or is it better for my husband and me to stay thus together, as two stone statues, because I can no longer adjust myself to fit his comfort as though I were nothing but his home slippers?

The pleasant bird with the white crown hovers around me and perches on my head. What next, Clever Hasan? What shall we do? Are we going to remain thus, two statues on Swan Isle?

A boy approaches us, jumping with vitality in the muddy puddles. His mother pushes a baby carriage with an infant. He contemplates us and tries in vain to draw his mother's attention to us. She appears to be concerned with something else and is preoccupied with her baby in the carriage. The boy plays with the edge of my petrified dress, then succeeds in breaking off a part of the petrified, thin scarf around my neck, having repeatedly hit it with a stone. He tries to take away Wafiq's petrified necktie but fails, except for a slim part of its lower edge that he chips off with a stone. I did not know that boys are enemies of statues. He now picks up a nail and tries to carve a letter with it on my leg, perhaps the first letter of his name.

The miserable fate of a statue like me that is still conscious has never occurred to me. I wonder: Is my husband conscious, too, of what is happening to him or has he entered the petrified state? Why am I still conscious? Is it because I still have a right to a third wish? If the swan genie returns, what will I ask of her? To change me into a statue that is aware of nothing? How will I then know that Wafiq and I are still together? Is that not like a suicide of two persons for the sake of remaining together? I wonder: Will tomorrow's newspapers bear the news of the disappearance of a Lebanese couple, the lady being forty-five years old and the man sixty? And on the same page will there be a story about a new statue of obscure origin that has been erected on Swan Isle? But who will notice an additional statue in a city, half of whose people are statues?

Will we remain thus forever, like Lot's kin who turned their heads back and became statues of salt?

Why didn't the myth say, Whoever looks back turns into a stone like my husband, and whoever does not turns into a stone like me? And why didn't it say that we are all sentenced to a curse under the very eyes of a fate that plays with our destinies and knows well how to uncover our fragility and egoism and transform them into a snare for us?

When will the swan genie come back, and what will I tell her, when I don't really know what to tell her? What is my third wish? What is it that makes me suffer? Is it love for this man whose weak points I know, having learned since childhood that the man loved by an Eastern woman should be a demigod, stronger and more powerful than her, and able to bear responsibility alone? He is the head of the family, and he is this, and he is that . . .

Does it trouble me that I love a man who is full of mistakes and weaknesses—like me; who is perplexed when making a decision—like me; in whose life there is nothing final—like me; who has fits of rejection—like me; who has moments of regret and perplexity—like me?

Is it a shame that he transcends nine years of his life in Paris and abolishes them? On the other hand, how can I abolish about thirty years of my life that I lived with loved ones in Beirut,

Aley, Brummana, Jizzin, Sidon, Shtura, Ihden, and dozens of
other places planted deep in my heart, such as woods, caves,
beaches, and mountains crowned with cedars and snow?

Clouds gather. Ah for the rain! Where are you, swan genie?

The horizon lights up with a giant zigzag flash of lightning
branching out in abundance, and the swan genie flies down
from it.

She sees me weeping without tears as the rain washes me
again, and I am unable to wipe my face, for I am a statue.

She says to me, "I've come to know you human beings. You
are like summer rains, never at rest. What do you want now?"

I tell her, "I don't know what I want. That's why it is pref-
erable that we return to what we were."

She says silently, but with a voice like thunder within my
head, "I knew that, from the beginning. You human beings don't
know how to deal with a miracle; you don't know what you
want and you lose the opportunity it opens for you. Fine, let it
be. Go back to your human forms."

Embracing me, Wafiq says, as though nothing has happened,
"It's exactly two o'clock and I'm not late." I look at my watch
and see that it is really two o'clock. I am amazed. What about
those hours that passed when we were both bewitched statues
under the sun and the rain?

Wafiq does not seem to be aware of all that. I hardly believe
all that did happen, in the first place. I don't dare tell him anything about those illusions or hallucinations.

We don't mind the wet bench, and we sit together under its
umbrella after he tries wiping a part of it with his handkerchief.
First we drink the beer, then we avidly eat the sandwiches with
the tomatoes he himself has sliced.

He does not ask me anything about my decision. From their
heights, the pigeons, the birds, and the seagulls alight on the
shore of the island. We feed them. I look for the pleasant bird
with the white crown but don't find him. My husband asks me
about it, laughing. I don't dare tell him about the hallucinations
I had as he arrived.

We are both happy, as though our separation is impossible,

whether we like it or not. We can wrangle and each can tear the other to pieces, but our being together is inevitable.

I rejoice because he has not asked me, "What have you decided?" Had he asked, I would have told him that I would never leave my job, that I would never give up my lifestyle here, that I would never abandon him, and that I didn't know how to combine these contradictions, on all of which I insisted!

A second bottle of beer, then a third. We laugh together for a long time.

Wafiq says, "In Beirut, we will always go out on picnics like this one when you have time for them. You will certainly be busy with your work, when you open a branch in Beirut for the fashion house in which you now work . . . Isn't that so?"

"Will I open a branch and become the head of a firm?"

"Certainly. This is a command of mine!"

"And are there other joyful commands, my lord?"

He does not answer, but he hums a song, "Ne me quittes pas . . ."[4]

Arab commands and French songs! I contemplate his Eastern face which must give "commands" even in circumstances of surrender, his face, which I've seen at the zenith of his weakness and at the nadir of his strength and which I loved in both cases, bare and without masks.

I remain silent. My affection pours out for him. I almost tell him about the hallucinations I had just as he arrived.

I feel a little pain in my leg, and I stretch it forward to look at the painful place.

Wafiq asks me, "What's this scratch on your leg?"

I notice the scratch in the place where the boy tried to carve a letter with a nail. Is that reasonable? Certainly not. Perhaps I scratched my leg when stepping on that broken branch, and the scratch became part of my hallucination, just as a light that is suddenly turned on when one is sleeping becomes part of one's dream. Everything has a logical explanation.

I am distracted as I toy with my silk scarf around my neck. I am surprised to find that a little piece is missing on the edge, as

4. "Don't Leave Me": a famous French song.

if someone has cut it off. Perhaps it got caught in the metro door as I got on this morning. These things happen daily and we take no notice of them.

We return home. Wafiq says to me as he is taking off his necktie, "Are there rats in our house?"

"Certainly not. Why?"

"Who then gnawed at my necktie? There is a piece missing . . . Look how strange this is!"

I remember the boy who tampered with us when we were both statues, but I don't answer.

I stare out of the window at Swan Isle as the summer clouds are gathering again and threatening with a storm. And when lightning flashes in a zigzag tree of light, I hasten in terror to let down the curtains.

Thirty Years of Bees

Reem stares out of the car window, her chest boiling with suppressed rage, like a hermetically sealed beehive.

It seems to her there is a quiet agitation sitting on Paris, its streets, its buildings, and all visible things, an agitation suffocated with heat and humidity.

The car leaves the city and the crowds like a boat trying with difficulty to plow ahead in dark, obscure, and viscous water.

Almost apologetically, Dr. Saduq says to his guest, as he partly turns to him on his right and continues driving the car, "It is rare that Paris and its suburbs have such oppressive heat; that's why the cultural center is not equipped with air conditioning. Sorry, Professor Rida."

Reem contemplates Dr. Saduq from her place in the back seat, where he seated her. *He ushered my husband to the front seat, heedless of French etiquette, but he is the one who has insisted on speaking French to emphasize his "progress."* Reem continues to stare fiercely at Saduq's skull from behind. *About a quarter of a century ago, he came for the first time to the office of the intellectual magazine that my husband and I cooperate on and produce. He was almost shaking with fear and hope. He had sent us many of his articles, but none appealed to my husband, so he neglected them. Saduq began to write us a letter a week, asking about his articles. I had pity on him, a young university student, because of his insistence and pleading. So I read them, despite my many preoccupations, and I found them to be good.*

They had a new but unfamiliar vision. I lied to Saduq and did not tell him that my husband did not see any good in him as a writer and would advise him to work in commerce. I rather wrote to him that my husband had not read them and that we would contact him as soon as he did.

I defended Saduq's writing at that time and my husband teased me and asked, "Have you begun to like young men?"

I smiled at his teasing. On that day, I was suckling my baby while my older son was playing with a writer's manuscript, tearing it and scattering its pages, as my husband chased him, laughing, and returned to me after saving the manuscript, saying in his sweet, playful jesting, "Let Saduq be your protégé. Publish his articles, even publish a book by him. I'll not interfere. But I bet you he will fail."

The book was published and had great success. My husband boasted of having discovered the author. When Saduq obtained a doctorate and became a university professor in France, the friendship between my husband and him became stronger.

Rida and Saduq converse with a great deal of warm intimacy, which Reem considers to be the bond between "important" men. She tries to get out of her suffocation and isolation by repeating to herself: *Be positive and take part in the conversation.* She gives her opinion on the subject of the conversation. They both fall silent as if a troublesome boy has interrupted the discourse of adults.

She hears the poor echo of her own voice as though it were a winter beggar's sock with a hole, no one responding to her either negatively or positively.

Professor Rida resumes his conversation and Dr. Saduq shares his enthusiasm. *It is as if my voice was not expressing my point of view but was mere women's chatter.* They burst out laughing together. She no longer hears anything.

The car continues to travel down the road. *My heart always runs alone in other paths and other times . . . I remember the day when Saduq began to shake with joy in front of me, like a pleasant little puppy wagging its tail, as he expressed his thanks to our publishing house for publishing his first book.*

He knew I was his ally, and he intuitively felt my husband's aversion to his writing and my husband's efforts to avoid meeting him. He knew the significance of the fact that a book of his was appearing in our city in North Africa at our publishing house which, year after year, was able through its books and its intellectual magazine to compete with other well-known Arabic magazines of the East of the caliber of al-Adab, al-Adib, Dirasat 'Arabiyya, al-'Arabi, Shi'r, Hiwar, Mawaqif, al-Katib, al-Tali'a, and others.

On that day, he said to me in French, I'll never forget your favor, Madam and great thinker." I accepted his flattering gratitude as an expression of his joy overflowing in kind words that were said but not all meant. I rejoiced at his thankfulness, but I was sad at his false and excessive flattery resembling lampoon or derision. For I have never been a "thinker" but rather a poet.

My literary beginnings were like my husband's. But I had a conjugal poetic "heart attack" and was no longer able to write poetry amid the whistling of the pressure cooker, the ringing of the oven bell, the crying of the children, and so forth. I was not afflicted with this conjugal literary "heart attack" all at once, for mine was a long and painful dying over thirty years, a slow and silent repression resembling torture by constant drops of water falling in the Chinese way until the drops succeed in time to perforate the skull . . . And by nature, my husband knows this way perfectly well, like all Arab men.

Love was what froze me in place under the torturing drops because of bonds of attachment to my children, my family, and my society, in addition to my husband's praise of my cooking whenever I showed him a new poem and his empowerment of our two children to ridicule my literary "genius." No . . . It was not love alone, but rather a mixture of urgings, frustrations, and threats, as well as my mother's commands to obey, and my father's ridiculing of any activity I indulged in other than motherhood, and his prayers, whenever I composed a few words of poetry, that the Lord might lead me in the right path when he, my father, had brought up my brothers and me to the music of military marches.

In my rare sweet moments with Rida, my heart wondered whether these were the sting of a circus trainer's whip taming a lioness or the smack of a spousal kiss.

The laughter of Dr. Saduq and Professor Rida is loud. They fall silent for a moment.

Saduq asks him, "Would you like to stop for a short rest and have a cup of coffee?"

Professor Rida answers in a voice that sounds to Reem as if he is eager to reach the celebration in his honor, "No, thank you. I'm not tired. Let's continue driving."

Reem says, in a voice that appears to them to be unnecessarily tense, "I need to go to the rest room."

Rida answers with his usual calm, "We'll wait for you in the car. Hurry."

She gets out of the car, her feet heavy and swollen. *I'm not in urgent need to go. Why am I acting like a child? Well, I admit, I'm trying to remind them of my presence.*

She enters the ladies' room, her knees exhausted. She washes her face that is always free of make-up. She contemplates it in wonder as though seeing it for the first time, with all its wrinkles. In her head, she hears noises like the buzz of bees. *I was beautiful and radiant when I went to him for the first time. I was not looking for a husband but for a magazine to publish my poems.*

He welcomed me warmly, for he knew several members of my old, respectable, religious family.

He said he did not expect much good from my plucky attitude, similar to that of the "cheeky" female writers who had started writing with me, but he praised the blush that reddened my face, as I blushed easily in those days.

In that first meeting of ours, my poems appealed to him very much. He read them aloud several times and promised to thrust me into glory, so he said.

In the period of flirting with our eyes before our engagement, he said to me in jest one day, "She who has such hair must certainly write the most beautiful poetry." I was thrilled to hear such flirtation from the great professor, whose magazine had successfully imposed itself on intellectual and cultural circles, despite its recent beginning. I was happy because he refused to publish anything by my daring and "cheeky" competitors. But I felt some embarrassment at the same time for this emotional kind of "literary criticism."

My poems meant a lot to me, but I felt they did not mean the same thing to Rida, as days went by.

One day, I insisted that he should read all the poems I took to him. He praised them a lot, but when I discussed some of them with him, I noticed he had not read them well. He said, "I've read as many as possible and found them publishable. I'm sorry, I was preoccupied with reading the book of your face and turning the pages of your eyes." How had I accepted such rotten nonsense that day and why did I consider it to be at that moment the most beautiful thing ever said since the Seven Odes of pre-Islamic Arabia?

He continued, "One cannot read the complete book of your eyes in a whole lifetime!"

Yet he seemed to finish reading it the night after the wedding, and he threw it out of the window with the screams of our first child.

Yes, I loved him from the first sting . . . since the time he said to me my hair was more beautiful than my poetry. I didn't understand that those words that made me happy were an introduction to that routine of numbing housework which he had in store for me without mercy. In the rare moments in which I tried to organize my time to write, he embarked on shaking my soul and making me doubt my writing abilities.

He made me understand from the beginning, in an indirect manner, that I had to negate myself and that I was deprived of the rights of the "artistic ego" because I was an Arab woman. I could, of course, work as an assistant to him, but I could not be independent nor have my own literary predilections. When he went away to attend conferences, I had to do his work and mine too; and when he returned and our child was sick, he slept and I stayed awake.

On the night I decided to run away, in a moment of full awareness, I realized my burdens were heavy: a baby in my womb and another on my arm . . . When I woke up the next day, I was transformed from a free bird to a docile sheep. But an invisible bee had started to buzz in my chest.

Reem continues to wash her face with cold water. She combs her hair and dozens of hairs fall out and are caught in the brush. She sighs with sorrow. She returns to the car. She hears Dr. Saduq say to her husband, Rida, "Local celebrations to honor you are not sufficient to mark a quarter of a century since your publications began and more than three decades since your magazine was established. It was inevitable that you should be honored outside your country, because the intellectual radiation of your magazine and your books extends from its center in North Africa to other continents. By honoring you in Paris, we strengthen the national thought on which your publishing house, of which I am proud, was founded. I am happy that you will publish my new book." And on and on . . .

Reem feels again the suppressed rage in her chest, like a hermetically sealed beehive. *The speech to honor Rida has just begun in the car, and everything has a price. I've become a neglected, black dot, a muzzled woman stuffed in a black sack enveloping her from head to foot.*

Dr. Saduq is silent. Reem is surprised, for she expected he would deliver his whole speech in the car. He appears to be occupied with chasing a bee out of the window. *What made him cut off the rehearsal of his speech? Was it the bee? I discovered too late, after he had become strong and thrown me away, that when such people are given the opportunity to speak, they jump on it and take off endlessly, trampling on the truth ignominiously, to resounding applause from the audience. In celebrations to honor someone, such people are—alas—numerous!*

In the last few weeks, I've done nothing but accompany my husband to celebrations to honor him. No one mentions me in a single word of thanks, except that I was the woman that stood behind the great man! They all forget that Rida and I always stood side by side, and that I often treated their writing tenderly and rubbed it with the balm of love.

I was stupid to antagonize the liberal female writers whom my husband called "cheeky." I was jealous of them. I worked in the shadows, like all the women of my country. I worked night and day, like a bee. I did my work as a mother and a wife, and I shared in my husband's work, taking half the responsibilities of the magazine and the publishing concern. They all know this truth. But no one remembers it in the celebrations to honor my husband, in which I am buried in silence and neglect by submissive agreement with social hypocrisy. For the man—as always—is the focus, he is the one to be honored. During these celebrations in honor of my husband, my chest becomes like a beehive buzzing with indignation. For I have always been a bee making honey for everyone, a stung bee.

Reem regrets having accompanied her husband to Paris. *At the hotel, I lay down on my bed to rest for a while. I thought of ordering a cup of coffee.*

I hate these honorific ceremonies, don't I? Fine. But I love hotels where I become equal to my husband. Let me then try to enjoy a few days without house chores. Only in hotels can I give rest to my body and set my thoughts free.

My husband opened the wardrobe, and suddenly shouted with joy. He found that the hotel room was provided with an iron for the use of occupants.

He asked me to iron his suit for the ceremony in his honor. Did he really want that or did he like to remind me of who I was, to put me in my "place" as is his custom, whenever there is an opportunity?

I took the iron, as an overwhelming anger boiled in my chest. I found it to be out of order. The chamber maid was summoned and she expressed her surprise because the iron was out of order. She said she had tested it and all other electric equipment before our arrival, as was her routine after every occupant left.

We went out of the hotel for a walk. I saw a beautiful car, the likes of which I had never seen. I stared at it and was filled with a desire to possess it. It awakened in me an adolescent dream of driving a convertible in bare feet on the moonlit beach, alone with music. I stood motionless looking at the car, opening its door in my imagination, with a strong secret desire. I was astonished to hear the car's anti-theft alarm go off at that moment, although I had not touched it, and nobody else had done anything to it!

The car stops. Saduq says, "Damn this bee!" He boastfully assures Professor Rida of his good judgment, saying that he is a cautious man and that he prefers to stop and kill the bee rather than drive on and be open to the risk of an accident.

Reem says to him, "Don't kill it. Let it go."

He assures her it is a big and terrible bee that should be killed.

He laughs as he crushes it on the glass.

Reem says to him to vex him, "Perhaps it is a queen bee and the beehive is in need of it."

He answers, "There is nothing that can't be dispensed with."

Indeed. There used to be something that I couldn't dispense with, even for the sake of my poems: Rida, whom I loved and hated at the same time. And the two children? All the words in the dictionary were not enough to describe my joy in having them—until they grew up and became strangers to me, like all other males of the tribe, talking to me in a tone like that of my father. They care for me, but there is no dialogue between us on anything other than food. On basic issues, they hold dialogues with their grandfather and their father. One of them migrated to Canada and the other to the realm of polite abandonment and silence, and I see him only on social occasions that suits his reserved behaviour toward me.

Indeed. There is something that cannot be dispensed with, poetry for example. Thirty years of domestication have passed, during which I have continued to write poetry secretly or in my head. Poems buzz in the space of my skull like bees, one poem after another, one bee after another. There are many poems that I wrote in my dreams and was unable to put down on paper in the morning. Since the beginning, Rida divided my time well for me. When he noticed me putting pen to paper, he invented a social occasion that would occupy me for several days until the spell of poetic madness died. He chose his goals with care and intelligence so that he would give a fatal blow—a banquet for members of my family or his, or for any passer-by. What are you doing? Writing a poem? But we have to invite our agent in Lebanon to dinner this evening, he is in town. Mobilized to do kitchen work, I still wrote silent poems in my head all evening long—buzzing bees that would not fall silent.

I was rushed between the office and the kitchen, attending to necessary repairs and house redecorating, whenever I told my husband of a new burning urge for writing poetry.

When I lie down, exhausted, in order to rest between one blow of love and the next, I see the spider weaving its cobweb between my fingers day after day, repression after repression, year after year. It is a spider that weaves its web with threads of silk and moonlight, but they bind my hands in a harsher manner than iron fetters . . . Meanwhile, the bees grow in number in my chest, day after day.

Dr. Saduq asks Professor Rida, "There will be many speeches honoring you this evening. Would you like to respond to them or not?"

Rida answers with humility, "I'll try, but I'll be embarrassed to say anything!" *But he is not embarrassed to participate in the coverup of the truth that everyone knows, namely, that I did half of the work at the publishing house and the magazine, in addition to my work at home. There is a collusion to conceal what a woman can do and it is a silent collusion that has continued through history. If my husband boasts that he fought unjust authority here and there in defense of his opinions and was defeated several times, I must say that I shared his fight, and at the same time I also fought my destiny as an Arab female.*

If he is repressed, I am doubly repressed: once with him and once by him! It never happened, in any conference honoring him, that he stood up in a moment of truth and gave a testimonial of truth, saying, "This woman did half of the work I am credited with, and she deserves half of the glory I have obtained." No, he never said anything. "A male shall have as much as the share of two females,"[1] even in work they have both done together, half and half.

Ah, my chest boils with repression like a crowded beehive. I am about to explode. A new bee joins others in my heart every moment, and the buzz rises and my silence deepens. On the outside, I appear as though I am sinking into my own body, which has become a mass of flaccid flesh, within which the folds of my suffering soul are lost to view, still sensitive, but repressed and buried under an external appearance like that of millions of women of my country: an obese mother, surrendered to the fate of flabbiness . . .

Dr. Saduq and Professor Rida cackle. They converse with one another, continuing a dialogue, the beginning of which Reem has not heard. *Whenever I was angry and thought of leaving him, he knew by intuition what I was concealing, as though he read my thoughts. He would not say anything. He would ignore me. But, from a private place in his desk, he would take out the love letters of the great poet Diana, dozens of letters that she had sent him expressing the burning passion of her heart; then he would take out her angry letters, coming after the announcement of our engagement, warning him*

1. This is a principle in the Islamic law of inheritance according to the Qur'an 4:12. Trans.

not to marry "the cow," meaning me, and then her letters that cursed
him after we got married and cut off her relationship with him and
withdrew her important poetic collection, which she took to another
publisher in order to harm him and me by her ruse.

Whenever I was angry, he would turn over his letters and my
vanity would be awakened.

The mere thought that I had snatched him away from her used to
make me happy. In time, I became aware of the snare: he had not
really given her up for me but rather for himself, so that he could
remain the front man and the crowned king, while I would always
be the shadow.

Diana would have never accepted being a shadow. She would
have never abandoned her inkwell for a kitchen pot.

Dr. Saduq stops the car and Rida himself kills another infil-
trating bee.

Reem thinks she has seen the bee come out of her own
mouth, shut up with silence.

She laughs aloud in disbelief at this irrational idea.

Dr. Saduq says, "The matter does not call for laughter. There
is a real problem concerning the bees in this suburb." *I sometimes*
feel ashamed of myself when I am angry with Rida. There are moments
in which I feel he is not responsible for my domestication but rather
the whole world is. And there are moments in which I wonder, if he
does not take part in the change needed, who will? And what is the
use of all the nonsense that we publish in our magazine and that is
discussed in conferences, so long as some men, like Shahriyar, go
back home afterward and lock up their women's minds?

Dr. Saduq continues, "A few years ago, a laboratory in the
neighboring district imported thousands of African bees to
breed and do experiments on, but they escaped from the laboratory a few months ago, and no one knows where they have
built their new nests. But it is certain that they have not gone
far because many of them still visit the district and annoy
people, as they have this evening in our car several times."

Professor Rida asks, indifferent to problems of bees and
laboratories, "Will the chairman of the department at your university be present at this evening's conference?"

"Certainly. And I'm currently translating one of his books, to have it published at your publishing house." *In the beginning, we used to communicate without words. Then something happened that spoiled our telepathic, spontaneous, and emotional understanding of each other.*

No, nothing big and sudden happened. And this is the frightening thing. Things were dying slowly by themselves, sinking gradually in a swamp of quicksand.

I tried to mend matters, but dialogue is not a ball to be tossed back and forth with Rida, nor can it be replaced when torn by another. Either there is communication or there is not.

I could no longer read his thoughts or dream the same dream with him at the same time, and he could no longer spy on my nightmares, my bees, and my suffering.

Several bees enter the car. Reem can hardly believe what is happening to her. *What a dreadful thing . . . It seems to me that they have come out of my ears and my mouth!* Saduq pulls the car to the side of the road and stops. He appears to be frightened by the return of the bees to the car. *It's not reasonable that the bees have come out of my mouth. My nerves are tired, but I'm not afraid, for the bees are my friends; they have lived within me and multiplied in my depths.*

After they repeatedly fail to kill them, Professor Rida and Dr. Saduq get out of the car until the bees leave it.

Reem insists on remaining in the car. She takes the bees in her hand, one by one, and sets them free into the air.

The two men return to their seats in the car.

They continue the trip.

Saduq says with assurance, as the suffocating heat increases, "A few more minutes and we'll be there." Then he and Professor Rida continue their conversation and Reem falls into the well of her silence.

The sunset appears to her to be sullied, and the bees buzz increasingly in her chest. *I was hoping that this evening's conference would be different, that the truth known to Saduq and others would be restored. But I felt nothing had changed as soon as I stepped on the ground at the airport.*

I saw Saduq after a long absence and he greeted me as though he was seeing me for the first time! . . . And why should this surprise me, for he and my husband have exchanged letters and interests since the beginning of his success.

In the beginning, he used to send me greetings and ask about my work and my poems in his letters to my husband. Then my name was dropped altogether from his letters and was replaced by the expression "My greetings to your wife."

Professor Rida says, "It seems the way is longer than I expected. Can we have a cup of coffee at some resting place?"

Dr. Saduq stops a few minutes later. Reem, distant and silent, sits down and sips her coffee. Seeking to ingratiate himself with her, Rida tries to draw her attention to the beauty of the place. He even picks a little wildflower from a flowerpot on a table in the middle of the place and offers it to her. *He can be gentle and sweet. He knows my weak points and how to treat the wounds he inflicts from time to time. But I am regretful. I should not have accompanied him this time. I'm afraid I'll explode and say what I really feel and cause a scandal. There's no scandal equal to telling the truth.*

In the last conference to honor him, I was about to rise and comment on the speeches of the panelists. I had noticed that all that was said in most of these conferences did not really praise qualities my husband had, but rather ones he did not have.

They invent virtues that they attribute to him when he really has their opposite, and they ignore vices they know well he has.

One of them stood on the podium that day and did not say a single word about our magazine or our publishing house, but rather seized the occasion to expound on his campaign platform and deliver a political speech. He had once vilified us when his interests conflicted with our national policy, which has never changed, and yet he found in this conference honoring Rida an occasion to announce his new positions!

On that day, I sympathized with my husband as they tossed him around like a ball in order to honor their own interests.

I almost regained my calm rationality, despite thirty years of bees buzzing in my chest. I decided to restrain my sympathy and be the devil's advocate. I said to myself, "In return for Rida's monopoly of

honors, he will be assassinated and not I, if the leaders of the oppos-
ing intellectual group want that. Rida is the object of honors, as a
man, but he is also the only target of murder and punishment, despite
my participation with him in all his acts and ideas. After his assassination, I'll become the martyr's widow, with all the qualities and
considerations that are implied in such a title and have nothing to
do with my personality. I'll become his representative. I will receive
a flood of sympathy and honors after his "martyrdom."

Leadership and its risks or honor are the lot of men. This is a
man's world, and Rida is not responsible, alone, for thirty years of
bees in my heart.

Besides, he is not without kindness. But matters have run in this
fashion for ages. He will not be the one to bell the cat. And nothing
will change so long as people like him are afraid.

He fears people's derision and misunderstanding of my poems or
their rumors about me if I was to give free rein to my pen and was
not a "lady of high society," polite, and cultured outside my duties
at home. Many are the rumors that circulate about poetesses, their
madness, their libertinism, and their alleged lovers!

If I were to explode, to publish, to dare to fly at night above the
roofs of the city in order to contemplate its innards, then write about
them, that would be a breach in the law that forbids women to visit
the planet of creativity—unless they do so within the conditions of
clownish social conventions.

In my head I began to write the speech I would have liked to deliver
at the end of the conference as a beautiful scandal. But I did not dare
go on and began trying to exonerate Rida from that swamp, claiming
to myself that he was not as guilty as my hatred of him would have
it, that he was the bullet and not the finger pulling the trigger, and
such nonsense.

That evening, I tried to replace my anger and jealousy with my
own store of patience, submission, motherhood, and tenderness. But
I was failing in the test of supine patience—and my anger rose.

I began praying that we might leave the conference before I exploded.
I listened with difficulty to a few truthful speakers and to many little
and big clowns honoring their own interests in speeches that were
supposed to honor my husband.

A charlatan pretending to be a genius told the story of his life, praising his innovations and using the opportunity of the honorific ceremony to survey his own glory. Another opportunist gave a veiled speech about our achievements. As for literature, thought, poetry, and truth, they were not among his concerns.

The face of the speaker began to appear double to me, as though I was drunk. Mouths opened and closed, and I understood nothing. I contemplated my husband. Sitting on the podium so as to be honored, he seemed to me to be worried.

It was as if all that glorification troubled him in a moment of truth with himself.

I began to see the speakers' faces plastering the walls and ceiling as they succeeded one another on the podium. Their succession had continued since the beginning of the ceremonies in honor of my husband. Their images followed one another on an invisible screen within my head, as in a nightmare. They all spoke at one time, as though they were tapes all blaring together. And I heard the applause and the buffoonery.

I almost went to the podium to deliver my truth and my bees. Then I heard a voice like Rida's coming from my depths, asking me, "Are you really disgusted by the scorning of truth or are you trying to find pretexts in all that is happening because you feel jealous?"

That evening, I remained silent. That voice saved me from the scandal of telling the truth.

They leave the resting place. They continue the journey in silence.

"Here, we arrive at last," says Dr. Saduq as he gets out of the car in haste to help Professor Rida. He holds the door open for him.

Reem opens her car door herself and gets out. She turns around as they both precede her on the narrow path toward the cultural center.

She contemplates the visible things around her as she gradually walks into the grayish dusk of evening. *The world appears strange to me and the evening is exceptional, as I wend my way to the conference to bury truth in this remote Parisian suburb.*

On both sides, I see giant curtains hanging from the sky down to the fields surrounding the cultural center and tied together at the horizon over a plateau that looks like a gigantic theater.

Two curtains of dark crimson velvet, in which I almost hear the hissing sound of bees.

The sky is well paved with cement, and the clouds are of baked brick and fired clay.

I hear the roar of underground rivers of boiling water.

The trees run in space with the scarecrows; the trees' dark leaves are gray saturated with black.

Behind them, a petrified river does not run but fills its bed, almost overflowing its banks.

There are overturned boats with worm-eaten wood on the riverbank; their desire to move and their memory of the water have passed away.

In front of the cultural center, there is an apple tree.

I pluck an apple. It has a mask, with carnivalesque eyes and a dangling mustache, like all the apples on the tree.

Under it, on the metallic ground, flowers of bright-colored neon and plastic are growing.

Do Saduq and Rida see what I see? Or am I alone stepping onto my own private planet?

All visible things bathe in suffocating, trembling shadows. Sunset invades the gigantic theater. The moon is just a memory of a moon. It is dark and surrounded by a pale, silvery halo like an echo.

There is hot congestion within me, like the inner part of a bomb at the moment of explosion, just before actual fission; it spreads out its electrons to join my depths to those of dark mysteries.

An inner river of obscure suffocation stretches its dark veins between me and the elements of the universe, joining me to the circulatory system of an unknown, mysterious planet.

A FLASH:

A bare train like a skeleton passes by us. Women fettered to its iron seats are screaming in the caravan of metallic litters.

A FLASH:

I see a woman lying down in a coffin, reading instructions to workers aloud, explaining how to close it firmly upon her.

A FLASH:

A hot Artesian fountain bursts out of the bowels of the earth. With it leaves from all the books I translated and the poems I composed, and the pages of all the magazines I reviewed.

A fountain bursts under Dr. Saduq's feet and raises him up in the air. He screams, then falls down to the ground. He rises and continues to walk, conversing with Rida, not saying anything about what happened to him and not believing it, lest he be accused of madness.

The world is logical and any deviation from the paths of logic is illogical and unacceptable! But he turns to me, behind him, with a cautious and accusatory look of fear in his eyes.

A FLASH:

Old women gather around a girl to circumcise her. They forget all about that when they discover she has little wings. They proceed to cut them off and curse the devil. But the wings grow again, so they cut them off again. This is repeated ceaselessly and endlessly . . .

A FLASH:

The two leaves of a wardrobe door close on a girl weeping inside. Her voice gradually dies down and finally stops when a huge, ghostly, floating, severed hand, turns the key in the lock. The hand is lacerated and wrapped in mummification bandages redolent of their embalming medicaments, which remain effective over the centuries.

A FLASH:

A fettered woman is dying and, far from her, a blimp flies in the air carrying medical equipment for surgical operations, and cotton, life rings, and carnival clothing.

The woman screams and asks for help, but fireworks are shot in the air to celebrate her dying.

A FLASH:

A thread is tied to my leg and I am a giant bee with a human head. A child, who has a mustache and a face like Antar's in the drawings of Tinawi and Rafiq Sharaf, toys with me.

He puts me under the burning sun so that I may fly like a cicada, which children play with and whose buzz they like. The buzz is not emitted from my chest alone. The threads are many and so are the bees, and the child has tied hundreds of them with threads to all his fingers. Angry buzz. Buzz. Threads. Buzz. I send out my calls for help to unseen swarms of bees . . . I communicate with them.

The ceremony to honor Rida begins.

Reem closes her eyes and opens them, exerting an extraordinary effort not to let some unknown element explode in her chest, trying hard to listen to what is being said.

The voices reach her with interruptions, like some nonhuman muttering, like the sighs and shrieks of creatures in cages at the zoo at night.

Reem tries in vain to be connected to human language. The terrible buzz returns to her ears, and she does not know whether it comes from her chest or from outside through the window.

She sees the audience wearing face masks. Some are not human. The person delivering a speech from the podium is a poodle with a horse's mask. Another speaker is a unicorn with a rabbit's mask. *My God, what is happening? The swarm of bees in my chest is about to explode. Thirty years of bees. Bees in my veins. A deafening buzz. I am not imagining things.*

The buzz deafens her ears.

It deafens the ears of all those present. They are astonished to see swarms of bees flooding the place from every direction, like a violent sand storm, and no one knows from where they come.

The bees rush in. Someone shouts, "Close the windows! The bees are attacking us."

Immense swarms of bees float about the hall. Reem is in a state of semiconsciousness, like one having a familiar dream over and over again. She sees what is happening with glazed eyes and does not know whether those bees have really come through the windows or have rather come out of her eyes, ears, throat, nails, and hair. She is frozen stiff, and all those present scream like crazy people while the bees sting them in a horrible long nightmare.

Her husband stares at her, terrified, as though he is seeing what he cannot believe. He screams with pain, then runs toward her and does not know whether he is doing that to seek her protection or to protect her.

She does not notice, in her semiconsciousness, that she bends over him like a womb.

Clouds of bees cover Saduq's face and sting him. He shakes with pain and points an accusing finger at Reem, as though wanting to say something. He falls on the floor. He trembles like a person who is burning; he points at Reem, but no one hears him screaming that the bees are coming out of the mouth of that witch.

Those present scream and twist with pain. Some of them try to escape through the windows and doors. Most of them fall on the floor in terror and pain from the stings of the bees and their terrifying buzz.

Gradually Reem comes to. She notices that she has no pain. No bee has stung her and she is not afraid. Only the buzzing and the screams deafen her ears. The bees cover the faces of those sitting at the table of honor, and their bloodied hands wave in the air like drowning persons before final collapse.

Screams . . . Buzzing . . . Swooning . . . A great exhaustion befalls Reem and she faints.

The sirens of ambulances. The police. She does not know how much time has passed. She opens her eyes: What a nightmare! It seems to her she has seen it before. *But where am I? Why am I sleeping in a field?*

She turns around. She sees her husband lying by her side. He trembles, having apparently been stung by scores of bees. Many people are lying in the field.

Nurses and ambulances come and go under floodlights. The police and doctors roam about among the bodies laid on the ground.

A young physician bends over her. Pointing to her husband, she asks him, "How is he?"

He says, "In bad shape, but his life is not at risk. You have fainted but you are all right. It is strange that the bees did not sting you. Perhaps your perfume protected you from them. You are one of the few who have not been stung by the bees."

She listens scornfully. *The physician is not at a loss when faced by an ordinary puzzle like this one. Scientists always have convincing answers.*

He repeats, "Your perfume is certainly what protected you from the stinging bees and drove them away from you. There are perfumes which are sweet to the human sense of smell but which some insects are driven away from and others are attracted to.

"These African bees are wild and poisonous. Swarms of them escaped from one of the laboratories a while back, and they have moved about. It seems they have been hiding in an abandoned house near the hall and were not found, despite a close search for them."

Reem falls silent. She does not say that she does not wear perfume because of her allergy.

She heaves a deep sigh. She breathes with ease and feels that her chest is like the atmosphere permeated with the evening breeze. It is no longer congested with a suffocating, obscure, and mysterious buzz.

The doctor asks a colleague of his, who seems to be puzzled, "But why did the bees sting some people in the audience and not touch others? What made them go crazy this evening in particular?"

The other doctor says, "Everything has a scientific explanation, and we will find the answer. Perhaps it is the heat."

Reem smiles in secret and says nothing.

They treat her husband with balms and injections. He turns to her and says, afraid of being accused of madness, "It seemed to me at one moment that the bees were coming out of you. I can swear that I saw them, in a glimpse, coming out of your mouth, fingers, eyes, hair, and nose . . ."

She does not answer.

Professor Rida continues, "But that is certainly impossible. It seemed to me later that you protected me from the bees. Motherhood was your talent always. You secrete tenderness as bees secrete honey. A woman is like a bee. For her, giving is a secretion she is never thanked for. *There is always a honeyed sentence to appease me, which implicitly insults me. Why doesn't he keep quiet?* He became a chatterbox like them. Reem feels a new bee buzzing in her chest. *This is how it started, a long time ago: a few bees and a low buzz. This is how I started thirty years ago— thirty years of bees!*

She contemplates the sky, dark with mysteries, and sees the moon as a mirror that has fallen on the ground and broken into smithereens that are strewn about.

The Other Side
of the Door

Snow is flying about as if it is falling upward to the sky from the earth. Darkness has also begun to pour its black flakes into Layla's eyes as she leaves the hospital in the Parisian suburb.

She pushes the wheelchair of her son, Shaker; its wheels sink in the snow that has been falling for one day and night. *I am a poor, tired horse pulling dozens of carriages, not knowing how or why.*

I used to be a rather happy pony on the beaches of light. I made my way as a writer for the cultural page of one of Beirut's newspapers, and I dreamt of success. And here I am, hardly able to move in the snow.

In those days, I was a passionate lover of Na'im's eyes, seeking protection in them, while hiding in the shelter, from the thunder of shelling and the terror of death. His warm, honey-colored eyes were windows to which I ran and through which I escaped to open fields, silent except for the chirping of birds, away from the sounds of shelling and the feeling of fear—I had known nothing else besides, since the age of ten when the war broke out.

In the shelter, two eyes armored me against fear, death, and pain, as well as against a mosquito as big as a rat and rat as big as a cat. Surrounded by our two families, amid dozens of other neighboring families, we both sat, our stealthy looks embracing in a pleasant plot to annihilate those present, to do away with them from the shelter one by one with an invisible eraser, along with their voices, the smell of their sweat, the stench of their walls, their rats, the sounds of their war, and their madness. And we remained alone together in those quiet, green fields.

How did all that end up with me in this sad, humiliating walk between home and the neighboring hospital three times a week for five years of poverty and repression?

In my adolescence, I dreamt of a conjugal nest, but it never occurred to me that I would choose one merely because it was near a hospital on another continent!

Shaker awakens her from her thoughts and asks her, twice, "When will Uncle Bobos come?" He repeats his question before she can catch her breath to answer impatiently, "He promised to come at half past six."

With difficulty, she raises the wheelchair in preparation to get off the sidewalk and cross the street. She feels the pain returning to her exhausted arms. *In Disneyland, when I raised Shaker from his seat in order to put him on the airplane seat of the merry-go-round, I suddenly realized that he was growing and that his tragedy was growing with him, and I did not know how long I could continue to bear them both.*

His weight is above normal. He was about to slip out of my hands, so he stretched out his arms to hold on to my shoulders, as though he was crucified on my body, which is crucified by exhaustion.

At that moment, a man I did not know stretched out his arms and carried him for me and put him on the seat. Contrary to his habit, Shaker smiled at the stranger, although he is a child who has not laughed once in the five years since he was hit by the shrapnel of the last shell of the war; it left the lower part of his body paralyzed.

I said to the man in French, "Thank you, sir."

He answered me in French also, "I will remain with you and help you carry him to the various games, then return him to his seat."

If it were not for my age and my ordinary looks, I would have thought he wanted to make advances to me.

I contemplated my son. He was a child who had grown up suddenly. His cheeks were bulging with candies stolen from his grandmother's box. His eyes were merrily looking at Disneyland's joys for children with innocent excitement and wanting to embrace them all at once.

The man and I conversed in poor French until we discovered that we were both Lebanese.

I asked what he was called, and he said, "Shaker."

I laughed. "What a coincidence! My son is also called Shaker."

He added, "But the children call me Bobos."

"Your children?"

"The children at the circus, where I work as a clown. This is at least the nickname that outsiders call my profession.

I asked him seriously, "And what is your profession?"

"A servant of Père Noël or Santa Claus. He distributes gifts in the Christmas season, and I try to distribute laughter all year round. Parents do his job for him one night, and I do it for the rest of the year."

I smiled with all my heart. The important thing was not what Bobos said, but how he said it. He had a talent to revive joy in one's heart.

He carried Shaker back to his seat, and my son did not show any dislike toward him, contrary to his usual behaviour with strangers.

He asked me, "Where is his father?"

I answered, "My husband, Na'im, works in a store that rents Arabic videos in Paris, and he cannot accompany us."

He shook his head incredulously.

I felt an irresistible desire to tell him the truth: "Well, we don't have enough money to pay for three tickets. Admission costs 250 French francs per person and our financial conditions are difficult and don't permit us to live in Paris. We have been obliged to live in one of the suburbs for the sake of the boy's medical treatment. They did all they could in Beirut and advised us to come here. My husband's salary is meager but we manage."

"Why don't you work and help him with your salary?"

"I could work as a writer in the emigrant Arab journals here, where I would earn double his salary. But Na'im refused that and said it was unacceptable that a wife work and her husband stay at home, even if her salary were double his.

"I said to Na'im that day, 'Necessities make forbidden things permissible, but I will not argue with you about the error of your decision.'

"Na'im said to me, 'Your son is in need of your tenderness. As a female, you have things I cannot offer him.'

"I wanted to discuss this myth with him, which men invented to bind us to the cribs of our children, but Shaker cried in his sleep and we both ran to him and never discussed the matter again."

I was astonished that day to hear my voice as I divulged these secrets to a man I had seen only one hour earlier, who worked as a clown and whose full name I did not know.

I felt ashamed and repentant at the same time, and I realized how lonely, fragile, and spiritually weak I was, thrown in my psychological wheelchair. Here I was begging for the compassion of the first person approaching me and making him push me a little. I was permitting myself to use him as a sympathetic listener to my complaints and I was even about to confess to him that I thought of suicide from time to time.

I wondered whether he read my thoughts when he said, "Don't regret having divulged to me what you did. I, too, feel you are close to me, for you resemble my sister's ghost. Don't you know that the loved dead ones have ghosts that don't leave us and that come to us when we are in need of them, not in memory alone, but in body too?" Then he asked me, seriously, "Have you ever seen a ghost?"

I was astonished, so he added, laughing, "For example, I am a ghost. I don't frighten people in the dark but am rather myself afraid of the night a little, and I love daytime. When I die, I will be transformed into a ghost that will make the children laugh and be happy."

He continued, "I love children, and everyone who has not known love is dead. Death is not the dying of the body. Most of those you see around you now are dead. Haven't you ever noticed that? Don't you see how the living, the dead, and the ghosts mix in the streets, in the hospitals, and everywhere?"

The ferris wheel stopped turning, so Bobos carried Shaker in his arms for me for the fifth time, saying to him, "I'll do anything for you, my love." And he did not return him this time to his wheelchair but raised him up onto his shoulders and was occupied with him and distracted from me for the remainder of the day, playing with him and moving with him from one game to another. He appeared to be very happy doing that, to the extent that he even joined him in some games and insisted on paying for the soft drinks and sandwiches we had, and then he took us home in a taxi.

My husband saw him through the window, carrying the wheelchair and seating my son in it, then saying goodbye to us. He asked rather angrily, "Who is this old man?"

I answered, "A Lebanese man who works as a clown in Cirque de La Rigolade in the St. Cloud district. He gave me three complimentary tickets to attend the parade and amusements that they offer the children on the weekend. He never married and has no children. He treated Shaker fondly, as if he were a son of his."

She continues plodding in the snow with difficulty, pushing the wheelchair and almost collapsing in the heavy darkness of a solid black sky without a single star.

Shaker asks her, "When will Uncle Bobos come?"

She tenderly repeats, "At half past six, sweetheart. It is half past five now. I'll prepare the sandwiches and the sweetmeats. Your father will bring your birthday cake from the confectioner's on his way home from work. Your birthday will be the best birthday ever."

He asks, "What shall we play with until Uncle Bobos arrives?"

She answers, "The children will come at six. By the time they all arrive, your Uncle Bobos will have come. He will not come later than half past six, don't worry. You and the children will play with your toys until he arrives." *I said to Bobos, "Shaker's birthday is next week, and we'll celebrate it for the first time since the war's end in Lebanon. Don't forget that you suggested this to us once. Can you come and spend the evening with us?"*

"That depends on my work schedule, but I'll certainly do my best to come."

"There will be no birthday without you, Bobos. Shaker smiles only when you play with him. At school, at home, in the street, even when he plays with his friends, he frowns constantly like a melancholy old man.

"A year ago, the doctor said to me, 'This boy is healed in body but still lacks the will to walk. If he does not smile and laugh, he will not be really healed. Medicine can do a lot. It can transplant organs, but it can't transplant joy.'"

Bobos said, "I swear by Shaker's life, I will come even if I am dying. This is a promise, and I will not be late."

I asked him, "By which Shaker are you swearing? By him or by you?"

He answered, "We are one."

Layla stops for a little while. She arranges the hat on her

son's head and wraps his neck well with the woolen scarf. The cold is bitter and freezes the snow into ice. She almost slips. She holds fast to the wheelchair lest it should slide away.

She continues her walk slowly. The grayish evening snow is still falling—in the air, in her heart, under her skin. Snow is falling in her blood system. Snow is falling in her throat, making her feel almost suffocated in the cold gloomy evening that became dark before five o'clock.

She pants and the cold air bites her lungs like the legendary wild white ants. *Here I am, a cripple pushing a cripple. How tired I am! But I must pull myself together. This is the first time we celebrate Shaker's birthday. The suggestion came from Bobos a few months ago. He said to Na'im, after the bonds of friendship between them had become strong, like between two stray cats in a forest they don't know, "This child lacks joy. Why don't you celebrate any occasion so that his heart may rejoice? Celebrate all the holy days of the various religions. At least, celebrate his birthday."*

I was preparing the tabbouleh *salad in one corner of the gloomy room that had been transformed into a kitchen, and I was listening to their conversation in silence while my heart was crying.*

Na'im said to him, "Celebrate, you say? I loved my wife in the shelter, and there I asked for her hand from her parents. On the wedding night, we were subjected to shelling and spent the rest of the 'celebration' in the shelter. One year and a half after that, she went into labor in the shelter also, and it was impossible to take her to the hospital because of the violent, close fighting between combatants on our roof and those on the opposite one. And so Shaker was born in the shelter; one of the neighbors present was fortunately a midwife, who helped. Here, we live in a room with narrow windows which is like a shelter. For three years, we laughed and were merry between one shelter and the next, because we were happy for having Shaker. And in spite of everything, we lived and we worked—I as a clerk and she as an editor—until the shrapnel hit our son in the back, and broke our back. You are not a stranger, and you know our conditions. How do you expect us to rejoice and make him rejoice? Don't you see how we have moved from shelling by fire to shelling by poverty?"

"I'll not lecture you on the philosophy of life, although I studied philosophy before becoming a clown. I know that intelligent, clever words don't remove a toothache. But I'll be frank with you and tell you a secret, then you can laugh at me.

"When I graduated from the Department of Philosophy at the university, I wanted to work as a professor of philosophy. On the day I submitted an application for a position, we were subjected that evening to shelling. So we went down to the shelter, which was dark except for a candle in the corner. I played with the neighbors' child and she laughed. A candle was lit in my heart. I repeat, I'll not lecture you on philosophy. It was not lit in my heart only; I actually saw it standing on the shelter floor near the first candle.

"I played with another child. He laughed. A third candle was lit. His mother said that I was talented in making children laugh. My mother was annoyed by these words said about her son, 'the philosopher.'

"I played with the children in the shelter. They laughed and their parents laughed with them. Light spread in the place, as it seemed to me, and the bad atmosphere changed. When a shell fell at the shelter's door and killed my mother as it exploded, I pledged to devote my life to making children laugh. I decided to work as a clown.

"I always wanted to increase the element of light in the darkness of our hearts, dense with hostility after a legacy of darkness accumulated over the mercurial years of the war in Lebanon.

"Ever since the shell killed my mother, who was the quintessence of transparency and light, I fled all that horror so I could make the terrified and wounded children of the shelter laugh. The neighbors said I had lost my mind because of the violent death of my mother in front of me, and also because of my abundant studies in philosophy! I ask you by God, my friend, do you think I am mad?"

Na'im answered, "You're mad and a thousand times mad. You spend your salary on toys and other gifts you buy for Shaker."

"The real madman is the one sharing the room with me. He spends his salary on women."

I intervened and said, "Everyone is a madman in his own way. We are all mad. What is important is that one should choose the madness that best suits one's reality."

Shaker begs his mother, almost crying, as he shivers, "Hurry up a little, I am cold."

She answers quietly, "I am afraid of slipping on the ground, sweetheart." She does not tell him that her fingers are almost frozen inside her woolen gloves that are wet and covered with snow. She is afraid his wheelchair may slide away from her grip and he may be hit by a car or may collide against a wall . . .

She does not want to tell him what may upset him. That's why she answers in a calm voice, "Yes, sweetheart." *I stood in front of the Champs Elysées store window as the warm, fur-lined coat called to me. The beautiful, warm clothes were exorbitantly expensive. How could I buy warmth? The pink dress called to me, too. I know I am not beautiful. My nose ruins the beauty of my eyes, hanging down almost to my mouth. I am short and plump and deprived of the rounded but pointed breasts that make one's figure desirable. But if I could buy this overcoat with its fur-lined warm hat, I would not suffer in the snowy nights. If I could buy this pink dress, my nose would appear a little smaller. And if I had the money for plastic surgery on my nose, I would become beautiful.*

The saleswoman came toward me asking, "May I be of service to you, Madam?"

It is the polite French way of chasing away penniless customers and reminding them that there is nothing here for them to do.

I said to her, "No, thanks."

I turned tail and left the shop, promising myself to continue saving on home expenses so that we could buy a battery-run wheelchair for Shaker and a car to facilitate moving about with him.

When I returned home, I had a fight with Na'im because he had bought a gross of cigarette packets, despite their high price. He smokes and wastes the money and suffocates us with his cigarette smoke in our apartment cell. Shaker and I escape to the little room adjoining our main room. It has no door but has a little, high aperture doubling as a window.

We argued for a long time, each barking in the other's face. I knew we were arguing with our own destiny and barking in the face of our own fates.

We continued to wrangle until we both turned into two flies struggling in a vast cobweb where there was no light. Bobos then surprised us with a visit and his philosophy, saying things about light and the darkness of hostility on his way to our son's nest-like, narrow room. We heard him play with him and make him laugh. Then he came out, half an hour later, when we had calmed down, and he said, "The poor boy is now sleeping like an angel. He will never stand on his feet and will never be healed as long as you keep up your wrangling and wretched life. How heavy his legacy of darkness is!"

We did not heed his words, and our voices rose again in quarrel.

He said angrily to us, "You are two ugly and frightening ghosts. If you quarrel again like this in his presence and if you awaken him with your hostility, I will punish you by kidnapping him and disappearing with him."

Na'im smiled, his fit of anger having subsided. His usual goodhearted nature returned to him and he tried to repair the damage he had caused around him, currying favor with us to the point of flattery, praising any stupid words we said, and laughing at the most trivial jokes. But he did not apologize.

As for me, I was really frightened by what Bobos said. What terrifies me more than Shaker's paralysis is losing him, losing that suffering and proudly patient, beautiful boy whose hair diffuses the scent of cedar trees, whose skin exudes the saltiness of the sea, and in whose sweet eyes loom the memories of my own childhood in those beautiful days before the war.

Ah, for lovely remembrances that my memory transforms by erasing all that was ugly and by doubling the beauty of what was beautiful. Memory . . . that ghost to which I cling, which I see and don't see . . . which I artfully invent.

Shaker says, his teeth chattering with cold, "At last, we've arrived."

His voice has a tone of eagerness and expectation due to his joy on his birthday.

Layla tries to say something to him but does not find her voice. I am overcome by pricks of conscience. The child begs me for a happy dialogue as in children's birthday get-togethers on television. But matters in real life are different.

I almost collapse under the impact of the night's darkness and my heart's darkness. I feel that darkness has weight in the cold, that it is as heavy as a tombstone; it has a sad smell, and a sound resembling that of my tired breathing. My breath is now frozen with cold.

In moments like these, I used to think of suicide.

But for a reason I don't know, I have stopped planning my suicide since I became acquainted with Bobos.

Layla carries her child up the high, timeworn, wooden stairs. She takes care not to slip and fall with him. She almost cries from exhaustion, vanquished and crushed by his handicap as she is.

The old lady who is her next-door neighbor opens her door and tells Layla that an employee of Printemps Department Store came in the afternoon in their absence and delivered dozens of gift boxes and toys for Shaker. When he found no one home, he delivered them to her and made her sign a receipt.

Layla thanks her and goes down the stairs to carry the heavy wheelchair up to the apartment. When she raises her eyes to look at the sky, it seems to her like a large, firmly-closed, black door. *Who sent this heap of gifts from the sumptuous Printemps Department Store when Shaker's friends are all poor like us and I expected no gifts better than crayons and the like?*

Shaker amuses himself by running his hand with pleasure over the colored wrappings of the boxes and their golden ribbons. Layla reads Bobos's name on the birthday greeting card. Who else but Bobos could have sent dozens of expensive gifts?

Layla leaves her son in the room waiting for his other friends to arrive so that he may tell them about the gifts. With him is Danny, whose parents have just brought him early.

She also leaves her apartment door open and goes to the apartment of the old woman living next-door. The latter had offered her large kitchen next to the entrance so that Layla could prepare the food there for the celebration of her handicapped child's birthday. More than anyone else, the old woman knows the narrow space of Layla's apartment, for it is her property and originally part of her own apartment that she had split in order to rent part of it and earn some money—and a large measure of companionship.

Layla gets busy making sandwiches and sweetmeats quickly. *Ah, if only I could set up a table for him like my mother used to do, with the help of my aunts, on the occasion of my birthday, before the war impoverished and humiliated us.* She rushes from the next-door neighbor's kitchen to her door whenever she hears the sound of a child arriving, and she receives him from his parents.

Signs of joy are all over Shaker's face whenever a child arrives and gives him a present, and then he begins to tear off its colored wrappings.

Layla goes back to making sandwiches.

The telephone rings. She rushes to answer. Na'im says that because of extra work, he will be a little late in arriving with the birthday cake. He asks her whether Bobos has arrived.

She suddenly notices it is half past six. She says to Na'im that Bobos has not yet arrived but that he has sent dozens of expensive gifts, which the neighbor received for her during her long absence at the hospital with her son.

Na'im says, worried, "I hope he will not disappoint us. We don't have anything to amuse the children with in our suffocating room if Bobos does not come." *At the circus, the children were laughing at Bobos at the top of their lungs, but many of their parents did not laugh at his painted clown's face with its cherry-like red nose. To adults he appeared touching, but to the children he was a source of real merriment. I never saw a circus as a child, like my son, from whom Bobos succeeded in getting a smile and nothing more. But gradually, Bobos infiltrated into my soul as I began to see him, as the children did, with my heart's eye and not with the myopic eye of logic. After a few minutes, I found myself laughing like the children, having become one of them. I became aware that I was still radiant and alive, because Bobos was able to make me laugh like the children.*

Na'im was content with a smile and said almost apologetically, "He is wonderful." But he did not laugh. It was as if he had forgotten laughter, like his own son.

The old woman asks Layla, "Where is the clown who you said would be coming to make the children laugh?"

She answers, "I don't know why he is so late. The important thing now is to prepare the food."

The old woman says, "If it were not for rheumatism in my fingers, I would help you." *There is no longer anyone to help me. Even my husband appears to be distant these days. I can hardly believe he is the same man I pined for. Those days seem to be so far away, they never existed. The whole city appeared to be allied against our love at that time, then it cast us into this pit of dark night and snow.*

There are days in which I feel the whole world is allied against me in a war I did not make. There are days in which I remember what I have written and said; I remember my biases, my applause for this party, my silence at the dishonorable practices of that party, my gloating over the death of one group, my grudge against another group . . . Can I really consider myself innocent of this war?

Have we not all been polluted by it?

Is this misery my punishment, the reaping of my sins?

Is there any redemption for me without confession, without reciting the act of repentance?

Didn't the shrapnel that hit my son come from a shell fired by a group with which I used to sympathize at one time? Oh, I don't know . . . It seems to me sometimes that thinking in this way is a luxury, sinking as I am in the deep snow of poverty and guilty feelings.

It is terrible when one feels guilty for dreaming of happiness for oneself, as I do . . . And these sandwiches, aren't they going ever to come to an end? A layer of butter, another of meat, another of lettuce, then mayonnaise, then silent weeping, and secret weeping, and weeping . . .

Laughter.

Layla hears laughter coming from her apartment through the open door. The children are laughing, and she distinguishes Shaker's laughter, which she has not heard for a long time, not since he was hit by the shrapnel of the last shell fired in the war and was turned into a handicapped child. But she knows with certainty that it is his laughter, and that it is Bobos alone who has finally succeeded in releasing it.

She also hears the voice of Bobos, who, it appears, arrived a moment earlier and has begun to spread a wave of joy over the children.

She hears his hums, his roars, and Shaker's laughter. *The doctor has often repeated, "Doesn't this child ever laugh? There is nothing* that medically impedes his recovery, and there is no organic cause for his handicap anymore. He is in need of an awakening of the will to live and be joyful."

The old woman says, "It seems that the clown has arrived."

Layla continues her work, the rock of ice having fallen away from her chest. *What remains is the arrival of Na'im with the birthday cake, and the first birthday in exile after the war will be a success.*

She leaves the sandwiches and decides to take a look at what is happening. *I want to see Shaker laughing. It is a sight that can make me forget all this misery, in which I fumble about as one walking in a nightmare and unable to leave it.*

Layla invites the old French lady to join her to see the clown, and the latter says she will follow her after doing her make-up.

Layla goes toward her apartment across the little corridor on the landing, her heart quivering. *Do I love Bobos? Yes, I love him. Without him, I would not have been able to pull myself together in the last two years. I have not known a more gentle, a sweeter, a wiser, a more affectionate man than he is. Yes, I love him. It's not the love of erotic desire. I never thought of embracing him or possessing him as a male. But I love his presence in our life, and without him we would have been all broken to pieces.*

The children's laughter is louder as she enters the room, and she sees her son, Shaker, laughing with great joy like the other children. It seems to her that she sees Bobos standing on one foot on a bucket; she does not know where he brought it from. He moves quickly, while laughing, and she does not clearly see whether he is standing on the edge of the bucket or in its middle, without having his foot sink into it, in one of his special and obscure tricks. He then moves away from it and rises gradually in the air, jumping and jesting and pretending to be afraid of falling down. Meanwhile, the children laugh, cheer, and applaud. Shaker's face is ruddy with health, as it has never been since he was hit. Bobos is moving around like a phantom, glowing with disembodied vitality, pouring out joy and merriment.

She has never seen Bobos alive with such a fiery energy, with such sprightly movement, as though he were a shadow on the wall or a ghost.

She decides to bring the sandwiches she has prepared and to ask Bobos to stay for supper.

She returns to the kitchen, the children's noisy joy and her son's laughter still filling her ears. This is her first happy night in exile. She says to the old woman, who now has her make-up on and is ready to see the clown, "I wish Shaker's father was here to see his son laughing so. His heart would rejoice."

But the children's laughter becomes less audible, without ceasing, as when someone turns a radio down, and the sound becomes less perceptible although the radio is still on.

Layla carries the tray of sandwiches, and the old woman walks with her to see Bobos's tricks. Layla does not see Bobos, but she sees the children playing happily. Shaker's face appears for the first time to be normal, not without innocence and hope, resembling the faces of Antoine, Danny, Julio, Hassouna, Ali, and his other schoolmates.

The old woman asks, "Where is the clown?"

In turn, Layla asks her son, "Where is Uncle Bobos?"

He answers indifferently as he continues to play happily, "I don't know. Perhaps he's gone to my room or to the bathroom."

A child shouts, explaining, "He was walking on the wall."

Another child continues, "He was walking on the ceiling. He was walking on the water."

A third child and a fourth say together, in mingled voices, "He was chasing a cat. He was chasing a star. He was chasing a rose."

The children's stories are numerous and joy reigns over the place. *I am dreaming. How have we come by a happiness like this?*

She rushes to her son's room and finds no one there. The bathroom is also empty.

She says to the old woman, her neighbor, "Perhaps he got tired and went home or perhaps he returned to the circus or . . ."

But she is astonished at not meeting him in the little corridor between the two apartments and not seeing him leave.

At that moment, Na'im arrives carrying a big chocolate cake. The children happily sit around the little table. Shaker blows out the candles that Layla has lit. *I will not be able to light a candle from now on without remembering the candles Bobos lit in the shelter.*

Na'im notices the atmosphere of joy and happiness reigning over the place and the laughter of his son, which he has not heard in years. He asks his wife, "Bobos has come, hasn't he?"

She says, "He has just left after making the children laugh. Even Shaker laughed for a long time. Look at his face and how it shines with joy as he laughs with his friends. This has not happened here in the past."

The children are cheerful. They eat the cake and the sandwiches, then return to play with the expensive toys given by Bobos. Shaker opens the last gift from Bobos, and Na'im reads his kind words on the card: "With the savings I made, I decided to buy toys for Shaker instead of a battery-run wheelchair, because I have a feeling that you have no need for any wheelchair."

Na'im asks his wife, "Why did Bobos go?"

"I don't know. I didn't have an opportunity to speak to him. I watched him for a while, and he was really wonderful and extraordinary. Then I continued my work in the kitchen, and when I returned with the old woman to invite him to stay for supper, to talk to him and thank him, he was gone."

After everyone has left, Na'im decides to call Bobos and thank him for his gifts and for his presence, which succeeded in making Shaker laugh for the first time since he was hit and became handicapped.

A roommate of Bobos answers the telephone, crying and saying in an extremely sad voice, "Bobos passed away an hour ago in the hospital; I've just returned from there."

Na'im exclaims, unbelieving, "My God, what are you saying? This is impossible."

The man weeps, "Bobos went out on his motorcycle this morning as usual. He said he was going to Printemps Department Store to buy toys for Shaker. Two hours later, they called us from the hospital saying he was dying."

Na'im screams, "What?"

The other man continues, "I've learned from the first-aid staff at the emergency department that his motorcycle slid across from Printemps Department Store and that it collided with the wall and that he was thrown off. The store's guards got in touch with the first-aid staff, who then took him to the hospital. The doctor told me that Bobos was seriously injured in his head and vertebral column."

"When did you say the accident happened?"

"About eleven o'clock A.M., according to what they said at the hospital. The poor man was in a deep coma from the moment of collision. He never regained consciousness and died in front of me an hour ago."

Still holding the telephone receiver, Na'im calls his wife. Trying hard to whisper in order not to upset Shaker, he asks her, "Did you say Bobos came here this evening?"

"Yes. I said he came."

"Are you sure of that?"

She answers, astonished, "I saw him with my own eyes. So did the children. Why are you asking?"

He does not answer her but continues his telephone conversation with Bobos's roommate: "It's not reasonable, my friend, that the accident happened before noon. Bobos was with us an hour ago."

"Impossible. I was next to his bed an hour ago. I even spent all afternoon with him in the hospital. I did not leave him until he breathed his last. The sight of him tore my heart. The poor man was unconscious and attached to dozens of tubes, coming out of his veins, his nose, and his neck. May God spare you the sight of anyone dear to you in such a condition."

"But . . . who brought him to us?"

"I don't know. I have no logical explanation now. I'm sorry."

"Do you think he sent us one of his colleagues?"

"I don't know."

"I swear to you he was here. My wife is not lying."

"Nor am I lying, my friend. I stayed with him as he was dying from noon until he departed this life an hour ago. You may go to the hospital, ask the nurse and the doctors, and verify the police report. Is it reasonable that I would lie to you about such a disaster?"

"Excuse me, my friend. The shock has made me lose my head."

"Me, too. So, please pardon me."

Na'im puts down the telephone receiver. His wife has listened and understands nothing. She turns to him for an explanation.

He says in a low voice, "Bobos died this morning, after having bought the gifts and asked for their delivery."

"But he was here . . ."

"He wasn't here. It does not stand to reason that he was dying and breathing his last at the hospital and at the same time jesting with the children at our home."

She falls silent for a long time, then she whispers, "Didn't he once tell us he would come even if he was dying? Do you remember?"

"Unreasonable. Perhaps before the accident, he agreed with someone to replace him."

"Unreasonable, too. I know Bobos well. I know his voice, his movements, and his laughter. It's unreasonable that it was not he."

"What is reasonable, then?"

"I don't know. I saw him. I did not see a ghost."

"Are you sure?"

"I don't know!"

"Do you really believe in the existence of souls?"

"I don't know . . . I don't know . . ."

They both sink into a stunned silence as they see Shaker, at the door of the room, standing on both feet and holding on to the door. He takes a few steps toward them, leaning on the wall, and asks them playfully, "What's the matter with you? Have you seen a ghost?"

An Air-Conditioned Egg

If her voice had not come out of that plastic box, I would have sworn it came from the depths of that dark water which I avoid swimming in and rush to flee from all day in my skyscraper office—that water, teeming as it is with demons, shadows, sharks, shiners, skeletons, and treasure chests, and echoing with songs of sea nymphs and corsairs.

Ah, that dark, shining water deep within me, I know well how to escape from it, but I am forced to visit it at night, when sleep takes me to it, handcuffed, on dream boats.

If her voice had not come out of the telephone, I would have sworn it called me from the bottom of that water to ask me to surrender and jump and follow its cadence to those coral corridors whose doors I firmly locked with seven locks, spending seven years—day and night—to do that, and lamenting, "Close, Sesame!"

Is it possible for a faint, quivering voice, coming on the telephone from a distant past, to explode in my face with its sound waves, to tear my soul and let my shattered self fly off, and to make a sea of obscure tempests drag me again into dark depths while I resist in vain?

She says in an old Damascene dialect, I am Maymana, mother of 'Irfan al-Saruji. Do you remember me?"

I begin to tremble like a cat, wet in a dark alley in winter. I recognize Maymana's voice, and I gesture to my male secretary to leave the room with the two female clerks, because I am afraid that my tears will find their way to my cheeks after many years and explode the myth of the woman of steel nerves.

I begin to repeat with confusion, like a stupid woman, "Mother of 'Irfan al-Saruji? Maymana Hanum?"[1]

She asks again, "You haven't heard my voice for a quarter of a century. Do you remember me?"

How could I forget the voice of the mother of my first great love? He was her only son and was, perhaps, my only love. What an unbreakable relationship between two women, Maymana Hanum and myself, loving one man. *She took me by the hand to face the mirror, framed in mother-of-pearl, in the reception hall of the Saruji family palace. She took off her splendid diamond earrings and asked me to try them on.*

Blushing with embarrassment, I put them on with trembling hands.

They made my cheeks reveal the fire in my heart, for I was in love, happy, and only sixteen years old.

I contemplated the earrings: two large diamonds, each like a magician's transparent ball, surrounded by a gold frame with eastern engravings, like the mysterious writings of an obscure amulet. Trying them on brought to my face the scent of al-Ghuta gardens and the delights of Barada evenings,[2] and it brought to my ears people's whisperings over thousands of years in the alleys of our age-old city. I was afraid, as though they were magical earrings. I took them off and returned them to her. She gave me a warm embrace, pressing me against her plump body wafting the fragrance of Arpège perfume mixed with the smell of fattat al-makdus,[3] and she said, "These two diamonds will be my gift to you on your wedding night. They have been an heirloom in our family from a long time ago, perhaps going back to the days when the Damascus city walls were built. I know you will take good care of them and will, in turn, offer them one day as a gift to one who will deserve them."

1. Hanum is a Turkish title of respect used in Damascus for women.

2. Al-Ghuta is a fertile oasis on the southern side of Damascus, and Barada is the river running through the city. *Trans.*

3. Fattat al-makdus is a Damascene dish offered at banquets.

*She returned them to her ears, and they hung on both sides of her
face and looked extraordinary. I trembled with joy and kissed her
with adolescent impetuosity, swearing to her that I would rather die
than betray her trust.*

My silence is long and my hand holding the telephone trembles.

Thinking my silence to be indifference, she says, "I'm sorry,
it seems you've forgotten me."

I finally find my voice. "No, I haven't forgotten you. You
certainly know that. Otherwise, you wouldn't have called me."

"Is it possible for us to meet?"

"Certainly, wherever and whenever you would like."

"Come, then, to my hotel in two hours. I'm at the Waldorf
Astoria Hotel."

"I'll be there. Until then, Maymana Hanum. And all my best."

I put down the telephone, almost unable to believe. My hand
on it is dead, heavy, like a fish that has just perished. It is no
longer my hand, it does not belong to me, and I don't know how
to make it go back to the computer keyboard in front of me.

The telephone rings again for an urgent matter that I, unchar-
acteristically, decide to postpone. I ask my secretary to tell the
clerks to put off the meeting we had begun.

I contemplate New York from my office window on the
eighty-fifth floor of one of the skyscrapers.

Once again, I am overcome by that feeling of suffocation,
and I feel I am living in a hellish egg, which sweats on the inside
on account of the crowd and the excitement, while the horizon
is closed in a semi-circle of noise.

In New York, I miss the easy breathing which used to come
like the sleep of a baby in the Mimas desert or on the giant heights
of Mount Qasiyun as we ascended them together, 'Irfan and I.
That beautiful breathing used to reach my deepest veins through
my pores, open to absorb life and joy. The love of the age-old
furrows in the face of Mount Qasiyun and its time-mellowed
wrinkles used to unite us and give our love a dimension that
transcended all times.

Since my early days in New York, when I began working as
a clerk at this bank, then rose in rank until I became deputy

manager, I have felt I was living in an air-conditioned but suffocating egg, whose hellish shell I did not know how to crack or
how to open a window through in order to leave it and go to
the world beyond it and live.

I lead a double life. My daily life as I work in the air-conditioned
egg seems to be a golden nightmare, from which I do not wake
up until I go to sleep and dream. At that time, my other life begins
as I escape that suffocating, huge egg and go to other worlds
that I have never succeeded in forgetting.

I continue to contemplate New York from the window. Hundreds of thousands of windows stare at me derisively. There is
a witch on a broom flying among the skyscrapers and helicop-
ters, ready to penetrate the wall of silence and go outside the
hellish egg.

My secretary, in his twenties, enters and asks me, with his
bright face, "Will you come to see me this evening?

I answer him like any businessperson with many worries and
burdens, "Not this evening. I'm tired, but if I change my mind,
I'll call you."

He says in a soft voice and with an Arabic accent that has not
left him, although he came to America as an immigrant with his
family when he was a little boy, "You treat me as an Eastern
man treats his lover. Say 'Yes, I'll come' or 'No, I won't come'
and leave me to dispose of what remains of my time. You know
that I love you."

Outside my window, a man is cleaning the glass on a movable
plank suspended by ropes. My secretary rushes in his direction
with some annoyance to let down the curtain, like someone
slamming the door in the face of another. I am filled with a
charge of hostility toward him. *This young man, two decades my
junior, loves me? The matter appears comical to me, if I do not think
of my friend Nadwa in Damascus. She loved the man for whom she
worked as secretary; he was two decades her senior, and because of
him she committed suicide. Why shouldn't a man younger than I am
love me? Is it merely because I am a woman and he is a man?*

I answer him calmly, "We'll discuss the matter outside the
office without any fuss. You know that I don't mix my work and

my pleasure, and I don't want you to accuse me one day of exploiting my position in our relationship. Now, I have to go out for an urgent matter. Please, cancel my remaining appointments."

"I loved you because I thought you were Shahrazad, and lo and behold, you are Shahriyar."

"Excuse me, but I'll not embark on a discussion of all this now."

"You're not an Eastern woman. You're an Eastern man!"

"Excuse me, but I'll not embark on a discussion of all this now."

"I'm a desert man, but you treat me as the harem used to be treated. Why have you chosen an Arab to torture? Why don't you have a relationship with Richard or Johnny?"

"Excuse me, but I'll not embark on a discussion of all this now."

"I no longer want all this love. I'll marry my cousin, whom I've never seen, and I'll submit to my family's will. I'll summon her from the other end of the world. That would certainly be better."

I hear my own voice, cool and as sharp as a razor on a winter morning: "Excuse me, but I'll not embark on a discussion of all this now."

I take the elevator to the basement garage. I drive through Wall Street and go uptown to Park Avenue, where her hotel is.

I drive my huge Cadillac unconsciously, like an automaton. Meanwhile, I run as a barefooted little girl in tatters in the alleys of Damascus of the past, weeping and searching for those I loved in the past who went away . . . "as in a dream, they went away."[4]

But the past does not really go away. It remains deep inside me like an engraving on stone that time cannot efface. No exorcist can expel the faces of yesteryear's loved ones who inhabit me like dear ghosts.

I reach the Waldorf Astoria Hotel, but there is still more time. I roam about aimlessly for a long, long time in crowded New York. I drive my car erratically in streets and on bridges, recalling all my past, beginning with the faces of my schoolmates. I almost hit several cars.

4. "As in a dream, they went away" is a song by the Lebanese singer Fayruz.

I return to the hotel entrance and leave my car to the parking attendant. I regret not having gone home to fix my make-up so that Maymana Hanum would not see my face after all these years without cosmetics as in Damascene funerals. She remembers me as one who cared for my appearance when I was engaged to her son and raided her compact and mauve lipstick, which was fashionable then.

I ascend the marble stairs to the grand entrance area with its floor embellished by a circular mosaic tableau that reminds me always of the mosaics of the Umayyad Mosque in Damascus. Oh, how I miss old times. I sit to wait for her in the Peacock Alley Lounge.

I've arrived more than half an hour before my appointment in order to empty my head of the noise of dozens of computers that inhabit it and to prepare myself for my inner celebration when I meet her, like a criminal who prepares the scene of his crime to the last detail.

I hope she will tell me something, divulge a secret, and thus give me a knife, so I can put an end to the past, mutilate its corpse, and hang it on the ramparts of my heart for seven days and nights, and rest.

The waiter comes. I order a double Glenfiddich, with lots of ice and no water. I take out a cigar and light it. I don't care for the sideways look of a man displeased with my usurpation of his right to a cigar. Perhaps it is the same look his grandfather gave the first woman he saw smoking a cigarette a long time ago. My scene will not draw the attention of his son or his grandson.

I will never understand these comical laws, nor will I ever submit to them. What is the law that forbids me to smoke a cigar as long as I have not stolen any money to buy it and have two lungs like any man? Lack of refinement? Why should refinement be limited to women?

What a contradictory woman I am, loving Damascus but not daring to return to it. A woman of steel in the daytime, who turns into a suffering adolescent at night, dreaming every night of 'Irfan and Damascus, running barefooted in the Damascene alleys, knocking on the windows of her sleeping loved ones, who think her knocks are the sound of the wind. Meanwhile, her spirit wanders near 'Irfan's tomb in the Dahdah cemetery between the Seven Pools and al-Qassa'.

How can I return? Can I live in Damascus and sit at its evening parties publicly smoking a cigar or a pipe?

How can I return, having become accustomed to being an independent person, like any male? This is a matter I am not sure my mother city will accept. Nor will it accept relations I may establish outside the frame of "great love," as is done precisely by some brokenhearted, heavily burdened, and disappointed persons, of whom I am one. Furthermore, I have never been able to master the art of embellishing my reality or concealing the worst part of it! *My father said to me, "You'll get married to the son of my friend Badr al-Din al-Saruji. His son is named 'Irfan. He's an educated and intelligent young man who has just returned from Cambridge University after having completed his studies in his specialization. His father is wealthy. His reputation is good. 'Irfan, furthermore, will inherit his father's factories. It's the ideal marriage."*

I said, "I don't want an ideal marriage but rather a marriage of love. I'll not marry anyone now, so please, tonight don't spoil my joy at having passed the baccalaureate exam. I'll marry only a man I love. He may be poor, but it's better if he's wealthy."

"But I've already agreed with his father."

"This is a matter between you and him. As for me, I'll not get married to anyone. I want to continue my university studies."

"He'll visit us with his family tomorrow, in an initial move. Why don't you just have a look at him before you reject him?"

"Because I'm not rejecting him, but I'm rejecting the custom. Father, you cannot just educate me until the bridegroom arrives, then cut off my education. Learning is not merely a "diploma" I boast of, for if it was, the matter would be easier. Learning transforms me from the inside. You can no longer make me marry anyone, as your father made my aunt, who neither reads nor writes."

My father was very angry but he suppressed his anger and said, "Well, I'll get in touch with his family and we'll postpone the matter."

He entered his office and I heard him speaking on the telephone. I tried to listen stealthily but only succeeded in hearing his laughter.

The maid caught me overhearing and I pretended to be passing by coincidentally! My father continued, almost in laughter, quoting a Damascene proverb: "Don't play hard to get, you're already unwanted." The man's son, too, refused to attend the initial visit of acquaintance and would only marry a young woman he knew and loved. He did not want a marriage contracted in what he called the old way. What a spoiled generation!

The waiter returns. I quickly order another Glenfiddich with a lot of ice. I put out my cigar firmly. I'll not smoke it in the presence of Maymana Hanum, not out of hypocrisy but because the Damascene little girl inhabiting me is afraid of hurting her feelings. Only love can control that little girl whom I did my best to kill, but who did not die. Here she is, getting the better of me while I am awake after having defeated me several times in the world of sleep and dreams. *O little girl residing in my depths, I offer you peace and co-existence. Daytime is mine, nighttime yours. Work is my kingdom, dream yours. I recognize you; recognize me. O little girl, who a thousand years ago at the age of sixteen sat at the edge of the table at the Four Hundred Stereo Nightclub in Damascus— her female neighbor Ghayda and Ghayda's fiancé took her there; then they got up and danced, leaving her at the table alone, staring curiously at the night life she had never known—please release me from memories and from the fragrance of Damascene jasmine diffused at night like a lover's sighs.*

From my seat at the Four Hundred, I watched Ghayda dancing with her fiancé in a reserved manner and I watched their friend, who had come with his sister, dancing with another friend's sister.

In those days, evening parties in the presence of sisters meant goodwill and a high moral standard. The young man would be "harmless" and would not do to others' sisters what he did not wish to be done to his own sister. It was a kind of guarantee for an acquaintance whose aim was honorable, ranging from eventual marriage to fraternal friendship.

An older man, more than ten years my senior, came and asked me to dance with him and I declined. He limped because of a defect in his foot, but that did not bother me. He fixed me with a sharp look of his eyes and his attractive but not handsome face and said daringly, "Do you refuse to dance with me because I limp? Everyone limps while dancing and becomes like me!"

I started laughing. How did I not notice this before? Did a lame person invent dancing so that everyone else would be lame like him? His frankness opened wide the doors of my heart, for I was a young girl who did not know the art of making masks. I said to him, "I declined because I have never danced with anyone other than my brother and my female schoolmates on their birthdays. I am more confused than you are and am crippled by terror."

He sat by me. An invisible secret current flowed between us, and we caught fire.

We were flooded by the inner fountains and obscure rivers which intervene in our destinies, unseen by us and uncontrollable, rivers which perhaps have their source in dreams and pour into the sea of madness, passing by art, poetry, hallucination, and fever— fever between my hand and his. A long conversation about everything and nothing followed, time being a fast cat on the run. Then came the language of silence, before which all language appears trivial.

Through two hours of night partying, I saw no one but him.

Something happened to me that did not persuade my mind: love at first sight. All others in the place were transformed into plastic dolls.

All loud sounds died and were overcome by the whispers our lips exchanged. He held my hand in his, and I trembled as though he was embracing me. We laughed at stupid jokes like two crazy people.

As we danced, he held me in waves that felt my pores and explored their way under my skin, and I flew on a violet, green, red, and blue cloud. He suddenly said, "I don't believe in love at the first dance but I do love you. Please believe this, because it is not logical but it is real."

We danced, fully embracing each other as an invisible power drew us closer and closer. We almost forgot all about dancing and nothing remained but our close embrace. I roused from that public cleaving together called dancing and said to him, "I have not danced a dance like this before. I believe Damascus is going to find a scandal about which to talk . . . This is my first scandal."

"And you are my love at first sight, at first laughter, and at first dance."

I was about to ask him his name when he said, "Imagine, my father wanted to marry me to a stupid woman I never heard of."

He continued, "Just like that. A marriage by the ID card, through matchmakers, by signing documents, like making a deal to buy fruits for conserves for our factory. A young woman I was supposed to seal in a can and print the expiration date on: 'The birth of the third son.' It had to be a boy naturally!"

I said to him, "The same thing happened to me. I was supposed to discontinue my studies and agree to my father's wish to marry a stupid man called 'Irfan Badr al-Din al-Saruji."

Without blinking or changing his tone, he said, "And I am this stupid man, and you are the young woman I refused to marry!"

"I am rather the young woman who refused to marry you!"

And we laughed for a long while.

Thinking our meeting had been prearranged, my friend Ghayda said, as we were leaving the Four Hundred, "I heard the rumor of your engagement to 'Irfan al-Saruji but did not believe you would marry a man chosen by your family and the matchmakers."

I said to her, "Nor did I believe I would, either."

The waiter comes and looks at me with astonishment when I order a double Glenfiddich and a big cup of coffee to be served at the same time, and quickly. *This is my life, moments between fire and ashes. Between the birthplace of my heart in Damascus and the birthplace of my success in New York. Between the open horizon and an air-conditioned egg. Moments between the bottom and the summit. Between extreme love and utmost indifference.*

The waiter returns. I drink the Glenfiddich in one gulp and begin drinking the coffee and sucking a lozenge to conceal the smell of alcohol, in fear of Maymana Hanum. The Damascene little girl inhabiting me, whose kingdom is my dreams, begins to spread her power over my wakeful hours, too. *On the evening of my engagement to 'Irfan, I seized the opportunity of our merchant fathers' joy at a forthcoming marriage, suitable to their business interests, and I asked my father to permit us to go out to the Candles Restaurant for dinner. My father said, "But you have both had dinner." 'Irfan said, "We did not have enough!"*

We sat on the second floor, usually more isolated, and we ordered a dinner, which we did not touch.

'Irfan said to me, "You don't need to discontinue your studies because of our marriage. You can first obtain your degree, and then we'll get married."

"Can you wait? Can I wait?"

"I love you really, and not in the sense of possessing you. The growth of your personality is a gain to me. I'm not a descendant of Shahriyar. I'm from a new breed. I'll not order Masroor, the executioner, to arrest you, and I'll not tie you like a camel to the tents of my tribe. You'll be my wife, not my bonded slave."

"I don't believe that this wonderful dream is happening to me and that you are a real man, not a dream. Yes, I want to continue my studies and not lose you. But your father will refuse, and so will my father."

"We'll refuse their refusal and we'll impose our will on them, for we're the children of another age. Don't worry, I'll convince them. Remember that I'm 'the man' and I'm free to do what I like with my wife, in front of them at least. But between us, you are free within our marriage as much as I am."

"Sometimes I feel that having been born a woman and an Arab at the same time is an unforgivable sin. It means depriving me of my civil rights. There should be a male to bear the responsibility of my acts before society, including my desire to study and work. He has the task of setting me aright, or else he'll be blamed before me."

"Rest assured, I'll never be the husband who will oppress you but rather the friend who will protect you and your desire to study and work."

That was unbelievable, too good to be true. Oh, did that really happen or is my memory embellishing the image of the dead in my heart?

When we left Candles, we went to a café suspended between the night and the water at Dummar. We drank coffee and River Barada was our witness. Then we went to the Muhajireen neighborhood and stood in the plaza, embraced by Mount Qasiyun.

He hugged me in the darkness, seizing the opportunity of the absence of passers-by. I stared at Damascus, my heart throbbing with love for it and him. Despite the darkness and the little lights here and there, I could see the contours of the city engraved in my heart as if it was bright daylight.

That night, the translucent moonlight opened an avenue of brightness into the city's ancient alleys and humble old homes, and it poured its liquid silver on its roofs, its minarets, and its domes.

Nocturnal Damascus, bedecked with a necklace of jasmine flowers, stretched out to relax in the moonlight. Damascus of the mornings, sitting on the throne of the empire of light, exhaled the smell of Arab coffee, cardamon, Arabian jasmine, lemon blossom, and orange.

I said to him, "I love you both, you and Damascus. I will complete my studies and return to you both."

My father did not permit me to leave the country for my higher studies without first having the marriage contract signed—which, as a conjugal legal document, was an insurance policy in his opinion— after which 'Irfan would bear the responsibility of any behavior during my further education that could be improper.

The important thing was that our Arab society should find a male to hold accountable if I erred and make him bear the responsibility of punishing me. His penalty would be gossip if he did not turn me into vapor or dust, and did not return me to my genie's bottle and seal its mouth with molten iron; then, instead of throwing it to the bottom of the ocean, he could keep it in his bed!

The marriage contract did not really matter to us, for we had married one another to the last throbbing artery in our hearts, our witnesses being the night, the apples, Mount Qasiyun, and the moon— madly beautiful as seen from a convertible.

The strokes of an antique clock in the middle of the hotel's lounge next to Peacock Alley announce it is six o'clock. A few minutes later, Maymana Hanum descends upon me like a cloud laden with the rains and thunderbolts of the past. *On the night I left, he said encouragingly, "It would be good if you decided to study finance and business administration at the same university I studied at. Pampered girls like you are usually satisfied with studying home economics at the Beirut University College and taking part in beauty contests.*

"When you return, we'll work together in the administration of our business and we'll cooperate in everything. You'll not be the lady of the house, in the sense of being the proverbial female deficient rib, but rather in the sense of being my sweetheart and my female."

I could not believe my ears. It was a dream to hear an Eastern man say such words to me and be my sweetheart and my husband.

He said goodbye to me, his anguished smile echoing the Arab songs in the heart-sick mode of Mayjana, 'Ataba, and Oof, and reminiscent of the traveling sighs of hearts that invented the art of sighing.

We had anxious telephone conversations and sent playful, thrilling messages in secret transcontinental codes. One month after I had left, I was about to tell 'Irfan that I was pregnant and that that night had not been transient, despite our efforts. But he spoke before I did and said, "Don't get worried if you hear that I am hospitalized. It's an insignificant nose operation to rid me of the pains of chronic inflammation in the sinuses. I don't want anything to spoil our honeymoon later on."

I later learned that he was anesthetized before the insignificant operation—but he did not come to.

He died, perhaps to prove that love disappoints everyone and that death disappoints no one.

I did not dare return to attend his funeral. I could not possibly land at the airport in Damascus without him to meet me. Nor could I walk in the Damascus streets while he lay in the Dahdah cemetery next to my home.

They sent my aunt to console me.

I had no need for consolation. I had lost my mind and that was the end of that. There was one thread binding me to life: it was the baby in my womb that he had unknowingly planted, before I left, despite all his precautions.

I decided to keep the baby, and I divulged my secret to my aunt, thinking she would rejoice that some trace of 'Irfan was left for me. However, she was astounded and decided for me, "You must abort that baby. Otherwise, you will lose your opportunity to marry again. It's true, you were legally 'Irfan's wife. But what's proper is proper. An honorable lady does not give herself up, even to her husband, except in accordance with proper ways."

She continued, "The daughter from a respectable family like yours ought not give birth to a child by her fiancé, even if he was formally her husband!"

Who really cared for such nonsense when 'Irfan was in the world beyond?

But my sorrow killed my baby.

When I miscarried, my aunt considered me very fortunate while I lamented both 'Irfan and our baby. Nothing but ashes remained.

'Irfan was as wonderful as a dream. And dreams have no right to live long or to die!

I raise my head. I see Maymana Hanum standing in front of me like a ghost. I did not hear her steps. *I am the ghost, not she. Perhaps I've died and everything came to an end a long time ago. We are not aware of our death until we meet those with whom we lived the truest days of our life.* I rise. She hugs me and I'm about to cry, and my wounded eyes are about to rain salty tears. I kiss her, slender and withered as she is. She sits with all her elegance and pride, her record of sorrows showing in her wrinkles. I know that what happened to her happened to me, too. In her old age, I see the chariots of time that have gone to and fro over my youthful radiance. We've both grown old in the court of sorrow over 'Irfan.

I hold her close to my bosom in silence, without moving from my place. I remember the moment she embraced me in front of the mirror as I tried her earrings on. *A quarter of a century of sorrow separates the two moments, but she is still as close to me as she was on that day. There is something common between broken-hearted women like us, and it may be a man who has gone and not returned.*

She sits as tears flow from her eyes, still beautiful despite the passage of time.

I try not to cry, but I take off my thick glasses and rub my eyes. I must not cry, for 'Irfan is the third person at the table. No lover like me can meet her sweetheart's mother without her sweetheart being the third person present.

I contemplate her lips, which kissed him as a baby, and her belly, which bore him when she did not know he was to die before her.

I stare at her silently, as the river of affectionate, tender looks we exchange sweeps us both away, and we float and sink.

*Oh, lady! Why did you call? Why do you open up both your wound
and mine? Leave me alone in my world, escaping to my work and to
my impossible oblivion. Since your son died, I've not trusted a single
man with my love, lest he should betray me. I've never trusted anyone but 'Irfan. There is a secret part of me that has remained a child
and a lover, who keeps newspaper clippings of old Damascene places
as though they were memories, who collects old picture books of
Damascus, street names of those days, photographs of alley houses
with their engraved wooden doors and of the Diyar Plaza, with the
pool in the middle and trees, flowers, and jasmines encircling it.*

*There is a part of my practical mind that earned profits for the
bank and a part that continued its irrational life in dreams, believing that the universe is a playground open between the past and the
present. All that one needs to do is to dare move around between them.*

*My father's fez sits on the table in the entrance hall of my New
York home. My ancient Damascene lattice hangs on the wall like a
window to the secret, and through it I leave the air-conditioned egg.
When I open it at night, I don't see the wall behind it but Damascus, as
the scent of jasmine blows in and 'Irfan's face looms in a twinkle. I
wish him good sleep, saying, "May you be well in the morning." And
I wonder: Why don't I see him in my dreams, not even once? I always
dream of Damascus with him in it, but I have not once seen him in
my dreams face to face and he has never spoken to me, not even once.*

Maymana Hanum says, as the scent of jasmine from evenings
at Dummar and al-Hama wafts from her and as moonlight flows
from her fingers, "It was not difficult to get your telephone number. You are a successful and well-known lady, and your news
continued to reach me even after your father passed away and your
mother moved to Paris to live with your married sister there."

I ask myself, Has she crossed thousands of kilometers to tell
me that? Exactly what does she want? I try to say something but
find nothing but silence.

She continues in her voice which time has not changed, "I
know that you've refused to marry any other man after 'Irfan
and that you've not visited Damascus since he died . . . Do you
still love him?"

I am about to say to her, "Memory is my daily bread and I've not been able to rid myself of the dictatorship of memories. It's as if my emotional growth stopped after that day and I've become handicapped. I continue to go to spiritualists in New York in order to call him to the world of dreams so that I may see him, at least one last time. I feel he is on a trip and has been away for too long, and I miss him . . ."

But I am aware of my inability to say a single word. Perhaps heroes in bad movies speak like that. In real life, however, dumbness is the master.

She repeats, "Do you still love him?"

I find no voice in my throat full of ashes. I nod affirmatively.

She says, "I know that."

The waiter comes. She excuses herself for not drinking coffee because of her ill health and orders mineral water.

She appears to be exhausted. She trembles like the last flame of a candle. My love for her flows over. Unable to find my voice, I try to say to her, "He does not visit me in dreams, and I don't know the reason. But I still live with him in some sense. He continues to be my husband and I've not yet become his widow. He is still alive in my life as he is in yours, despite a quarter of a century of separation."

I cannot speak. Infernal thorns grow in my throat.

I feel she reads my silence. There is a special language between two brokenhearted women who love one man.

She says, "My daughter. I'm on my way to a hospital in Houston. There is a serious surgical operation that may save my life, but I'm dying and I know I'm dying. I've come to bid you farewell before I die and to give you a trust."

My tears flow inside and my pores lament. The death of anything related to 'Irfan is a new death for me. I resume my exercise of dying in her presence. Her power to read my thoughts astonishes me, for my silence does not bother her and it is as though we communicate through it in a better manner.

I tremble in her presence and imagine what my colleagues, the men at the Exchange and my male secretary and clerks, would say if they saw me reverting to a child in the presence of 'Irfan's mother, as I tremble and run in dark corridors and open all the old coffins.

She resumes, "I've come only to see you and give you this trust that I've carried for you for a long time." *What is the trust? Is it a letter from 'Irfan that I've not been worthy of until now? A letter from Damascus?*

She takes out two diamond earrings from her handbag. I make an effort not to sob as I immediately recognize them.

My mind recalls that unforgettable moment in front of the mirror, framed in mother-of-pearl, when I tried them on one day when I was a butterfly of joy at the age of sixteen. My God, it is as if that happened yesterday and a thousand years ago at the same time.

She says, "I know that you are faithful to his love, and I want you to keep them. These are no ordinary diamond earrings. They are magical earrings. They have extraordinary power which I leave you to discover by yourself. Their magic is very powerful, on condition their owner has true feelings, and I know you do."

In order to avoid being affected by the Damascene magic of the earrings, I take refuge, as I usually do, in the language of the steel woman. I try to speak with her in the language of New York, the banks, material things, and the modern age. I try to tell her that they are worth a fortune, not to be sneezed at in the language of banks and finance, that ten grams of diamond, five to each earring, surrounded by old gold and antique engravings, are not to be thrown away easily, but that I feel also that they are nothing compared to 'Irfan's love, that their price is nothing compared to their value.

I take them from her hand and conceal them in my bra, as my grandmother used to conceal her valuable things. I take them as though convinced I deserve to be entrusted with them.

I tell her, all of a sudden, "I beg you, don't die, too."

She rises from her seat opposite me and sits beside me on the sofa, as if I were her daughter going on a trip.

She hugs me and says in the clarity of those dying, "At the beginning, I was jealous of you because he loved you. My beautiful little baby was attached to another woman, young and beautiful and not fat like me. That was something I could not bear at that time. Then the infection of my love moved on to you when I learned how much you loved him."

Time passes quickly as we converse about 'Irfan in an extraordinary session, recalling his spirit in the heart of Manhattan, next
to the skyscrapers, the Pan-American, the Empire State Building,
the World Trade Center.

Maymana Hanum pants and exhaustion appears to take hold
of her little by little. I wish I could keep her.

She repeats her advice, "Keep the earrings, they are no ordinary
diamonds. They have exceptional magic power. Remember that."

I escort her to the elevator. I hug her and say goodbye.
When the metal elevator door closes on her with quick deter-
mination, like the falling of a guillotine, I wish she was in a slow
train and I could wave to her until the smoke disappeared on the
horizon, so that I could take in the farewell, drop by drop, and
become accustomed to it.

When the elevator goes up with her, I feel another invisible
elevator going down with me, to the bottom of dismember-
ment and isolation.

I am terrified of going back to my nearby apartment on Fifth
Avenue, where I will not find 'Irfan. But I go back. I always go
back like a tortured ghost chased out by all haunted houses to
face its own demons and sufferings.

I press a button at the door of my apartment. The lights in
all the rooms are turned on simultaneously, according to the
system I asked the interior decorator to install, in fear of the
moment of returning home every evening and in fear of the
darkness awaiting all those who live by themselves. It is as if the
darkness says to me, room after room, "I'm empty and you're
alone. Nobody is waiting for you. You can die and nobody cares."

The second step I take to break the desolateness of the place is
to listen to the tape of my telephone recording machine for voice
messages. There are invitations to evening parties that begin with
dinner and end with business deals, passing through backbiting the
other gossip circle that simultaneously backbites us. Emptiness.

Jogging in Central Park and emptiness.

Expensive clothes and perfumes, men carrying invisible lad-
ders to climb on to glory, women like them, and bored wives,
and emptiness in the air-conditioned egg.

The third step to break the desolateness is to press two buttons at the same time, that of the television set and that of the music system, so that I may escape from noise to noise and not hear the voice of my depths.

Tonight, I'll not listen to Michael Jackson or Madonna. I take out the tape of my secret tunes, and the voice of Muhammad 'Abd al-Muttalib rises from the stereo in Egyptian Arabic:

> Bid farewell to your love,
> Forget it and forget me.
> Time will never bring it back again.
> It was a dream and it went away.
> Forget it and rest.
> Bid farewell to your love.

I sing with him as I contemplate New York from my window on the fiftieth floor. It was a dream and it went away? Not for certain.

Life is gone but the dream remains. The former gets smaller and the latter bigger.

I move about in the apartment, almost laughing, like one seeing it for the first time. Perhaps it is a home that reflects me. My father's Ottoman fez sits in a central place of honor—and next to it the fax machine. There is champagne in the fridge— and next to it my old Damascene amulet, which my grandmother advised me never to abandon, but the suffocating heat of New York forced me to put in the refrigerator in the summer because it was beginning to deteriorate. Old photographs are on the table: my picture in a fig-leaf bikini next to that of my cousin wearing a scarf and long sleeves, together with my aunt in a black veil and Arab clothes and my grandmother in a pelerine.[5]

5. In Damascene Arabic, it is called baralin and refers to the type of outdoor clothing worn by women of the middle class in Damascus more than a quarter of a century ago. It consists of a black fabric that covers the head tightly and hangs down to the waist; it is worn over a long black frock, along with a black transparent veil that covers the face, called a *fisha*.

That's the mosaic of my life, stretching between the present and the past, between two continents, two lifetimes, two modes of wakefulness and sleep.

There is a picture of me with 'Irfan, in which I am wearing a necklace of jasmine that he bought for me from an insistent boy. I wonder, Where is the boy today? Did he grow up? Or is he still selling jasmine to lovers, forever a child, unchanging like love itself?

I take a quick warm bath, a jigger of Glenfiddich with a few bites, a calm seat on the balcony overlooking the city.

I prepare myself for sleep, almost terrified. What dreams will I have after this visit, which planted turbulence in my soul?

I don't know why I contemplate the diamond earrings before sleeping. For the second time, I put their hooks through my pierced ears; a quarter of a century separates the two times. Something strange happens when I wear them and they hang down the sides of my tired face with my short hair, dyed blond.

Little by little, it seems to me, I look younger. The wrinkles in my forehead are reduced. I laugh at this thought. I decide I should go to the unknown world of sleep.

Every night, I fear the adventure of going to sleep, I the one who in the daytime takes financial risks that earn great profits for the clients and the bank. A success in the daytime. A failure at night when dreams pounce upon me and return me to Damascus. I keep the old diamond earrings on, as amulets hanging from my ears, and I decide to sleep without taking them off.

I sit in my bed. The telephone rings. The answering machine comes on and I hear my secretary's voice saying in all the impetuosity of his youth, "Please, get in touch with me. I'm sorry."

I must take a double dose of sleeping pills tonight after cutting off all telephone calls. I reset the alarm for early next morning and notice it is called the Dream Machine.

I turn off the light. I gradually descend into a deep well, gliding to I don't know where.

I wake up. I find myself outside the air-conditioned egg, sitting in a red convertible parked in the Muhajireen Plaza in the lap of Mount Qasiyun, wearing my brocade dress, in which I shone on the evening of my engagement to 'Irfan. My sight is not clear. Perhaps my glasses are dirty. I take off my heavy glasses and am surprised that I am able to see without them, as though I returned to being a young woman. I feel my short hair, dyed blond, and find it is long and black as it covers my shoulders and my chest. I turn the car mirror in my direction and find I have returned to being sixteen years old. At first, I can hardly recognize my face, but for its great resemblance to my face in old photographs. I turn left and find 'Irfan sitting in the driver's seat; beyond him and below us stretches the Damascus of old times. That does not surprise me. I am certainly dreaming, and dreams are a journey across ages and places. I am overwhelmed with joy: for the first time, I see 'Irfan in my dream. But am I really dreaming? Usually when I dream, I don't know that I am moving in a dream. In my nightmares, on the other hand, I become aware I am having a nightmare, especially as it approaches its end.

But I seldom dream with an awareness, as in my wakeful hours, that I am dreaming.

I contemplate 'Irfan and try to absorb his presence with my eyes. My thirst for him earnestly pleads for the unusual, the exceptional, the impossible.

I look at the city of Damascus, which has been petrified in my head along with the loved ones of yesteryear who don't grow old and don't die. My astonishment increases. How can I be aware that I am a mature woman who has become an adolescent? Perhaps I am not dreaming but in some magical way I have escaped from the air-conditioned egg in order to wander in other times and live again moments I desire and be aware of that illogical wandering. Or is that what is called dreaming? 'Irfan's hand on the seat is next to mine. I don't dare hold it lest I discover he is a man of clouds. I am afraid of touching him or talking to him lest I wake up, if what is happening to me is a dream. I look at the passers-by and it seems to me they don't see us. We both contemplate our city below us. I tremble with joy at having him and being in Damascus. The city's raiment appears to be embroidered with green gardens, and the domes of the Umayyad Mosque swim in the molten gold light of sunset, surrounded by little houses packed in alleys of many gentle turns and curves, like one being folded in on one's own secrets, joys, and tears. To the right on the heights, I see the popular coffeehouse with its stairs dug in the earth and supported by primitive pieces of wood. Its tables, I know, shake under the weight of a cup of coffee and a glass of water because its earthen floor is not level. 'Irfan does not say anything to me and I don't utter a word. Language appears to be a comical thing. He stretches out his hand and holds mine, and I'm afraid the dream will vanish. Nothing happens. Holding hands unites our blood and forgotten happiness flows from my veins into his, back and forth, as time passes in a wink of an eye and the moon rises, crowning the surrounding thin air. Its light pours in silvery transparency like a flowing, shining mantle over the streets lined with homes that are architectural poems. Here is my school at al-Jisr al-Abyad, and there, my home. On the other side is 'Irfan's home at al-Halbuni, and next to it is al-Takiyya. Nearby is the university encircled by gardens, and River Barada is flowing silver crossed by bridges. It is the Damascus that I know. It changed and grew with time, but it appears as it used to be when it was petrified in my head, and nothing can erase it. I have a pervasive desire to ask 'Irfan many questions. Where has he been? How has he come to meet me? Is he dreaming, too, or has time gone back a few steps in honor of us?

It is sufficient for me to think of a place or yearn for it, and I instantly find myself there with 'Irfan. I remember our dance at the Four Hundred. Here we are at the Four Hundred, dancing again our first dance, by the music of that time and among the friends of those days. I wonder, does he know, like me, that all this exists no longer? I remember our dinner at Candles. Here we are at Candles of that past, whispering to each other. I remember our sitting together at Dummar after dinner at Candles. Here we are at Dummar, on the wooden balcony suspended above River Barada between the moon and sighs, his nose next to mine like a kiss masquerading as common breathing.

Moments later, we return to our favorite place on Mount Qasiyun, overlooking our beloved lady, Damascus. There is a sweet voice in the distance singing Fayruz's song "A Hundred Good Evenings." Here we are at al-Ghuta, at al-Rabwa, at al-Hama, at al-Mazza Airport. We are in places which, in the opinion of some, no longer exist; but they are always there except they have become invisible. I tell him that I miss him. He does not answer. I tell him that I want to remain with him. He gestures with his finger that I be quiet. I remember the story of Orpheus and his return with his sweetheart in a boat from the caves of death. But I miss him. There is a step I must take to cross the river to the other bank so that we may never again be separated. Until that happens, dialogue seems forbidden.

As we leave the airport restaurant, the boy selling necklaces of jasmine follows us. 'Irfan takes one necklace and puts it around my neck. I desire to tell him that I will forever remain with him, wandering in times and in places, so that we may never be separated. It is a simple walk that only real lovers know well. I desire to confess to him of having betrayed him with my male secretary and others, and I wish to hear him say to me that these are the needs of the trivial body, which I will take off one day, needs that he knows as a man . . .

I desire to tell him that love disappoints everyone, that death disappoints no one, and that we'll meet one day. But I remain silent as he feels the earrings suspended from my ears—with an exceptional smile on his lips like one who has discovered a secret.

I tell him that his mother visited me in New York and considered me to be worthy of them, and that I put them on before I fell asleep, or before I woke up, I don't know.

His smile widens and he turns his back to me in order not to say anything. I weep and beg him to turn to me. I ask him, "Where are you? Why have you gone away? What happens where you are? What is there on the other side of the door? What is the shape of the moon in your sky? How can I meet you again?"

He does not answer, nor does he turn to me.

I repeat with insistence, "Please, turn to me. How can I meet you again?" I repeat my question, crying.

He turns to me like one who wants to say all that he knows.

He whispers, "The earrings."

He hardly finishes saying these words when I wake up. I open my eyes to see the sun's light filling the room. *Why did I wake up? What crime did I commit?*

I stay lying in bed. I close my eyes again, recalling the dream moment by moment. Slowly, like one turning one's tongue around a candy, I remember one detail after another. I feel the magical earrings hanging from my ears, and I smell the jasmine.

Again, I recall my dream like a miser counting his gold coins, one by one, as he feels the surface of each, one coin at a time: 'Irfan . Mount Qasiyun. Al-Ghuta. The scent of lemon blossoms. The boy selling jasmine necklaces. The necklace 'Irfan took from him and put around my neck in the dream. Al-Rabwa and Dummar . . . and al-Ghuta . . .

Again and again, as I lie in bed with closed eyes, I recall the dream from its beginning, like a video tape that does not bore me, repeating it on the screen of my closed eyelids, as the scent of jasmine is diffused around me . . . But, how in the world has jasmine come to me in New York?

I remember he held my hand in the dream. I smell it. It diffuses the unforgettable fragrance of his perfume mixed with the scent of jasmine. No, I'm not imagining things. Everything seems to be real. I'm certainly imagining things. Real? Unreal? Dream? Wakefulness? Illusion? Reality? Do things have to happen to us only in one of those two aspects?

The alarm rings. The Damascene dream ends. The bell summons me to return to my other world in the air-conditioned egg.

I get up from bed while the fragrance of jasmine still envelops me. I hardly dare to look in my mirror.

In the dream, I was a young woman of sixteen. And here I am a woman on whose face the wheels of time have rolled.

I feel my face in front of the mirror, then my neck. As I do, I am surprised to find a necklace of jasmine around my neck, its petals a little yellow!

The Brain's Closed Castle

I was in bed with her, riding her like a boat to the islands of wonder, pleasure, and oblivion, when her husband entered. In the beginning I did not believe my eyes. The door of my house was locked and I did not hear the sound of anyone breaking in. How did he enter?

He saw what condition we were in and did not say anything. But he began to come closer to us, sobbing aloud, gasping like a dying person, and holding his head in his hands as though his neck could no longer carry it.

I noticed that he did not have any knife or revolver, so I felt a little relieved because he was not armed.

He continued to advance toward us, tall and stout. He stretched out his hands to my neck, now gasping like a person about to reach orgasmic ecstasy, and he started to strangle me as I struggled for breath. My God, he was killing me. I was being choked. I was dying. I was dying!

I died. Leaving my body, I stood by the bed while he continued to strangle me. The matter seemed odd to me, and I told him to stop strangling me because I was dead and finished and he did not need to exert any further effort.

I expected he would now turn to Nahid, who was silently trembling in the corner of the bed with terror in her eyes, covering herself with the white sheet like a ghost. I expected he would strangle her as he had strangled me.

I was afraid he would do that and Nahid would become a ghost like me and forever stick by me. When she paid me a visit, I was always at a loss for ways to get rid of her after completing our journey in bed.

However, he did not strangle her but rather collapsed on a seat and buried his face in his hands, weeping and trembling and repeating, "Curse you, Nahid. He was my friend. Couldn't you find another man instead?"

She did not answer.

She got up and began to put on her clothes quickly, hiding partly behind a seat as though her husband had not seen her naked before, or as though nakedness in unfaithfulness was different from nakedness in marriage. It was as if she was now another woman and he might assault her and rape her like any desired stranger.

I can observe all this with neutral calmness, or rather with curious calmness, in my capacity as a ghost.

She says to him, "Stop crying. Perhaps he is still alive. Let us call an ambulance, for he may be saved."

The stupid woman. Does she not see the pale color of my body and my tongue dangling out of my mouth and my glazed eyes looking like a doll's?

He answers her, "He died. I know that he died. I killed him."

He continues to weep, covering his face with his hands.

I contemplate my body. It is rather ugly. How did I ever see it as beautiful, play the dandy in front of the mirror, step on the scale, and pat my hair with pleasure?

For the first time, I see myself clearly, with slender, white, and almost hairless legs resembling the legs of a chicken—my mother used to pluck the feathers from chickens when I was a child in the village. I used to watch her in terror, perhaps because I had a feeling in those days that I would die like the chicken, and my body would shake and flutter as it did on being slaughtered. My belly is large and hanging down on my trunk. I don't know how such slender legs could carry it. Perhaps this was the cause of my knee pains. On my chest is soft hair, here and there, in bad distribution and without abundance, like the tousled chestnut-colored hair on top of my head. My hairdresser would dye my white hair and that would please me, although I pretended to object and blame him. Our dramatic dialogue was part of the dyeing process, and, hence, I used to tip my hairdresser generously.

Now I can see how ugly my face is, narrow, long, little, and mounted on a body that does not suit it. My nose is swollen and large, much unlike the falcon's beak that I used to imagine it to be and that would normally give a face the look of a powerful personality. However, women used to claim they fell in love with my handsome looks. Now I clearly realize that the matter was rather related to the handsome figures in my bank account.

Here I am, dead. I have become a ghost and have no need for all that wealth of mine. I am happy because I spent much of it like a madman, repeating like a parrot, "No one takes anything with him. We all die tomorrow." But, of course, I did not mean what I used to say and never thought that it would happen to me. Now I am happy because I willed my wealth to those who deserved it before I died.

In a voice that appears to be too much in control for a woman who has just lost "her first and only great love," as she used to call me, Nahid says to her husband, "Well, what are we going to do now?"

I notice she does not cry over my body, she does not lament my death, although she would call me dozens of times a day on the telephone, claiming she would die if she did not hear my voice.

She will not hear my voice from now on, and yet she does not appear to be about to die!

She repeats, "You killed him. We are in a mess. Let us run away from here."

I become angry a little because she does not try to contact the police so that the murderer of her "first and only great love" may meet his punishment.

His crying ceases as if he is waking up. He says to her, "Let us contact the police. What happened happened."

She fixes her hair in front of the mirror and does not see me.

I don't see myself either as I stand next to her and my image is not reflected in the mirror. She says, "If people know, scandal will be my lot and prison yours. Let us get out of here."

He says weakly, "They will know."

She says, "No one will know. We'll make it appear like a robbery."

He asks, "What about the fingerprints?"

She answers, "We spent last evening here with friends until dawn, as is usual when his wife goes to visit her mother. We entered the bedrooms and took drugs and other things in all parts of the villa. Traces of the evening party, its dirty glasses and plates, its remaining food, are all left in their places, including the fingerprints of the other members of the clique, not ours alone, and that is most important."

He says, "What if they investigate carefully? Admitting to the truth is better than having it uncovered by them later on, when I will be accused of killing him with the intent of robbery. Everyone knows that we have been poor since the war destroyed us and that we now live by profiting from him and his money."

She answers, "Uncovering the truth happens in stories and on television, not in life. The police investigator will not care very much about the death of the murdered man and will prefer to close the investigation and go back home for dinner."

Naji has now transcended the shock. He, too, has begun to think and this is not surprising. What is surprising is that Nahid is calm and clever. I had not seen anything alive in her other than her beautifully enticing body. Truly, ghosts see clearly. They are not like poor living creatures.

I used to imagine that only I knew the truth. Now I see that I knew nothing. My death is exciting because I can now know the truth of things; I can now see them in a better way. The problem is that I did not become mature enough to know until I became mature enough to die, I mean, to be dead.

Naji rushes to the safe in the corner of the room. He tinkers with it looking for money and perhaps for the jewelry of Carmen, my wife.

She says to him, "Don't tire yourself. The safe is empty. It is there only to mislead robbers. It is camouflage, nothing more. He puts his money and her jewelry in this paltry plastic box, in a secret compartment at the bottom, under his wife's pins and combs. He gave me money from it and let my try on her big diamond necklace."

She quickly empties the contents of the box into her handbag, jewelry worth tens of thousands of dollars in addition to a variety of foreign currencies. He goes to the glass door leading to the garden. He opens it, goes out, and closes it behind him. He then breaks the glass from outside and enters after wiping his fingerprints.

I have seen similar scenes in movies. Truly, movies teach one everything. He says to her proudly, "The police will now think a robber strangled him in his sleep."

She makes the bed, in part only, so that it looks as if one person slept in it and as if it was not the arena of passion. She says, "Let us now get out, one at a time. Nobody will see us in the dark, but precaution is better."

He chides her, "You are the cause of this misfortune."

She says, as though reminding him that he was my killer, "Thank God you killed him here in his country home, and on the day of his servants' holiday, in the absence of witnesses— except for me."

So she is happy that I was killed here and not in my well-guarded villa in the city. This is unbelievable.

He repeats angrily, "You are the cause, you . . ."

These revelations overwhelm me. How beautiful it is for me to be a ghost and see those I have known but did not really know.

I decide to follow them to their home. The whole affair has aroused my curiosity and is almost entertaining. I will follow them in the dark and frighten them. I have been afraid of ghosts since childhood and I shake in the dark. But here I am, a ghost who can frighten people today.

I stand in her way as she is leaving the house and I scream in her face in a terrifying voice, but she doesn't notice and asks her husband calmly, "Did you just hear the sound of some movement in the garden?"

He answers, "It's the wind. We'll meet at home."

I decide to go to their home to watch the moment when he reproves her for her disloyalty.

I am not as angry with Naji, who strangled me, as I was with her. I want to see her suffer. "Angry" is not a suitable word, for my feelings now are of a different kind, less sharp and more profound, like a dark light.

I hardly decide to go to their home when I find myself there. This happens with extraordinary speed, like the movement of a point of light on a wall. When I was a child, I was fond of playing with a mirror and the sun; I would hold my mother's mirror inside a shady room and let the sun rays fall on it from the window, then I would cast that point of light on the wall. With a little movement of my hand, the point of light ran in the wink of an eye, like an insect of light.

I played with that insect of light and made it run madly from wall to wall and on the ceiling. I inhabited it and spoke in its voice. When its voice became too loud, my father would come and rebuke me tenderly. He knew he did not have the money to buy me another plaything. My beautiful, beautiful father—if he could only see me now, as a ghost moving like a point of light, he would be surprised and would cry because I died. Now I myself feel the need to cry and lament.

Nahid enters, talking aloud to herself. I see her clearly in the dark until she turns the lights on, and then I see her less clearly. She heaps abuse on this cursed night, in which her husband had claimed he would go to an evening party with his friends but surprised us instead.

Most likely he had been observing us. He stole her key to my house and made a copy of it before he surprised us and caught us red-handed.

She heaps on further obscene abuse in a loud voice, "Damn this evening party. What are we going to do now? Who will pay our expenses? My husband knew all the time and yet pretended not to. What demon took hold of him tonight? What a miserable life we've been living, since the sons of bitches destroyed us in Beirut, the sons of whores, the sons of . . ."

Her vulgar language surprises me. I thought she was beautiful and tender like a butterfly, not even needing to go to the bathroom to do disgusting things like me and the rest of humankind.

I thought beautiful women were like wonderful porcelain dolls and did not go to the toilet. But it seems they are like the rest of humankind and, furthermore, they use vulgar obscenities and try to conceal crimes.

Naji enters, raging like an angry watchdog, having now regained his power at home. He attacks her. He slaps her face.

She impudently spits in his face, saying, "Don't play the role of the aggrieved and deceived husband. I know of your relationship with Carmen, and I saw you both at an evening party a month ago, doing it excitedly while standing, and I watched you carry her and possess her with all your virility. I had followed her to the bedroom to fix my make-up. Were you not afraid her husband would catch you doing it?"

He is stunned and says nothing. He falls into a seat and buries his face in his hands. I try to do likewise but have no face to bury.

My wife, Carmen, doing it with this ugly pig? What does he have that I don't? And I am the one she called "the most handsome," the stupid man who carried out all her requests.

Well, she once caught me with her ugly maid. What's wrong with that? I tried to explain to her that when a woman is naked there is no difference between a maid and a scientist and that when the light is off Claudia Schiffer and Whoopi Goldberg are equal in beauty. The important thing is changing the kind of skin, its smell, its touch, and so on.

She did not say anything that night. She remained silent. I said to her that a man needed that, he needed change, even with an ugly maid. It's unfortunate but true. And I am no better than Emile Zola who had children by his wife's maid.

I had expected her to respond, "A woman needs that too." Then we could have quarreled and I would have beaten her and reminded her that I am a man and she, a woman, and there is a difference between us. Then we would make peace, and I would swear to her that, truthfully, I would not do it again. This would end the matter, but, truthfully, I would do it again.

But Carmen remained silent that day.

Nahid says, "Why is it permitted to you and forbidden to me? Why did you kill him when you do to his wife what he does to me?"

His chest rises like a cock's and he screams at her, "Shut up. I'm a man and you're a woman."

She says, "The time when such an answer was the final word on the subject is gone."

I am afraid she will start a lecture on women's liberation and double standards and other ideas that some female writers have published, to my great annoyance—I have reviled these female writers at evening parties and related imaginary stories about my adventures with them, or about their chasing me and my resisting them. Fortunately, Nahid remains silent.

After a long silence, she calmly says, "And now, where are we going to get money for our expenses? This jewelry should be buried in the garden until the rent period paid for by the late victim passes. Then we'll study the matter. The important thing is that we cannot sell it before the passage of a long time . . . On television, the thief is always caught when he tries to sell the stolen goods."

He answers, "For our expenses, we'll use the cash and the various currencies we stole. We'll do that carefully so that our living standard will not suddenly rise and attract the attention of the investigator, as happens in movies."

"And then? We're both displaced persons and you are jobless. May God destroy those who destroyed us. What shall we do after that?"

He answers, "After that, I'll divorce you and marry Carmen, his widow."

"What?"

He continues, proudly, "She's madly in love with me."

She asks him, calmly, "And after that? Like her late husband, she's fifty years old. She's an old woman and we are both young, in the prime of our lives. What will you get out of that marriage?"

He replies, sarcastically, "And you, what will you get out of me? I'll marry her for her youth and I'll betray her with you for your money!"

"Come off this nonsense! After you marry her, I'll kill her and you'll inherit her wealth and return to me. One crime for another, but you're the one who started it."

I am afraid when I hear her. Wily women are disguised by their fragile bodies and apparently think better than men. They dissimulate, conceal their clever minds so that they may not be annihilated, and wait for the suitable day to reveal their real selves all at once; then they rule the world. How evil they are!

I am terrified of both of them. Ghosts are supposed to frighten human beings, but it seems the contrary is what happens. When Nahid begins to plan the murder of Carmen so that the matter will appear to be an accident, a matter of fate, with Naji certainly far from the murder scene and surrounded by witnesses, for an alibi, I begin to scream in terror.

Her husband asks her, "Did you hear a noise?"

She answers, "It's the wind."

No! It's not the wind. It's my voice. I try to shake the curtains and the chandeliers, open the doors and slam them, turn on the faucets and color the water in the bathtub red like blood, shake the bed and the chair under the person sitting on it, and I try to break the flower vases and do the other things attributed to ghosts by humans. But I can't. I have no physical mass. Things penetrate me, just as my father and I used to penetrate the light in the village cinema when we entered after the film had started and made the spectators scream at us. I used to bend over in fear, but my father could not sufficiently lessen his height, which resembled that of a pine tree he planted in front of our home. He used to love planting pines and cedars. Whenever one of us was born, he planted a pine or a cedar tree for him. My brother's cedar died and my father considered that a bad omen. Strange enough, my brother died soon afterward.

My pine tree grew taller than I am. Now that I am dead, will it die too? Will it become a ghost of a pine tree? Do trees have ghosts?

Naji now lies with Nahid and fiercely sails into her, my own saliva not yet dry on her rocks. It is terrifying, and I am a poor, terrified ghost.

They both frighten me as they remove one mask after another, revealing the truth in layers, one underneath the other.

My fear of them attracts me to them at the same time, and I am unable to leave them. She appears to experience real ecstasy with him. As a ghost, I observe her now, and I discover that she lied and faked her spells of ecstasy with me. Yes, indeed. He does have what I don't. I was not really the most virile of men, as I surely believed, nor was I the most experienced.

She says to him, "We must try to sleep now. I learned from him, before your arrival, that the maid will return in the morning, at dawn. This means that his corpse will not be discovered before then."

They converse like two intimate partners. Just like that, my name quickly becomes "his corpse"!

These living human beings do not cease to surprise and frighten a poor ghost like me. I become sad and I wail to frighten them.

Nahid says, "Have you forgotten to turn off the faucet?"

I leave them and go out to the fields. I feel lonely. The night bleeds and my heart—do I still have a heart?—is dying in the emptiness of the dark, infinite space.

I sit on a rock and cry without knowing why. I try to beat my head on the rock, I beat it and beat it until blood flows. My father sees me and has pity on me. He carries me home, but I know this will not happen to me.

I decide to live in one of the houses so that it may become a haunted house and I can try to frighten the people in it as much as they frighten me. But I don't know which house to live in, uprooted as I am from my village after my house has fallen to ruins.

It is true that I went abroad and became a wealthy man, but ghosts cannot build houses destroyed by shelling and buried by earth-moving machines.

What a miserable ghost I am, without a childhood or boyhood home to live in and haunt. I am a poor terrified ghost who does not know where to go, and I am lonely to the extreme.

I remember a house in the village which was haunted by ghosts, or so I was told when I wanted to buy it. I decide to go to it. I find myself in front of its door. Apparently ghosts are not in need of means of transportation. They are insects of light who run, reflected by a mirror in a playful child's hand in the sun. No one knows where they come from.

I move in time and space, faster than light. I discover myself as a ghost and explore my powers, such as seeing in the dark.

"Ghosts' Inn." I read the sign in letters of colored darkness on the door. I enter. The place teems with ghosts. I see them, and I don't see them, but I know they are there. None of them wears a white veil or bedsheet (as Nahid had done, for example). They are all naked in their sadness, and they reel with fear and perplexity.

I greet them: "Good evening, ghosts."

One answers, "And peace to you. You seem to be new here. Welcome."

How kind they are, like the inmates of a mental sanitarium, inmates who have been tortured by electricity under the pretext of a healing treatment; tamed in rooms with silencing rubber walls like silencers on murderers' handguns; given shots of forgetfulness in their blood, in which swim cedars, pines, lemon blossoms, tobacco, figs, olives, and loved ones who betrayed them or whom they betrayed, and the past, the past, the past, and the impact of the past that killed the present and the future—and the hellish blood system burdened with sufferings that have lost their face, their voice, and their memory and yet have remained in the veins, and burdened with the radioactive waste, and the Mexican television series, and the food that rotted in the heat, and mosquitoes, and the moving ashes in the tubes of the heart betrayed by time and women . . . The blood knocks, knocks, knocks on the rubber walls.

Nahid screams and wakes up from her sleep "What is this knocking?"

Naji says, "I haven't heard anything."

I move again to the Ghosts' Inn, quickly, as if I were in two places simultaneously. I head toward that ghost bent on himself like an apricot dried under the sun for ten years and I say, "I'm suffering and afraid."

He answers, "Let's look at the filled half of the glass."

I laugh.

He continues, "Ghosts have many possibilities, limited and broad, like all self-government. For example, you can move in time and space like a point of light, to and fro, on condition you don't come near the beginnings, the endings, and the red lines."

"For example?"

"You can now go to cast a farewell look at your corpse and attend the meeting in which your will is opened and read."

"But . . ."

"There's no 'but' either in the world of the living or in that of the dead. 'But' has been hanged in the garden and is hanging from the city walls. Look out of the window and you'll see it in the neon light illuminating the darkness, where it is being pecked by predatory birds. Give up 'but' as well as 'wonder' and 'surprise,' and you may perhaps be saved."

"But . . ."

"Shut up and be gone from my sight. Walls have ears even in ghost houses and punishment is eternal. Learn about your limited abilities and use them instead of fighting the impossible. Otherwise, ghosts will cast you out and allow their tribes to shed your dark blood."

"Yes, my lord. I'll leave eternal issues to your wisdom and return to my private affairs."

"Why don't you visit your corpse and frighten the living? Standing at the remains is advisable, even if they are the remains of your own corpse. It is important not to ask many questions."

"I'll do that. I'll visit my corpse."

As soon as I intend to go, I find myself there.

Here is my corpse, and the police photographer is taking pictures of it. Damn! I always like to have my good, left side in photographs because that conceals my large mouth, gives my narrow eyes some amplitude, and hides the bald right side of my forehead. Nobody cares for the feelings of corpses, let alone ghosts.

Here is Carmen lamenting my death: the beautiful, tall, wonderful, and withering red rose I picked from the nightclub and crowned as a queen on the throne of my heart. I forgot the world for her sake—I forgot my father's pines . . . Oh, my father!

Here is Carmen weeping over my corpse: a wonderful dramatic scene.

The lawyer says to her, "The poor man died young!"

He knows that I was past fifty many years ago.

It was a world of monkeys in a zoo, but they had cars, clothes, poems, tales, novels, buses, large stores, neon advertisements, supermarkets, lawyers, banks, airplanes, wars, television sets, and fathers, some of whom no longer loved us.

Oh, my father! How beautiful and tall he was. We returned together from the field and I swore to him I would return from abroad a wealthy man and build him a palace. But I forgot him as Carmen was dancing and dancing, and I lost my head.

They move my corpse. The investigator says, "Take him and perform an autopsy."

I would like to see my own autopsy but they wrongly move my corpse to the lunatic asylum. Stupid. All they do is wrong. I alone am right.

The condolatory visitors leave. Carmen is beautiful in black. How entertaining her appearance was before they arrived as she put on her widow's make-up with an effort to make it invisible. She put on a line of kohl, then erased it with her fingertip wetted with her saliva. She wiped off the extra powder with her palm, then tried a hat with a black, lace veil hanging down from it. Finding that it increased her beauty, she smiled to the mirror. She did not see me standing next to her and went on applying further layers of lipstick. She let down the lacework over her face as though adding a layer of powder, as in an important rehearsal for a play. Now, she takes off the hat, as though casting off a mask under which are many others. Naji remains with her after Nahid apologizes and goes home, pretending to have a cold, like any faithful friend never tempted to doubt her friend.

I wonder, did Carmen know of my secret relationship with Nahid? If she knew, she would have seized the opportunity to kick her out. A widow becomes a queen after her husband's death, kicking out his weeping mistresses, even those he loved more than her.

Perhaps she does not know that Nahid was one of my mistresses, but has suspicions about the others.

Here I am, trying to find justifications for her disloyalty to me with Naji, so that I do not hurt my ghost's ego, as if I were still a human being and a liar and had not been transformed into an authentic and real ghost.

It seems that being healed from the past is difficult, even when we turn into ghosts, for pain continues to chase us in the inner corridors.

I run in the corridor, like a mercurial ghost terrified by living human specters chasing me. Ah, there's no escape. But my state as a ghost is better than it would have been if I were alive and knew all their lies.

I run away. I turn into an insect of dark light and wander for a long time in a trance in timeless nowhere.

It is time for the probate of my will and I do not want to miss that. Here is my wife, I mean my widow, in resplendent attire, ready to go and inherit my wealth.

She diffuses the fragrance of perfume. I did not know that ghosts have a sense of smell. I thought they only wore white sheets and roamed in palaces.

Carmen does not know. Naji does not know. Nahid does not know. How happy I am to deceive them. They don't know that none of them will inherit me, and that others will not benefit from the inheritor. I have been more cunning than all of them and here lies the glory of ghosts.

Before Carmen leaves home, a delegation of notables in mourning clothes arrives. The head of the group surprises her by an abundance of eulogizing words in verse and in prose, the upshot of which is the hope that the gifts of her late husband (that is, me) may continue to flow to them.

Well, I used to fund one of those "charitable" groups, which only the Lord knows what they did, whom they served, and where their money went—other than in their pockets. Carmen assures them very firmly of her commitment to my "legacy" of good deeds and of the fact that the check will continue to reach them at the appointed time. They praise her character, her generosity, and her Estée Lauder make-up. And the meeting ends with a photograph taken for the newspaper.

Carmen rides in the Cadillac and goes to the lawyer in the company of Naji and Nahid. I am burning with eagerness to watch her after she arrives at his office, as he reads the will to her and the two young and faithful friends of the family who are bonded to her in good and bad times, in evening parties, and, more importantly, in checks.

Here she is, coming out of the car, her feet hardly touching the ground as she walks like me, almost flying. It is as if joy transforms the living, too, into ghosts floating in their own space.

She sits, with Naji on her right and Nahid on her left.

The lawyer reads the will and everyone is stunned, including the lawyer himself, who will no longer have the opportunity of administering my estate, nor that of flirting with my widow, my spokeswoman who thought she would distribute my wealth to those she wished and those who knew how to thank her.

It is an unhappy surprise to them all, for I gave away my estate and I deprived her and them of any inheritance.

In the beginning, Carmen can hardly believe it. I jump for joy and go through the ceiling and the walls when she opens her lovely mouth in surprise, then loses consciousness.

Nahid, too, falls unconscious. Naji, on the other hand, is afflicted with muscle cramps, and his cockiness contracts because his old hen will not lay golden eggs, as he expected, but rather only sighs and ecstatic moans, like the rest of the poor women.

What a happy ghost I am. Yes, indeed. I was somewhat crazy to will all my wealth to old people's homes to improve the conditions of the elderly so that each of them might have a little bedside table on which to put pictures of the real past, like me and like the rest of the nation of ghosts.

I am the leader of "The Front for the Liberation of Ghosts" and have dedicated my wealth to its service. There are no better allies for the elderly than ghosts, for the elderly are on the threshold until they join us. They have the right to choose the pictures that torment them and to put them near them at their bedside. They have the right, when dying, to call the loved ones who do not hear as they exhale scents of pines, lemon blossoms, tobacco, dust, and gunpowder—loved ones who leave the stories told about them and disavow some of the false tales told in favor of the living.

Yes, indeed. After the reading of the will, most of them fainted and that was beautiful, beautiful. Ghosts with weak shadows left their bodies when they fainted, and they were about to see me and converse with me, but they were unconscious ghosts and had to wait a little longer until their ghostly selves would assert themselves in death. Oh, how happy I am to see this pleasant scene of those I knew, standing on the brink between the illusion of life and ghostliness.

I see two executioners in white clothes coming toward me, a man and a woman. I am a ghost and they cannot see me.

The man says to the woman, "This is your first day as a nurse and you must be introduced to the patients. Are you tired?"

"No. Who is this poor one, bent over himself like a ghost?"

"This is precisely what may be said of him. You've described him well. If the previous patient thought he was Jamal 'Abd al-Nasir, and the one before, Yitzhak Rabin, this one thinks he is a ghost."

"Strange!"

"There is nothing strange in a lunatic asylum. We are the ones who are strange, for they have their own world and their own logic and their own heads that are as impregnable as castles."

"Whose ghost does he think he is?"

"The ghost of himself. He is an expatriate who made a fortune and returned to Lebanon, then became crazy."

"Why?"

"This is not a question to be posed in cases of madness. What causes one man's madness may be passed by another with indifference. You know that the soul has dark corridors. Jumping out of the window of mysteries is risky and may lead one to the other, unknown shore . . ."

"Well, but what is the cause of his madness in our opinion?"

"No one knows exactly. I've tried to gather some information about him because of his strange case. I was told that, on the night of his return from expatriation after long absence and with a great fortune, he was surprised to find his father in an old people's home. His poor father was dying in a miserable bed among dozens of other old people, in a hall crowded with them and their crutches. His father apparently did not recognize him before dying. The poor man was dying and may have recognized his son but was unable to express his feelings . . . or perhaps he wanted to punish him, who knows? The death of his almost demented father, who ignored him or did not recognize him as he lay dying, shook the returning expatriate to the core and apparently created in him a terrible feeling of guilt and remorse."

"And how did he arrive here?"

"His lawyer brought him to me one day. He was suffering from terrible pains that moved from place to place in his body and had no physical cause; he was also the victim of a break-down and chronic dejection, which is understandable in his case. I treated him by giving him some agricultural work to do with his mates. I also treated him with drugs and assigned him some drawing and poetry writing, for I was told he began his life as a poet."

The nurse laughs, "Every Arab thinks he is a poet. This is a general case and is not limited to crazy people. Every Arab starts his life as a poet, then he becomes a struggling fighter, and then a realist or a madman!"

The physician laughs and says, "I tried to penetrate into the folds of his soul by reading his writing. He wrote a very painful poem entitled 'I'm a Ghost.'"

"And what then?"

"He became convinced he was a ghost as much as the patient sitting next to him thinks he is Prince Fakhr al-Din al-Ma'ni."

"What happened next?"

"He went astray in the corridors, away from me, and moved to the other shore. All electric shock therapy and drugs were of no use. I think he suffers from megalomania and feelings of guilt at the same time. Perhaps he thinks the world has perfidi-ously betrayed him. Perhaps he feels he neglected his father and so he tries to perform an act of repentance. He is now a citizen of the other shore and I cannot make him hear my voice, nor can I hear his. He thinks he is a ghost, says nothing, talks to no one, and thinks no one sees him."

"Poor man. It's not easy for you to return with a great fortune to pamper your father and then find him dying and unable to recognize you, at least to tell you goodbye or forgive you."

"It is said also that while he was an expatriate he was in love with a dancer of legendary beauty and great persuasive abilities; she was of Arab origin and was named Carmen. She betrayed him after having made him forget even to write letters to his father. It is as if his feelings of guilt broke him asunder . . . But who knows. Medicine is still very primitive in the face of the mysteries of the corridors of the soul, and the soul's courtyards open to unknown winds. For this is a man, not a computer."

They are plotting against me. They don't know that I am a ghost and that I can hear and see them.

Oh, how happy I am because I am a ghost and can listen to everything without being seen by anyone, including the two executioners who claim they are the physician and the new nurse.

Enemies disguise themselves in a variety of clothes, most important of which are a doctor's frock and a nurse's uniform.

As for the previous enemy, who disguised herself in the uniform of the old nurse, my ghost killed her by crushing her under the branch of a pine tree during a storm. They thought that a thunderbolt hit the tree when she left her car and that the branch fell on her head and killed her.

Living human beings understand nothing. They don't know that ghosts are more terrified than they are, but ghosts do not die, and they have their own ferocity and know how to avenge themselves.

Here is my father, waiting for me on the other shore, as he does every day. He knows me and is happy at my return. I'll join him and we will resume planting pines and cedars in the garden in honor of the birth of ghosts, many as they are. We have planted a tree for a young woman not yet born and we put up posters for her in the avenues of the heart, hoping she will be born a ghost all at once without being polluted by first being a human being.

The two executioners are still in their white clothes, chattering and making the rounds of the place. I will wait for them in the garden on a stormy day and I will help them be born as two innocent ghosts like me after I crush their cunning heads under the branch of a tree, give them rest from their own poison, and be of service to them. Peace be on you . . . I am an insect of light, going to the dark side of the moon. Who will follow me?

I was in bed with her, riding her like a boat to the islands of wonder, pleasure, and oblivion, when her husband entered. In the beginning I did not believe my eyes. The door of my house was locked and I did not hear the sound of anyone breaking in. How did he enter?

He saw what condition we were in and did not say anything. But he began to come closer to us, sobbing aloud, gasping like a dying person, and holding his head in his hands as though his neck could no longer carry it.

I noticed that he did not have any knife or revolver, so I felt a little relieved because he was not armed.

He continued to advance toward us, tall and stout. He stretched out his hands to my neck, now gasping like a person about to reach orgasmic ecstasy, and he started to strangle me . . .